"It seems you are determined to know all my secrets, my lord."

"The important ones, to be sure."

"So then, what did you decide?"

Julian shifted to better see Miss Vance's face. "I've decided you will continue your criminal activities."

"My lord?"

"As directed by me. I'll provide you with the information, and you will pass it along to your contacts. You will start by informing your contact Lord Chambelston has called upon Sotherton."

"I, ah, already have. Yesterday afternoon."

"You are nothing if not efficient. I should have expected nothing less, I suppose. Did you include any other details I should know about?"

"Only that you are newly come into your title, it would seem."

"Indeed, quite recently." And perhaps not naturally. But then, she knew that from his anonymous note. A new thought struck him. If his father's death were indeed the result of the radicals, she could have gleaned nothing from the note their leadership didn't already know. Was she as she said, only a governess earning a bit of coin and not well-connected to the radicals? Or was his anonymous source sending him spurious information? To what end?

S0-AEG-280

Books by C. J. Chase

Love Inspired Historical

Redeeming the Rogue
The Reluctant Earl

C. J. CHASE

likes to make her characters solve mysteries, wrestle with the difficult issues of life and faith, and fall in love. All wrapped up with a happy ending, of course. Like a character in one of her novels, C.J. took a circuitous route to her own happy ending as an author. Armed with a degree in statistics, she began a promising career in information technology. But after coworkers discovered she was a member of that rare species—a computer programmer who could also craft a grammatically correct sentence—she spent more time writing computer manuals than computer code. Leaving the corporate world to stay home with her children, C.J. quickly learned she did not possess the housekeeping gene, so she decided to take the advice of her ninth-grade English teacher and write articles and stories people actually wanted to read. Her procrastination, er, hard work paid off in 2010 when she won the Golden Heart for Best Inspirational Manuscript and sold the novel to the Love Inspired Historical line. C.J. lives in the swamps of Southeastern Virginia with her handsome husband, active sons, one kinetic sheltie and an ever-increasing number of chickens. You can visit her cyber-home (where the floors are always clean) at www.cjchasebooks.com.

The Reluctant Earl

C.J. CHASE

⟨H⟩ **HARLEQUIN**® LOVE INSPIRED® HISTORICAL

Recycling programs
for this product may
not exist in your area.

™ LOVE INSPIRED BOOKS

ISBN-13: 978-0-373-82953-8

THE RELUCTANT EARL

For I know the plans I have for you, declares the Lord, plans to prosper you and not to harm you, plans to give you hope and a future.
—*Jeremiah* 29:11

To Sarah Chase
For all her support and shared love of stories

Chapter One

Somerset, England
31 December 1816

Snow drifted softly onto Julian DeChambelle's shoulders, so unlike the crushing weight of his newly acquired responsibilities. He stared at the cavernous hole of the open mausoleum while the rector's voice rolled over snow-blanketed graves and echoed off distant monuments.

Chilly summer had given way to frigid autumn and even more bitter winter—a winter of despair and deprivation, of desperation as the poor harvest brought scarcity and strife. Julian shoved his freezing hands into his greatcoat's pockets, his fingers fisting around the anonymous note that suggested the "accident" which overturned his father's carriage had been something more than accidental.

Something…intentional?

His gaze shuffled around the shivering throng gathered to pay their last respects. Did the author of the note even now slouch among the mourners where a few local gentry huddled in woolen cloaks and brushed shoulders with yeoman farmers? The late Earl of Chambelston had been universally loved by the common folk.

Or not, as the letter—delivered only this morning—testified.

Indeed, even his eldest sister Elizabeth had scorned the opportunity for one last chance at reconciliation.

"Ashes to ashes, dust to dust..." The clergyman's familiar words carried Julian back to countless burials at sea, all those services on all those ships during his two decades of war. Death had struck with unnerving unpredictability—taking young powder monkeys and experienced sailors equally and respecting neither the lowliest seamen nor the great Admiral Nelson himself.

"Our Father, who art in heaven..." The rector led the people in a cold, wavery recitation of the Lord's Prayer.

Julian's youngest sister Caroline followed as best she could, her reedy voice lagging a word or two behind the others. She was twenty years old, but with a mind forever childlike. Another burden bore down on him as he glanced at the top of her head. Caro was his responsibility now, for the rest of her life.

Of the six DeChambelle siblings, only three—Felicity, Caro, him—mourned here today. His brother Kit lived in America now and wouldn't even learn of these events for weeks. Elizabeth preferred her resentment to her relatives. And Gregory...

The rector snapped the prayer book shut, the clap of pages echoing as loudly as a cannon salute.

His father had been proud of Captain DeChambelle the officer, but what about Julian the man? The new earl? Anxiety once again closed around his mind with paralyzing fingers.

Baron Trethewey, his sister Felicity's husband, paused before Julian, hand outstretched. "He was a good man, Chambelston."

Julian blinked as he mechanically shook his brother-in-law's hand, only now realizing that with his father's death he'd inherited not only the properties and responsibilities but his father's very name. The title fit him with all the discomfort of his civilian wardrobe. "Yes, he will be much missed."

"If there's anything you need, anything I can do to assist, send for me."

"Thank you."

Felicity wrapped a black-clad arm around him in an embrace of sympathy and shared sorrow. "Have faith, Julian."

"I…" The frigid wind stung his eyes, causing Felicity's features to waver. It wasn't supposed to be this way. Julian knew everything about commanding a frigate and nothing about overseeing an estate. His older—and now deceased—brother Gregory had been raised for this position, had been trained for the responsibilities of managing the Chambelston holdings. He would have known what to do to ease their people's suffering, what steps Parliament needed to take to becalm the brewing unrest as the poor and hungry petitioned—sometimes violently—for the government to intervene in the intensifying crisis.

"I know you'll make the right decisions when the time comes."

"Thank you." With an equanimity achieved by years of practice concealing his emotions from the men under his command, Julian squared his shoulders and fixed a resolute expression on his countenance for Felicity's benefit.

A few other intrepid mourners paused to offer their respects. Julian accepted their condolences with murmurs of thanks, then sent them on their way to escape the bitter conditions.

Maman touched his sleeve. Flakes of white glazed the top of her black bonnet. "We must get Caro home before she takes ill."

Julian glanced at his sister's pinched face, her nose reddened from cold and sorrow, her eyes reflecting the confusion of one swept up in events she didn't understand. "Come.

There is nothing more for us here." He grasped his mother's elbow and escorted the women to a carriage with its Chambelston coat of arms on the door. The waiting horses stomped their feet in the packed snow, their harnesses jingling as they shook their heads.

Maman climbed in first, then Julian assisted Caro while Maman held her hand. His little sister tottered once, and Julian tightened his grip while she regained her equilibrium. Steps had always been—would always be—difficult for his sister. Like most other things in life.

Julian kicked the snow off his boots and hoisted his weary frame up behind them. As he dropped onto the plush upholstery, the paper in his pocket crunched, demanding answers. Demanding action. Demanding he travel to the one house in England where he was least welcome.

Maman tucked a woolen blanket around Caro. "A pity Felicity could not stay, no?"

"Indeed. It would have been nice for you to have some feminine companionship during my absence."

"You are not staying in Somerset with Caro and me?"

"I must go to Northamptonshire." Rowan Abbey, to be precise.

Maman's lips tightened, her only betrayal of how keenly she felt her eldest daughter's antagonism. "You do not need to defend me, Julian. I made my mistakes and offered my apologies. There is nothing more I can do. I have made my peace. Elizabeth knows she is welcome whenever she wants to put aside her grudge."

"Actually I'm not going to see Elizabeth. I'm going to meet with her husband." The undersecretary to the Home Secretary, the man whose job it was to ameliorate the people's suffering during this winter of famine before hardship and hunger drove them to outright rebellion. Perhaps he was aware of the relationship between Julian's father and the petitioners.

"Sotherton?"

"We have…business." Business involving an anonymous letter and a mysterious death.

The bare branches of a nearby rosebush shivered forlornly as the bitter wind whipped across the dormant garden and through the threadbare elbows of Leah Vance's coat. The gust whisked up snow from yesterday's storm and chafed her face with the sharp crystals. She leaned toward her warmly dressed charge, allowing herself to feel a bit of envy for Lady Teresa Sotherton's heavy cloak.

"Mother says I am to go to London in the spring—if the situation calms." Enthusiasm beamed in Teresa's eyes of sparkling blue-violet. A few of her inky curls escaped her hat and framed her smile.

"If the situation calms." A state of affairs Leah was doing her best to prevent. Turmoil would extend her earnings from both employers.

"Helen says the city is filled with handsome men."

"Which you hope to meet."

"Of course. As many as possible." Teresa threaded her arm through Leah's elbow and pulled her along a freshly shoveled path.

"How distressing to learn your enthusiasm doesn't stem from the city's many prospects for improving your mind such as museums and libraries."

"My dear Miss Vance, what could I possibly have left to learn after all these years in your tutelage?"

"Comportment, patience and French conjugations."

"My poor teacher, consigned to an indifferent pupil like me. Perhaps you should come along to keep my conduct above reproach."

"Truly, you do not wish for my company. I would force

your focus to pursuits such as literary societies and philosophy studies."

"No, I would see you introduced to so many gentlemen so as to not allow you time."

"At my age? A ridiculous cake I would make of myself."

"An older gentleman, then. Older and scholarly and a bit mysterious."

Like Leah's father, a gentle and intellectual man who'd failed to adequately provide for his daughters. Or like the one upon whom she'd once pinned hopes...until adversity had driven him away. The wind shifted, carrying with it the acrid scent of the coal smoke that belched from Rowan Abbey's many chimneys. In her thin coat Leah shivered, longing for the fires that added a modicum of warmth to the drafty manor. "I would be content with meeting warmth come spring." Her future stretched before her as endless as the snowy landscape and as bleak as the leaden winter sky, a lifetime of caring for others' children but never her own.

Eight years she'd been here. When she'd arrived, Teresa had been a girl of ten and Leah scarcely twenty. What would she do when Lord and Lady Sotherton carted their daughter to the metropolis and its many eligible men? No doubt Lady Sotherton would write Leah a satisfactory reference that would procure her a position elsewhere. But where would she find one near her unfortunate, mind-damaged sister with the unique...situation that allowed her to earn the extra funds she needed for Phoebe's care? Asylums were expensive. Good ones—where the staff didn't abuse or exploit the inmates—especially so.

The jingle of harnesses rang through the cold stillness as a pair of matching chestnuts pulled a carriage along the snowy drive.

"I didn't know your parents were expecting a visitor." Leah had made a practice of knowing her employers' business.

Alas, the cold and frequent snowfalls had kept many a traveler at bay this winter.

"Probably another boring politician come to confer with Papa. I don't know why they can't wait until after Twelfth Night."

The carriage rounded a curve, revealing the emblem on the door. A nobleman, then. "Perhaps one of your fine gentlemen couldn't wait until spring but thought to sweep you away before his rivals had chance to make their intentions known."

"A lovely thought." As the conveyance drew to a halt before the Restoration-era house, Teresa's lips straightened and her eyes grew thoughtful. "But this is no overly eager suitor. That is the Chambelston crest."

Leah stumbled. "Your grandfather?"

"Yes." Teresa paused while Leah regained her balance.

In all Leah's years of service, Lady Sotherton's father had never called here. Nor had the lady ever ventured south to see him. Rumors about the long estrangement had titillated the servants for years. Rumors that increased in intensity and frequency only last month after Chambelston purportedly visited Sotherton's London town house. Rumors that Leah, as a proper governess, had once tried to avoid. At least until the day she'd realized that sharing the gossip about her employers could provide a better income than the meager salary allotted to a governess.

The coachman opened the door, shielding the Chambelston crest from their curious stare. Then a man descended the step. His dark hat covered his hair and hid his face, but not even the navy blue greatcoat could conceal the broad shoulders unbowed by years. As he strode to the house, his movements conveyed surprising determination and vigor for a man of Chambelston's advanced age. "Are you certain that is the Chambelston crest? Perhaps you are mistaken."

"No, I saw it on correspondence that arrived for Father once. Let's go inside. Perhaps we will get a glimpse of him."

"You mother will disapprove."

"Surely you do not intend to tell her, do you? Why, Miss Vance, consider this a secret quest of discovery, like… searching for the heretofore lost tomb of an ancient Pharaoh."

"I doubt your grandfather would appreciate being compared to a long-dead mummy."

Teresa's laugh chimed again, and Leah's heart lurched with love and pride. The shy, lonely girl had blossomed to a beautiful young lady on the cusp of womanhood. Would Leah develop the same relationship with her next students, or was this one—this relationship, this child—special? As Teresa steered them around the corner to a back door, a gust of winter blew one last shot of cold at them. The chill sliced through Leah's coat, and her heart. What would become of the sensitive Teresa in London? Leah feared the undemonstrative Lady Sotherton marked her daughter's romanticism and goodness as weaknesses. Would Teresa retain her gentle character or would disappointment and disillusionment harden into cynicism and make her into someone more like her mother? Like…Leah?

Once inside they paused to remove their heavy, snow-festooned boots. Leah wiggled stiff, aching toes as she unbuttoned her coat.

"Come." Teresa tapped her arm. "I want to see him."

"But we must retrieve our shoes and—"

"No one will notice us." Her charge focused wide blue eyes on her. "Please, Miss Vance. In all my life I've never so much as seen my own grandfather. He may leave at any moment. Surely it wouldn't be wrong to sneak a quick look."

Against her better judgment Leah followed Teresa until they paused in the doorway of a salon that allowed them an unimpeded view of the entrance hall.

And of the visitor—the visitor who was most obviously not the older nobleman of their expectations.

This man's presence overwhelmed the grand entrance that long-ago Sothertons had designed to impress—and intimidate—guests. Even larger in life than he'd appeared from a distance, their caller held his hat in gloved hands, revealing a full head of tawny hair. The chandelier's glow gilded those strands with a gold that rivaled the patterns on the elegant wallpapers. Matching brows arched over cynical eyes of brilliant blue. And yet, despite the intensity smoldering therein, lines serrated their corners—lines of hard weariness that marked him as a few years past a young man's idealism.

Lines that cut even deeper with the sardonic twist of his mouth. "I thought we might at least see you at Father's bedside. He lingered long enough for you to see him one last time. But not long enough to outlive your rancor, it seems." Barbs edged the visitor's deceptively soft baritone.

Lady Sotherton's eyes glittered with all the wintry chill of the January cold. "So his sins finally caught up with him."

"Or someone else's."

"I fail to see why that should concern me."

Tension tightened along the square jaw and in the sharp, chiseled angles of the man's cheeks. "My dear sister, surely even your hard heart feels a twinge of sorrow at the passing of a man who'd provided so generously during your first years of life."

"His faults were more memorable than his generosity."

"Fortunately, so was his willingness to forgive."

"If you've come to judge me because I refuse to feign feelings I don't possess, you've misjudged my scruples."

"Actually I'm not here to see you at all, Lizzie." Scorn darkened his eyes and broadened his derisive grin. "I came to meet with Sotherton. Your husband."

Awareness prickled along Leah's spine, like the ache that

radiated from her warming fingers. Was it important the new Earl of Chambelston—for such he must be—should call on Lord Sotherton at a time like this?

Lady Sotherton's jaw dropped, her gaping mouth reminiscent of a dead codfish. And with the same degree of comment.

Beside Leah, Teresa stifled a giggle with her palm. But not well enough. Lady Sotherton's head jerked toward them, her hard eyes farther narrowing with even greater displeasure as she peered at the salon doorway.

"Teresa? Are you eavesdropping?"

Teresa swallowed and stepped into the entrance hall. "Good afternoon, Mama. I only now returned from my walk. I heard voices and waited so as not to interrupt."

Leah hesitated, wanting to flee but refusing to leave her charge alone to face the coming reprimand. Her prospects for receiving a good referral from Lady Sotherton dimmed as she slipped into the entrance hall and paused beside Teresa.

Lady Sotherton folded her arms across her chest, her perpetually present frown amplifying the wrinkles around her mouth. "Now that you have indeed interrupted, you may continue to the schoolroom. No doubt you have studies to complete."

"Yes, Mama." Teresa scurried to the stairs, mortification coloring her face a deeper red than the cold.

Leah offered her employer a hasty curtsey and hurried after her student.

"And Miss Vance." Lady Sotherton's frosty tones cut short Leah's retreat.

She froze, then turned—slowly, deliberately—gripping the remains of her composure as tightly as her fingers wrapped around the bannister. "My lady?"

"How do you expect my daughter to comport herself with proper conduct when you participate in her wayward behavior?"

"My apologies, my lady." Despite Leah's best attempts to control her response, the blistering words of public censure—in front of her charge, the servants and a stranger—scorched her cheeks. A stranger whose brilliant blue gaze softened for the first time with an expression akin to…sympathy. Her embarrassment melded with rebellious anger, and her spine stiffened at the added indignity of a stranger's pity.

Julian's jaw ached with the effort to keep silent. Only twenty years of naval service—of remaining aloof whenever a fellow officer disciplined his subordinate—prevented him from intervening. He cared nothing about Elizabeth's probable reaction, not when his uncivil sister hadn't even bothered to introduce him to the niece he'd never seen until this moment. But the other woman—whose wide, hazel eyes flickered to him one last time as she turned her scarlet face away—deserved no further humiliation.

"Return to the schoolroom, Miss Vance." Elizabeth's toe tapped against the floor. "And see you don't permit my daughter to run rampant about the house without shoes like the veriest hoyden. I insist she comport herself in a manner that will secure her future."

"Yes, my lady." Miss Vance dropped into another, more subservient curtsey like the most menial scullery maid. The chandelier flames gleamed on her hair—straight, severely styled and commonplace brown. It complemented her other features—unremarkable except for the spark of defiance glinting in her eyes.

Certainly not beautiful. Not even striking. But… interesting.

She followed her charge up the grand staircase, the skirt of her dark, humble gown swaying with her steps.

The governess, obviously—a woman trapped by circumstances in a nebulous world between classes, never quite belonging anywhere. Rather like his own feeling of entrapment at finding himself thrust into a position for which he'd had little preparation and no inclination. Compassion, even connection, stirred within him.

"Why do you want to see Benedict?" Elizabeth's strident voice pierced Julian's musings and drew him back to the matter at hand.

"Business."

Her frown tightened. "How…coincidental. So your father claimed when he called last month."

A frisson of excitement ricocheted along Julian's spine as he let her disdain pass without comment. "Father was here? Last month?" Such news lent credence to the letter writer's claims. His father had been involved in the recent unrest— but in what fashion? Had he worked with the government to stem the rising tide of riots?

"Not here, of course. We were in London. He called at our town house to see Benedict—on business, he maintained." His sister lifted her chin. If she hoisted her nose any higher, she would be staring at the friezes on the ceiling. "Rightly, I suppose, since he didn't expend any effort to visit with me."

"How strange he would rebuff his own daughter after all his attempts at reconciliation. Or was it you who discouraged any familial discourse?"

Elizabeth tilted her head toward the hovering butler. "Hawkesworth, find out if Lord Sotherton is receiving visitors."

"Tell him Lord Chambelston wishes to know." Julian added when it was obvious Elizabeth refused to offer him even that courtesy. The butler nodded and withdrew, his steps muffled by the plush rugs that swathed the parquet floors. Julian shifted inside his heavy cloak. How like his sister to scorn even the offer of a warm drink before she tossed him out into the cold afternoon. "I understand your animosity toward our parents, but why do you spurn the rest of your family?"

"And see that constant, simpleminded reminder of our parents' debauchery?" Twenty years of rancor had not been kind to this, his eldest sister. Silver streaked her once golden hair, and discontent now congealed in the same eyes where once delight had danced. Lines of complaint aged her countenance beyond her forty years, making her appear a bit like the swags of yuletide greenery that still decorated the entrance hall—old, dry, tired. And ready to be torn down. "I don't know why Maman didn't put our youngest sister in an asylum where she belongs."

"Perhaps Maman thought committing another wrong to save herself the embarrassment of a previous wrong was... wrong?"

"So instead she chose to humiliate us all."

He glanced at the stairs where his niece and her beleaguered governess had so recently fled. "Poor Lizzie, who believes humiliation is permitted to flow in only one direction."

The butler's reemergence saved Elizabeth from delivering yet another cutting response. "His lordship will see you now, my lord."

Julian passed Hawkesworth his hat and gloves, then swung his cloak off his shoulders. "With your permission, Lizzie?" He bowed to his sister. Then without awaiting her response, followed the butler.

The pine-scented hallway whispered to him of happier times, when six eager children anticipated the holidays. His mother had left Chambelston Manor unadorned this season, except for the black the servants put up after his father succumbed to his injuries. At least Caro's future holidays wouldn't be tainted with reminders of this year's tragedy.

The butler paused in a doorway and announced, "The Earl

of Chambelston, my lord." Then he moved aside to let Julian sweep past.

Sotherton laid aside his quill and rose from behind a mahogany desk. His heavy brows and sagging jowls gave him a squirely appearance—as if he were a man given only to his horses and hounds—but the keen edge of his gaze warned Julian not to discount this man's observations. "Chambelston." His gaze slid over Julian, as if his brother-in-law were too small for the title he bore.

Julian understood. Would he ever grow accustomed to the name? The loss? "Sotherton."

His brother-in-law gestured to the chairs that flanked either side of a marble fireplace. Flames blazed on the hearth and threw cheery light onto the paneled walls of the masculine study. "A nasty time of year to be traveling. I heard about Chamb—your father's accident. He was a good man. I'm sorry for your loss."

Not sorry enough to persuade his wife to attend Father's funeral, or at the very least, be man enough to bring his children in the face of his wife's refusal. "He will be missed."

"How is your mother?" Sotherton waited until Julian dropped onto a chair before settling on the adjoining seat.

"Weary. The last few weeks have been demanding. Maman was nursing Father while I was overseeing the estate." Thank goodness Felicity had arrived to tend to Caro. But now Felicity had returned to her home—and Julian was here. How would Maman fare so far from her support and so close to her grief? "I've been trying to settle the estate affairs. I understand Father called upon you in London a month ago." A very long month ago.

"I own I was rather surprised to see him as we haven't been particularly close. And imagine my astonishment when he confided that several leaders of the radicals had requested his assistance in petitioning the Regent."

Julian's fingers tightened around the chair arms. "Do you mean my father was working with those who instigated the Spa Fields riots?" Not the government? But...the letter in Julian's pocket had suggested the rioters had caused his father's injury and subsequent death.

"Not those who fomented the disturbance so much as those who believe the people have legitimate grievances. Chamb— your father functioned as a mediator between them and the government. He was uniquely respected by both the aristocracy and the common people."

So Julian had once also believed. And yet, the author of his mysterious letter averred otherwise. "Did Father tell you what he expected to accomplish?"

"Beyond trying to prevent the unrest from spreading to every corner of the country? The looting and destruction only increase the overall suffering. Your father wanted to use his leverage to convince the people that the government is not insensitive toward their needs."

"Only impotent?"

"What can we do?" Sotherton tapped templed fingers against his chin. "There is simply no more food to be had. The famine is even worse on the continent."

"But a man with starving children isn't oft given to reason."

"Worse, many are willing to follow anyone who promises them relief. Unfortunately while some of your father's, er, friends have good intentions, others are dedicated radicals who seek the destruction of the monarchy. The current hardships have provided them an opportunity to advance their cause."

At the cost of his father's life, it seemed.

Leah finished her note with a flourish and sprinkled sand over the wet ink. As she shook off the excess, the crackling parchment echoed the blast of winter that shivered against the schoolroom window. A draft pushed through the frame, causing the curtains to stir and the candle to flicker. Teresa had gone to dinner with the family—including her newly met uncle—leaving Leah alone with her thoughts and schemes.

Business, Lord Chambelston had claimed in his mesmerizing baritone. What business brought a man so far from home in the depths of winter to visit an estranged relative whose primary interest was politics, not commerce? A pity she couldn't have lingered longer on the stairs to find out. Once she finished informing her cousin of her discovery, she'd set out to learn more.

She folded the note, leaving the seemingly blank side exposed, and she poured a dollop of hot wax onto the parchment seam. Once she had the innocuous words sealed, she tucked a candle stub into her pocket and marched to the hallway, message in hand. Despite the dangerous nature of her errand, she smiled as she made her way to the narrow staircase that threaded through the back of Rowan Abbey. Approaching footsteps clattered against the treads, then a chambermaid's face materialized in the dark.

"Posting another letter, Miss Vance?" Molly offered a deferential nod and a shy smile that glowed despite the windowless, airless stairway. Even her hair—a bright, carroty red—defied the gloom. A tiny wooden cross hung around her neck on a thin leather cord. "You should have rung for me. I'll take it for you."

"Oh, no. You work hard enough already. Besides, I, ah, also have another message to deliver," Leah improvised. "But thank you, Molly."

Where did the loyalty of the other servants and staff lie? With the powerful who paid their meager salaries? Or with the common folk who couldn't find food in this winter of famine and despair? Leah reached the ground floor and a door that led out the back of the manor. Cold slammed into her as she crossed the snow-covered grounds to the stables, but grabbing her coat would have raised suspicions. At least the deepening darkness—and her governess-plain brown gown—hid her from curious eyes.

The wind tossed snow against her face. Just when her fingers began to numb, she reached the stable. As she pushed open the door, a blast of warmth swept over her cheek. The strong odor of animals filled her nostrils, carrying her back to long ago memories of happier times. She seized her skirts and hiked them above her ankles so as not to return with any telltale bits of straw—or worse—stuck to her hem. "Wetherel?"

The groom appeared from a stall. "Miss Vance, you shouldn't have come out in the cold."

Or at all, his narrowed eyes and drawn brows warned as she passed him her note. But who else could she could trust with such an errand? "If you could see to the matter as soon as possible?"

Once she'd returned to the house, she pointed her feet toward Lord Sotherton's study. The chink of silver and drone of desultory conversation drifted from the dining room. Hopefully Lady Sotherton's vanity had overcome her animosity, and she would keep her guest—and the servants—busy with an extensive repast.

Once by the dark paneled study door, Leah lit her candle stub on a sconce and let herself into the room. A quick examination of his lordship's desk revealed nothing new since her foray here yesterday. She blew out her candle and leaned back on her heels, surrounded by darkness. If the new Lord Chambelston had brought anything useful—any information that might advance the cause—he wouldn't have carried those documents to dinner.

Which meant she'd have to search his bedchamber.

Did she dare?

Gentlemen usually lingered over their drinks and discussions. Long enough for Leah to make discreet…inquiries? She reached for the doorknob.

The click of passing heels set her pulse pounding until the sound faded away. Hurriedly Leah slipped into the hallway and crept up the steps to the floor above where family and guests slept. But not glorified servants such as herself.

Lady Sotherton might wish to consign her brother to the dungeons, but doubtless her husband would insist that so august a guest be situated in one of the best rooms. Had Lord Chambelston brought a valet? His greatcoat had hidden all but his boots, and yet, she couldn't imagine him the foppish type. A former sea captain, so the rumors claimed and so the lines around his eyes confirmed.

Leah tiptoed past the dowager's bedchamber—just in case the elderly lady had tired of dropping acerbic comments and retired early—to the premier guest chamber. She glanced over her shoulder, grateful to find the hallway empty. Grateful? To whom? She ignored the implications in her question as she pressed her ear against the door.

Silence.

She tapped against the oak.

Still nothing.

She twisted the knob and pushed. The door swung silently on its hinges. A fire burned in the grate but revealed no life within. Leah pulled the door shut behind her, the latch catching with a gentle click. She would have to hurry—but where to begin?

A massive bed in a blue coverlet—a shade lighter than Lord Chambelston's eyes—dominated the room. Hardly a place for a gentleman to hide important papers. She crossed the plush Axminster carpet to a mahogany wardrobe and tugged open a drawer. Only clothes. Would he hide documents among them? She riffled through the lawn shirts and cravats, ignoring—or rather, trying to ignore—the uncomfortable sensation of touching a man's clothes, of inhaling the subtle scents of horses and smoke. And a stranger's at that.

How different from her clandestine forays into Lord Sotherton's desk.

And with a different outcome. If Lord Chambelston's business included documents, he hadn't left them in the drawers. She'd learned nothing of interest other than that he liked well-made but unostentatious clothing.

She slid the last drawer shut and leaned back on her heels as she surveyed the room. His greatcoat hung on a peg, the sheer size of the garment covering a large portion of wall. She moved closer, catching the smells of still-damp wool and the outdoors. And that same elusive scent of…male? As she ran her hands along the fabric, she fought back the array of memories that assailed her mind and conscience—of assisting her father into his cloak, of threading her arm through her fainthearted suitor's elbow.

Of struggling against another man's smothering strength.

Just as the maudlin thoughts threatened to overwhelm her, the coat crackled beneath her fingers. She searched pockets and located her first success, a folded piece of foolscap. Her heart raced forward even as she warned herself it was probably nothing more exciting than an invitation from an actress or a bill from Chambelston's tailor.

Leah edged closer to the low-burning fire, unfolded the parchment and scanned the contents to learn who had sent the missive. No signature at the bottom. What did that signify? She started at the top again, more slowly, her interest growing as she realized the note's import.

Murder.

Her pulse pounded against her temples, shutting out the gentle snaps and sizzles of the fire.

Did her cousin Alec know the movement was accused of

such a heinous crime against a peer of the realm? To judge by Chambelston's words to his sister, he believed the allegations. Such a personal note, anonymous or not, would be missed should she confiscate it. Her cousin would have to be satisfied with her word on the matter. She read the letter again, determined to commit its contents to memory before—

"Learn anything interesting?"

Leah's heart fell to her stomach and the note fluttered to the floor. She whirled to face the owner of that acerbic baritone as he latched the door shut behind him. Lord Chambelston blocked her only escape.

Chapter Two

Trapped—again—in a gentleman's bedchamber. Nausea churned in Leah's stomach and hurtled to her throat, propelled by an onslaught of terrifying memories. Would Lord Chambelston take advantage of her person or see her dismissed? Or…worse? And what would happen to Phoebe? A frisson of fear shuddered along Leah's spine as she stared into the deadly calm on the earl's implacable face. As he folded his arms across his chest, the fabric of his fine blue sleeves bunched over a sinewy strength that alluded to his previous livelihood as a sea captain. He leaned against the door, feet braced apart as if still on his ship's deck. "Dear me. Don't say I've mistakenly entered the wrong chamber."

"I…I…" Leah's mind spun, but the pounding of blood in her temples drowned out even her nonsensical excuse.

"I believe at the very least, introductions are in order. Chambelston at your…service, Miss…"

She willed her dry mouth to speak. "Leah Vance."

"Have you come to stoke the fire? You seem rather well spoken for a maid, Miss Vance."

Surely even Leah was not so insignificant he'd forgotten the awkwardness of witnessing Lady Sotherton's public censure of her only hours ago. Despite an urge to lie, she gathered what courage she could find. There was no point misrepresenting her position in the household. Not when he held her livelihood and her very life within his power. "I am Lady Teresa's governess."

He arched a patrician brow of the same tawny hue as his hair. "The education of young ladies must be quite changed from my sisters' youth. I don't recall their governess making any similar nighttime forays at our house. Have you long been Lady Teresa's governess?"

"Eight years."

"Long enough, then, to know my sister's faults. Probably better than I, after all these years."

Their gazes met, clashed—and Leah's concentration sank into that deep blue stare. Oh, he remembered her, all right, but where pity had lingered this afternoon, anger now burned, scorching her cheeks with its heat.

His gaze traveled the length of her homely gown until it focused on the incriminating note at her feet. "However, I can't imagine why my personal correspondence should be of such interest to a governess—unless you sought to escape certain spinsterhood by entrapping me in marriage."

"Of course not!"

"Oh? You are in my bedchamber, Miss Vance." Lord Chambelston studied her below eyelids that drifted down to a lazy, dangerous half-mast.

"Don't be absurd. No one would force you into wedlock to defend the honor of a mere governess."

"Then if it is not marriage you seek, perhaps another arrangement? It won't work, you know. I am not so green as to be tricked into matrimony nor so desperate as to need a... provincial governess for feminine company."

A plain governess, he meant. Too late, Leah realized she should have agreed to his first suggestion, no matter how preposterous and ridiculous. And obnoxious. Better to feed his conceit than let him guess the truth.

But he already had, were she to judge by the cold hard smile that twisted on his mouth below the proud edge of his aquiline nose. "Not an illicit affair, either? Then if you haven't designs on my name or my person, I can only assume you want something else from me. Information, perhaps?"

"What information could you possibly have of interest to a provincial governess, my lord? A correct French conjugation? The proper stitch for an embroidery sampler? Beethoven's latest piano sonata?"

"Or the details about the government's response to the recent troubles sweeping across the country?" Despite the stillness on his jaw, his eyes blazed blue fury as he leaned forward.

She retreated an involuntary step before she realized what she was doing. She steeled her spine, but her heart yet pounded in her chest. Could he hear it? "What would a mere provincial governess know or care about world affairs?"

"Come now, Miss Vance. As I recall, you were present when I told Lizzie I'd come not to see her, but her husband. Surely you don't expect me to believe one hired for her intelligence would miss the significance of that statement."

Leah glanced over her shoulder, but the room revealed no hidden escape. No, she was trapped by his astute deduction as surely as by his stance in front of the doorway. Her anger melded with fear and yielded resignation. How ironic—she wouldn't have to wait until spring to worry about her future after all. She focused on the portal's carved trim above Chambelston's gilded head. Was this how her brother David had felt as his ship sailed into Napoleon's fleet at Trafalgar? The stomach-churning premonition of impending doom, of waiting for the coming collision. "What do you want from me?"

His mocking smile cut deeper into the lines around his

mouth, below which the carelessly knotted cravat supported her conjectures about his lack of a valet. The snowy white linen contrasted intriguingly with the bronzed jaw that bespoke a life spent outdoors. "It seems I have you at my mercy. Do you fear for your virtue, Miss Vance?"

His coat stretched across broad shoulders and hugged the hard form of a man accustomed to action, to exercise, even to manual labor. Authority and strength radiated from him, held in check by a weariness—a vulnerability even—that he couldn't quite hide behind his sardonic mask. She wasn't a small, fragile woman like her younger sister, yet he could easily overpower her if he chose. Which he wouldn't. "No, I think not. You are a hard man, but not an evil one, my lord."

A fearsome stillness settled over his features. Shadows darkened the blue of his irises, concealing the emotion flickering therein. Sympathy? Bitterness? He held her stare several long moments more before he jerked his gaze away to stare at the fire. There was an uneasiness, a strain in his arrogant posture, as if he hadn't yet accustomed himself to civilian life or his new station. "A rather rash assessment based on our, what, ten minutes acquaintance? What would a mere provincial governess know of evil?"

"Evil exists wherever one person uses a disparity of power to harm another. Unfortunately one can find it anywhere."

A triumph born of knowledge flared in that intense gaze. Too late, she realized she'd said too much. "And is it this 'disparity of power' that prompts you to assist those creating unrest across the country?"

How many others would she bring down with her folly? Alec? Wetherel? Her sister? "Are we back to your wild accusations?"

"You haven't yet answered my question."

"I could say the same of you."

"But surely as the aggrieved party—we are in my bed-chamber, after all—I have the right to be satisfied first?"

Not that it much mattered what he believed. She was powerless to escape, to stop him, to change his mind. The mere accusation of treason by one of his rank would lead her to the same conclusion as a confession—a quick execution. And even if she found someone to believe her denials, what could she expect but a slower track to the same end? No respectable woman would hire her as a governess now. Without her position in Sotherton's household, her usefulness to Alec's... friends would come to an end along with her ability to sell information.

And as Lord Chambelston had so inelegantly reminded her, she didn't possess the physical or financial attributes necessary to enter into a liaison—licit or illicit—with a man. "So then, my lord, it seems we are at an impasse."

"Come, Miss Vance. Surely you don't mean to keep us at this impasse, as you say, all night."

Why not, when it was plain she would get no sleep anyway? Besides, here a fire danced merrily on the hearth. She doubted she'd feel so warm once he'd dumped her unceremoniously on the street on such a cold winter's night.

Tense moments of interminable silence ticked by as Julian waited. And waited. Alas, wintertime travel, compounded with the stresses of the past month, had left him too exhausted to appreciate the intriguing notion of being stuck in his chamber with a woman—a woman whose life he now held in his hands.

And she knew it also, as evinced by her continuing silence.

He released a dramatic sigh. "Very well, then." He reached behind him and wrapped his fingers around the doorknob.

"Wait!"

He paused, admiring her composure. Despite the tension

coiling through the room like whorls of smoke, she maintained her regal carriage. No fidgeting or fluttering of hands marred her apparent serenity. Only the faintest tightening of her jaw suggested disquiet. "Yes?"

"Where are you going?"

"Why, Miss Vance, what choice have I but to confer with my esteemed brother-in-law, the undersecretary himself? Unless you can give me a reason why I shouldn't."

"What do you want from me?" Did desperation append a squeak to her otherwise unruffled alto?

He released the knob and folded his arms across his chest again. "Let's start with a confession. Why are you in my chamber?"

Resignation softened her cheeks, and yet her gaze met his, direct and unashamed. "Very well. Yes, I entered your chamber seeking information."

"Information about...?"

"The government's response to the people's complaints."

Satisfaction whizzed through his veins. Here at last, someone who could get him the answers he sought—someone who *would*. Or else. "Tell me what you know about my father's death."

Brown brows arched softly over her wide hazel eyes. "Only what I read in your note."

"Ah, yes. My note. I'll take it, if you please."

She crouched down to the floor, her skirts billowing out around her, retrieved the missive and rose gracefully to her feet.

He held out his hand, refusing to budge from his defense of the doorway and forcing her to sidle closer. The subtle scent of lavender pulled at his senses as his fist locked around the parchment. "Thank you. Now the rest, if you please."

"My lord?"

"I want to know how—and especially to whom—you've been transferring your...discoveries."

"I—I don't know." She retreated farther into the room—farther from him.

Warning bells clanged in his head. Despite the still-proud tilt of her chin, her gaze focused once again on a spot above his head. So, she would yet lie. Sympathy for the cause? Or did she protect someone, someone with a complaint about the government? She herself did not suffer unduly like most of the truly poor. "Oh, I think you know."

Another pause, another hesitation. Then she said, "I leave notes in the stable."

"And you haven't so much as an idea who retrieves them?"

"Whenever I've returned the next day, I find my note gone and my fee in its place."

"Your fee." He lounged against the door, feigning a nonchalance he didn't feel. He could ask who recruited her to spy on Sotherton, but no doubt she would lie again. Why would someone pay for details about the government's responses? The truly desperate had no money for food, let alone espionage. Julian sensed a sinister hand behind her involvement. "So you would sell your country for a few pounds sterling?"

Stillness settled over her shoulders, like a shroud cast over the room. She stared into the flames of the fire, offering him a view of her face in profile. "A French shell destroyed my idealism a decade ago."

Her father? Brother? Long-dead fiancé? Another burst of sympathy lanced through his lingering anger, but he thrust it away with reminders that no matter her reasons, she was a traitor to her country and the family who employed her. He shifted away from the door. "I ride at first light. Come to the stable at half past eight."

"Ride?"

"We can't continue to meet this way, Miss Vance." He

swept an arm toward the room in a grand gesture. "My sister won't allow it, and you'll be of no use to me unemployed."

"My lord, as you yourself have remarked, I am a mere governess. I haven't sat a horse since…"

"A decade ago?" He echoed her subdued words of a moment ago. "I'm sure the groom can find you a suitably passive mount."

"Nor have I the proper attire."

"This is not an occasion to display the latest fashions, Miss Vance—nor is this a request. Unless you wish to conduct further conversation in my bedchamber tonight or before Lord Sotherton on the morrow, I suggest you meet me at the stable. You seem the resourceful type. Use your ingenuity."

"But what are you going to do about—"

"I'll inform you of my decision then." He yanked open the door and waved her into the hallway. "Good night, Miss Vance. And pleasant dreams."

The next morning, Julian was stroking the nose of Sotherton's favorite bay stallion when Miss Vance shuffled into the stable. He checked his watch—precisely twenty-six minutes past the hour. Punctual, as he would have expected. A dark velvet hat, its nap displaying its age, shadowed her face, and her drab coat hung loosely on her frame, as if this winter of scarcity affected even her.

In the dawn of a new day he pushed aside those feelings of connection and concentrated on his anger and indignation. "Good morning, Miss Vance. On time, I see."

"As you commanded." She nodded but refused to meet his gaze.

Bothered by a guilty conscience? He scoffed at the notion. In his experience, traitors didn't feel such regrets, not even when they were a trusted friend and colleague. But this time would be different. This time he would not be the victim. This time he would use her as surely as she'd sought to use him.

"I trust you rested well, my lord?"

"Not particularly."

She flinched, as if she interpreted his denial as being about her, her situation.

It wasn't. He'd gone to sleep plotting ways to discover the truth from her and awoken in a cold sweat, dreaming of Trafalgar. He hadn't relived that particular nightmare in many a year. Even now, a decade and more beyond that fateful day and in a very English stable, the memory, the very name—Trafalgar—brought back the horror. The stench of smoke. The screams of fallen men. The rivers of blood that slicked the deck and coated his breeches, his hands, even his tongue.

"I'm sorry you suffered such a restless night." Miss Vance's voice called him back to the present, from the embarrassing reactions that haunted him so many years later. "Perhaps your mind agrees with mine this outing is a mistake."

"It is true the thought of finding commonality with you would give me nightmares."

Brown brows rose above the eyes that at last focused on him—eyes wreathed by dark circles, and yet not muted by remorse so much as glimmering with ill-suppressed challenge. An answering warmth flared through him.

"My lord, are you certain you want this old mare?" The groom appeared at that moment with the oldest, most lethargic nag in three counties.

Julian regathered his dignity. "Ask Miss Vance."

The man caught sight of Julian's companion and stumbled. The ancient mare didn't blink at the momentary tightening of her reins while the groom regained his footing, if not his composure. An interesting response. Surprise to see the governess ride? Or more? After all, the lady had claimed to leave her ill-gotten information in the stable—which made everyone from the coachman to the greenest stable boy a possible accomplice.

Julian glanced her direction again, noting the skepticism cooling the subdued greens and browns of her eyes, so at variance with the hard edges of her attitude. "What think you, Miss Vance? I'm sure even your impaired skills will prove sufficient to handle this animal, but perhaps you would prefer a mount with more, er, life?"

"The poor thing does appear in danger of imminent demise, but I believe it will be fine for a *short* ride." Miss Vance's shoulders stiffened as she tugged the reins from the groom and stalked outside, her fine fit of pique somewhat impaired by the nag's ungainly plodding. The groom hurried after them, but when he paused to assist Miss Vance onto the horse, Julian stepped between them and thrust the stallion's reins in the man's hands.

"Hold these, please, while I assist Miss Vance." He moved closer, the faintest whiff of lavender once again teasing his senses as she planted her foot in his cupped hands. For a woman of her height she felt unexpectedly light, and she mounted with surprising grace—especially for one who'd claimed so long a dearth—onto the nag's swayed back. As she hooked her leg over the sidesaddle, her movements exposed a bit of boot-clad ankle to his curious gaze.

"We'll start slowly," he said as she arranged her skirts.

"I doubt we'll have much choice on the matter." She threaded the reins around her fingers, drawing his attention to her carefully mended gloves.

Julian swung up on his mount, and the groom disappeared into the warm stable. "Take heart, if she expires before we complete our business, Sotherton's prize bay can carry us both back."

Her wary eyes scrutinized his mount as the spirited animal pawed the snowy ground, impatient to be free. "Should such a tragic event befall us, I'll walk."

"Or run away?" Did she balk at such an energetic horse, or at sharing the saddle with *him?* A rusty chuckle escaped his throat.

She prodded the placid animal into a reluctant walk, and Julian followed.

Last night's storm had passed, leaving a fresh layer of snow blanketing the world. They traveled side by side, the stillness of the winter morning broken only by the muffled clomp of hooves. The barren fields around him, the gentle rocking beneath him, and the rush of fresh air against him pulled him back in time, as if he once more trod the decks of his ship.

As if he once more knew what was expected of him, and how to fulfill those obligations.

The bay tossed its head and strained against the reins, drawing Julian's attention back to the ride. "Now be truthful with me, Miss Vance. I know you would rather spend such a fine morning enjoying your freedom here than locked in your schoolroom." He swept his arm in the direction of the village below. The sun shimmered on the snow-clad roofs like candlelight on the finest silk.

"It seems you are determined to know all my secrets, my lord."

"The important ones, to be sure."

"So then, what did you decide?"

He shifted to better see her face. A gust of winter stirred the ribbons of her humble bonnet and tossed them against her cheeks. "I've decided you will continue your criminal activities."

Her brows drew together. "My lord?"

"As directed by me. I'll provide you with the information, and you will pass it along to your contacts."

"You want me to betray those who hired me?"

"I thought your services were for sale, Miss Vance. Surely your life is fitting compensation for what I ask of you?"

She fidgeted with the reins, her gaze level. Weighing him. "What would you have me do?"

"That wasn't so difficult, was it? You will start by informing your contact Lord Chambelston has called upon Sotherton."

"I, ah, already have. Yesterday afternoon."

"You are nothing if not efficient. I should have expected nothing less, I suppose. Did you include any other details I should know about?"

"Only that you are newly come into your title, it would seem."

"Indeed, quite recently." And perhaps not naturally. But then she knew that from his anonymous note. A new thought struck him. If his father's death were indeed the result of the radicals, she could have gleaned nothing from the note their leadership didn't already know. Was she as she said, only a governess earning a bit of coin and not well connected to the radicals? Or was his anonymous source sending him spurious information? To what end?

Compassion shimmered in the hazel gaze that met his. "I'm sorry for your loss, my lord."

"Thank you." The now-familiar connection once again snapped between them. "There is a Vance family baronetcy not far from here, I believe. A relative of yours?"

"Not close."

"Ah." Not close enough to support a dowerless female for the rest of her life. "So who is your father?"

"Was. I lost my parents some years back. My father was only the minor rector of a small parish."

Her words hung in the air, an awkward reminder of the stark differences between them. He wanted to despise her for the traitor she was, and yet, unwilling sympathy welled in him. He might be trapped by his responsibilities, but he was bound by gilded chains. No doubt Miss Vance would gladly trade her tenuous position for his comfortable prison.

He was of a mind to mention a man of the cloth might not appreciate his daughter's activities, but thoughts of his own father held back the words. The former Earl of Chambelston had been a man of steadfast faith while Julian was too cynical to place his trust in an unseen God.

"Is there anything else you require of me?"

He stared across the fields where a few skinny cattle huddled together for warmth. "Inform your contact I'm here to consult with Sotherton about the recent Spa Fields riots and will remain here for the while." That would give them time to set in motion any plots they might be hatching.

"Why would you trust me to do as you ask? I may betray you instead."

She was right, of course. He'd never know her true loyalties—if she had any. What if another offered more gold for her…special assistance? Unfortunately he had no skill at subterfuge. He needed his brother Kit. Kit had survived ten years of war playing a far more dangerous game than Miss Vance now dabbled in. "You're an intelligent woman—"

"Evidently not, or I wouldn't be here with you."

Another chuckle escaped Julian's throat, his second of the morning. How surprising and unexpected coming so soon after his father's death. "You were clever enough to get away with your duplicity until now. Surely you are smart enough to recognize your limitations and realize a woman in your position has no other options."

"Thank you for that reminder of my indigence."

"I mean only the truth, not an insult. You have made your own way in life." Unlike the many spoiled misses who'd jumped into his path ever since his older brother's death had propelled him from second son to an earl's heir.

"Unfortunately we can't all be born to wealth and privilege."

"You are quite the republican. And rather outspoken for a mere governess."

"You already know the worst about me. Will protestations of my loyalty change your mind?"

The bay stomped impatiently, forcing Julian's attention back to the restless horse. He'd made a mistake taking such a spirited animal on such a sedate outing. He studied Miss Vance from under his hat, noting her precise posture and the ease with which she propelled the recalcitrant nag to continue their walk. Perhaps next time he should see her better mounted and not deny himself—or Sotherton's bay—the exercise they both craved. "I wasn't always an earl, you know. I once worked for my sustenance the same as you."

"In a considerably more lucrative profession."

"And more dangerous."

She tilted her head and considered him. A few wisps of her hair caught on the breeze and whispered against her face. "Yes, you are correct. And undoubtedly you began your labors even younger than I." Soft respect smoothed the sharp edges off her voice and tugged his mind back to her assertion a French shell had ended her hopes and dreams. How often had he feared the same would happen to him?

"I was thirteen. And while life on a ship is more dangerous, it isn't necessarily more difficult." The thought of perpetual servitude to his sister was nearly as daunting as a French ship-of-the-line on the horizon. "My family connections, my education and my gender offered me options unavailable to you. While I don't approve of your treasonous behavior, I do admire your independence."

Surprise and suspicion flickered in her eyes. "Thank you. But my vocation wasn't by choice. I'd have happily lived on some inheritance from long forgotten forebears who'd stolen the wealth and labor of the local peasants."

"Are you casting aspersions on my ancestors?"

"I don't know you well enough to draw any conclusions. If you see yourself in my comment, perhaps it is your conscience speaking to you."

"Very conveniently—if not convincingly—deflected. And what would you have done with unlimited time and funds, Miss Vance, beyond what you needed for your life of leisure?"

She blinked. "Ah, I suppose…I'd use the excess to care for others. To help the needy." Vulnerability tightened on her cheeks. Did she think of someone in particular? Someone close to her who needed her ill-begotten gains?

"Very noble. And not so different from what you do here."

"Here? I teach Lady Teresa, who—as you may have noticed—does not go hungry or cold this winter."

"There are needs beyond the physical. It has not escaped my notice that my niece does not enjoy an intimate relationship with her mother."

"Difficult dinner last night?"

"I don't know who is worse, Elizabeth or her mother-in-law." How had his sister transformed into a woman so different from warm and loving Maman? If her own daughter suffered from Elizabeth's hard and haughty ways, how much more so her staff? A man less personally involved in the recent unrest could almost find a justification for Miss Vance's actions. Much as Julian hated disloyalty, he'd long ago learned honor traveled both directions—only those officers who respected their men earned the esteem and allegiance of those under them.

"If we are finished here, my lord, I really must return to my duties. That self-sufficiency you profess to admire comes at the cost of my freedom."

He steered his mount back toward Rowan Abbey. "Forgive me. I did not intend to see you in trouble."

Golden glints sparked in the depths of her eyes. "More trouble, you mean?"

"Just so."

With the promise of the stable before it, Miss Vance's nag increased its speed. Julian curbed the bay's eagerness, letting his companion take the lead for a moment. Despite her old coat, he admired the graceful curve of her spine as she adjusted to the horse's ungainly movements.

One could easily imagine Miss Vance's reaction under fire—calm, intelligent, rational. More so than many officers with whom he'd served. She'd make a formidable opponent and an even more impressive ally, if only he could be assured of her loyalty. Or at a minimum, her cooperation.

As he stared at a patch on her elbow, an idea niggled. A means for purchasing her allegiance. He urged the bay forward until he drew beside her.

Her glance slid askance his direction. "My lord? Was there something you wished to add?"

"Yes. I offer you not only a chance to retain your freedom, but financial remuneration, as well. Assist me, and I'll see you paid double for your efforts."

"You don't know my fee."

"A respectable amount, I should imagine, given your position and the risks you take."

She nodded her concession. "A goodly offer, my lord."

"But not kindly made." His fists clenched around the reins as new doubts about her character and cooperation assailed him. "Cross me, and I'll see you regret that decision for the rest of your life—however short that may be."

The soft threat whirled around Leah's lungs like a cold wind, squeezing the breath from her body. With Lord Chambelston's promised funds, she could support Phoebe for many a month. But would she condemn Alec?

Dear, faithful Alec, who'd been such a blessing these past two years. He'd given all he had for others—her, Phoebe, the men who'd served under him. Whatever she did, she must deflect suspicion from her cousin.

As they neared the stable and the promise of a meal, the old nag charged ahead with something approaching a trot. Leah's teeth still rattled, even after Wetherel grabbed the harness and drew the mare to a halt.

Wetherel. Another person to protect.

She started to dismount as Lord Chambelston moved closer. Awareness flooded through her even before he clasped her around the waist and drew her off the nag. Despite the many layers of winter protection—her gown and coat, his gloves—heat radiated from his touch, warming her more than any fire. She slid from the saddle, determined to put enough distance between them so the intriguing—and frightening—combination of soap and leather no longer teased her senses.

As soon as her feet met the ground, she jerked away, earning a revival of that mocking smile for her efforts.

"Afraid, Miss Vance?"

When she stood so close to a man—other than her cousin—for the first time in three long years? When his threats hung over her head like a noose? When she faced a choice between her sister and her cousin? She waited until Wetherel led the animals away. "I'm no fool."

"No, you aren't. Impulsive, greedy and perhaps even a bit idealistic, despite your claims to the contrary. But no fool." He was still far too close, the brilliant blue of his eyes kindling not with anger but with…interest?

In spite of the nausea churning in her belly, she fought the urge to retreat, to show weakness or fear. "If we are finished,

my lord?" She lifted a brow in the same patrician manner he
was wont to do.

He slid her arm through his crooked elbow, his broad chest
bumping her shoulder, and nudged her toward the manor. "I'm
certain my sister's cook will have a fair repast awaiting my
return. Won't you break your fast with me?"

"Thank you, but I haven't much appetite."

"It is a rare person who foregoes food this winter." He adjusted his long gait to her shorter steps. "Surely your strength
is greatly depleted from your dual ordeal of meeting me and
riding a horse. Please, I insist."

"One missed meal won't sap my strength. But one missed
day of instruction will surely end my position here. As you
said, I will be of no use to you unemployed."

"Very well, Miss Vance. Flee to your schoolroom." Lord
Chambelston's grip tightened around her arm and his eyes
chilled to match the cold blue sky. "But remember, deal fairly
with me and I'll see you rewarded beyond your imaginings.
Deal falsely with me, and I'll see you suffer more than my
father did during his last days."

Chapter Three

A cold draft skated through the village lending library. Leah smiled as Alec pulled the door closed and removed his hat. Her cousin's impatient glance swept the room, softening only when it encountered her. He sidled closer, his green eyes alight with a humor unperturbed even by the current difficulties.

"Milton?" He gestured to the book in her hands. "I thought surely you'd be reading Wollstonecraft, at the least. Or maybe Paine or Locke."

"Not in public." Not if she wanted to maintain her position in Lady Sotherton's household.

"Someday we will be rich enough you can scandalize the harpy with impunity."

She closed the volume of poetry and replaced it on the shelf. "Hush. For now, we are poor enough we can't afford to scandalize anyone." Most especially not her arrogant employer.

He proffered his arm. "Come. Let us not waste such a beautiful day."

Dread knotted her stomach as Leah placed her hand on the coat that had once been part of Alec's army uniform. Countless campaigns had frayed the hems and worn the wool to a dull shine. She adjusted her steps to Alec's limp and stepped out into the cold. The sun glinted on the mahogany highlights in his chestnut hair before he covered it with his well-worn beaver.

"My apologies for my tardiness."

"The wait afforded me the opportunity reacquaint myself with Milton." Her father would have approved of her choice—if not her motivation.

Alec's quicksilver grin flashed across his face, then his lips tightened into a sober line as he escorted her along the snow-covered street. "New developments delayed me."

Leah waited, but he gave no more details. It had ever been thus on their regular Wednesday afternoon meetings. Alec plied her for details while disclosing as little as possible about his activities. She'd never appreciated his caution—gained during ten long years of war—as much as she did this moment. At least she wouldn't face the dilemma of choosing between Lord Chambelston's gold and her cousin's life.

He leaned closer until his breath stirred the hair at her temples. "Rather shocking the new Lord Chambelston should come to see Sotherton."

"Yes, the rumors among the servants suggest an estrangement of nearly twenty years duration between the two sides of the family." The rhythmic ring of the blacksmith's hammer echoed off the stone walls of nearby cottages. Where did her loyalties lie? She couldn't betray her kin—nor could she reveal too much. Not if she hoped to collect Chambelston's payment. Payment. Who, in this winter of deprivation, compensated her for her reports? And why might those people wish to see an earl dead? A chill owing nothing to the wind slid along her spine. "Alec, have you considered some elements of your group may not have altruistic motivations for driving the unrest?"

"You mean a radical overthrow of the monarchy? It's not

going to happen. We only want the government's cooperation in doing more to provide for the people. No one wants
the kind of chaos and destruction France suffered."

Sure, France lay in ruins now, but only because of Napoleon's vaulting ambition to conquer the world. What if the
little despot had only sought to rule France, rather than dom-
inate the whole of Europe? Who would have stopped him?
"Then why do you need the details of Sotherton's business?
Of what use are they?"

"We want to know if the government will cooperate with
our requests or if the officials are taking steps to block our
petitions."

They strolled past St. John's stained-glass windows. Beyond the parish gate a collection of old and new gravestones
denoted the final resting place for centuries of village life.
Childhood memories assailed her. Once she'd found peace
in her father's church.

The sun hung low in the winter sky—the afternoons were
short this time of year—and gray clouds gathered on the
western horizon. Leah's steps slowed, her too-short minutes
of freedom at an end. "I need to return." She released her
cousin's arm. If Lord Chambelston should hear of her relationship with Alec... She glanced over her shoulder toward
the village green and the happily empty whipping post. Perhaps the earl would be kind enough to see them assigned to
side-by-side gallows.

Alec slipped a few coins into her hand. "I fear for you,
Leah. If only I could do more, you wouldn't have to take
such risks."

Leah dropped the money into her reticule where the silver made a halfhearted chink against the rest of her meager
stash. "We appreciate all you do." Or, at least, Leah did and
Phoebe would—if she understood. But Phoebe would never

understand, never respond, never again so much as recognize her own family.

"It's little enough."

"It's more than you'll ever know—and most unfair to you to assume this burden. If my father had better managed his finances…" Resentment swelled in her throat that her father had been so concerned with heavenly matters, he had neglected his responsibilities on earth. "He failed in his obligations, not you."

"Another man's shortcomings don't excuse mine."

"Nor do they compel you to atone for the rest of your life for his mistakes."

"Dear Leah." Alec reached for her hand again, but Leah retreated a step. "You've carried this burden alone for far too long."

His words called to mind Chambelston's professed admiration for her independence. How strange the sensation felt— unless he only claimed so to manipulate her?

Alec settled a gloved hand on her shoulder and drew her back to the present. "We could marry."

"We—what?" She halted and stared at her cousin, unable to construct a complete sentence.

"I see my proposal renders you silent. I said we could marry."

Marry? *Alec?* "But we're family."

"The law allows for marriage between cousins."

She smiled to ease the sting of her rejection as she slipped away from his touch. "Wisdom forbids the marriage of *these* cousins. Alec, you are like a brother to me."

"And you were very fond of your brother, as I recall."

She studied his countenance but saw no eagerness, only the same determination that drove him to assist with Phoebe's expenses and the same familial affection she felt for him. "Be serious. How would we survive? We can barely support our-

selves even now. Besides you might meet someone and I—"
Warmth invaded her face. How silly that a woman of her age
and station would wish for a quiver of the anticipation she felt
whenever she was with… Once she'd thought a man loved
her. And perhaps he had, at least until he'd learned Leah came
encumbered with a sister confined to an asylum. She glanced
at the stone church, again feeling the pain of rejection.

"I am being serious. At least wed, you would be safe." Dear
Alec, always trying to protect others. "I fear for you, Leah.
A defenseless woman, your livelihood tied to the whims of
that dragon and your very person at the mercy of any males
in the household."

Fortunately Alec didn't know the worst, lest his vola-
tile, half-Scots temper lead him into trouble. More trouble
than Leah even. "But I need my income—both of them—for
Phoebe. I fear for her. If something should happen to me—"

"Now my proposal renders you morbid. I liked it better
when you were mute." His smile flickered, then disappeared
behind a somber examination of the darkening sky. "You
know I'll ensure Phoebe gets the care she needs, no matter
what. Now it is time for you to return to the dragon's lair. I
fear we may see more snow tonight."

"Will you come to the asylum Sunday?"

"If at all possible."

With a final wave she pointed her feet toward Rowan
Abbey and a return to her responsibilities. By the time she
reached the door, the cold had numbed her nose and toes,
and the churning gray clouds had nearly swallowed the last
of the day.

"Ah, Miss Vance." Molly appeared as Leah unhooked her
scarf from her neck. "I feared you wouldn't return in time."

"In time?" Why did Leah's every encounter with Molly
seem to coincide with her…second career?

"Lady Sotherton requests you join the family for dinner."

An invitation Leah couldn't refuse, of course. Not even on her afternoon off. "I presume Lady Sotherton has guests?" Why else would she demand the governess's presence for dinner but to even the numbers?

"Viscount Killiane and his brother brought a friend."

The cold in Leah's extremities radiated upward and circled around her heart, and the blood drained from her face, leaving her light-headed and weak. "Lord Killiane's brother is here? Now?"

"Aye. Mr. Fleming."

Dinner. With Reginald Fleming.

The man who had attacked her in this very house three years earlier.

Julian paced before the salon's fire as he waited for dinner. The blaze highlighted tapestries cloaking the walls, their once-bold colors of ancient Sotherton triumphs now muted with age. One such scene shivered, bringing the knight and charger momentarily to life as they danced to a winter draft.

"Another cold night." As if to punctuate Sotherton's words, a gust of wind whistled along the glass. "You know my nephew Killiane and his friend Mr. Warren, Chambelston?"

Julian nodded to both gentlemen. "I believe we've met at my club." Briefly.

"My sister married an Irish title, but I have great hopes for my nephew's career in politics," Sotherton said.

The young lord ambled closer to Julian, drink in hand. Despite Killiane's age—four or even five years below Julian's—the viscount schooled his face in the careful ennui of the London set. "Sorry to hear of your loss, Chambelston."

Julian answered with a polite nod. "How is the situation in Ireland this winter?"

Killiane's lips flattened. "Worse than England, I fear."

"I'm sorry to hear it."

"We hope for some promising news in the future." Killiane withdrew a snuffbox from his coat. "I shall be traveling to London for the opening of Parliament's new session. I assume you will be taking your father's seat?"

"Ah, yes. Parliament." Another duty Julian could scarcely avoid. "Perhaps we shall encounter each other again there."

"A necessary obligation, Chambelston." Sotherton chuckled. "But perhaps you will grow to enjoy politics the way Niall and I do."

Or perhaps not. Julian hadn't Sotherton's...enthusiasm for power. "War is so much more straightforward. I prefer enemies who shoot me in the face to friends who stab me in the back."

The quip produced an outright guffaw from Sotherton and even earned a smirk from Killiane.

"Will this interminable winter never end?" The Dowager Countess Sotherton marched into the room, her cane tapping against the parquet floor that framed the plush blue rug. The heavy odor of her perfume reached Julian before she did. "A drink, Benedict. And one for Miss Godwin also."

"Just so, Mama." Sotherton rose from his chair and moved toward the sideboard.

"Good evening, Niall." She helped herself to Sotherton's fireside chair. Her companion followed glumly in her wake, then halted, sentinel-like next to her mistress.

"Grandmother." Killiane leaned closer and offered the dowager a peck on her cheek.

"You look well." She patted his arm, then peered at Julian as if she were inspecting her linens for flaws. "Good evening, Chambelston. For a minute, I thought you were your father. You really do have the look of him, you know."

"Thank you, my lady." Julian accepted her words as a compliment, whether meant as such or not.

"Unlike some in this household, I was sorry to hear of his

demise." Her watery blue eyes focused on her grandson's friend. "Will you be staying long, Mr. Warren?"

"Only until Friday, my lady." He offered her a bow, then returned to his silence.

"Here you are, ladies." Sotherton approached the two women with goblets.

The dowager sniffed her appreciation as she accepted her due. Though of an age with Julian's mother, the woman's years sat heavily on her face in wrinkles and frowns and discontent. Despite some three decades of widowhood, she yet wore unrelieved black that contrasted harshly with her pasty skin and rouged cheeks. Her fierce countenance found an echo in the sour features of the companion who hovered behind. A niggling of sympathy fluttered through Julian for his sister Elizabeth's lot here. Perhaps surrounded by such disagreeable dispositions, he would have developed a like aversion to familial relationships.

A feminine giggle echoed from the hallway. The dowager's frown lines deepened as Lady Teresa and her governess slipped into the room.

"Ah, Teresa." Sotherton ignored his mother's grumblings of annoyance. "Chambelston, you know my daughter. Allow me to present her governess, Miss Vance."

"Miss Vance." Anger and awareness warred within him as he drank in her gleaming tresses, her perfect posture, her subtle—and now familiar—scent of lavender. The rich chocolate of her dress complemented the variegated browns and greens of her eyes while an ivory shawl found a counterpart in the creamy glow of her cheeks.

"My lord. I'm delighted to make your acquaintance." Cynical amusement flickered in the gaze that met his before she dipped her head and dropped into a deferential curtsey, as if they were strangers only newly met.

"Miss Vance." Killiane edged between Julian and the governess and offered her a bow. The bored indifference fell away, replaced by genuine interest and…admiration? "It's been too long since I last saw you."

"Lord Killiane." Surprise and pleasure softened her lips into a smile that revealed an intriguing dimple on her right cheek. "How pleasant to meet you again."

Irrational jealousy fed Julian's frustration. At her. At Killiane.

A feminine hand tapped against his sleeve. "I fear the storm worsens. We may be blessed with your company until spring, Lord Chambelston." Lady Teresa's words drew Julian's stare from her governess—and that ever-present, ever-treacherous bond he felt. His niece's black hair gleamed with fiery red sparks in the candlelight, and mischief danced in her violet-blue eyes. Bands of painful memory constricted around Julian's heart as he looked into her face, so like that of his sister of twenty years ago, before disillusionment had hardened her heart and attitudes and features.

"Teresa is anxious for spring," Sotherton explained to Julian with an indulgent smile. "This year, she travels to London for her presentation to the queen."

"And eligible young men, of course." The dowager sniffed again. "A lot of expensive nonsense, if you ask me. In my day a young lady's father chose a suitable match for her, and that was the end of it."

An easier option than the elaborate rites of the aristocracy's Marriage Mart—which were as foreign to Julian as the deserts of Araby. An impecunious younger son, he'd left home, school and family behind for the navy at the tender age of thirteen and never learned to navigate the subtleties of polite society. Or women.

Senses drawn once again to Miss Vance, Julian watched as she sidled away from the family and found a chair alone by the window. Careful indifference almost—but not quite—

masked an aura of loneliness as she drew her shawl more tightly around her shoulders.

"Ah, Elizabeth. There you are." Sotherton left Teresa to greet his wife as she joined them in the drawing room.

Elizabeth's grimly pursed lips echoed the dowager's dourness more than Maman's serenity, as if such expressions were contagious.

Perhaps they were. Already tension tightened along Julian's jaw.

His sister's gaze brushed past him without acknowledgment before alighting on her daughter. "Don't slouch, Teresa."

Insecurity wavered in Teresa's violet-blue eyes as she whipped her shoulders to attention like a new recruit. The wind rattled against the window, memories carrying Julian back to his first days as a midshipman, to the uncertainty and anxiety and loneliness of an ignorant boy trying to please a demanding captain.

He glanced over his shoulder in time to see Miss Vance's jaw tighten. Julian's reluctant respect for her rose.

"Where's Reginald?" Elizabeth's querulous tones set his teeth on edge.

"I'm here, aunt!"

Miss Vance flinched, as if trying to make herself smaller inside her shawl.

"Finally." The dowager's cane thumped against the floor as she rose from her chair. She tottered for a moment, then clasped her son by the elbow.

"Late as usual, Reggie." Disgust darkened Killiane's eyes as a young man with black curls and an apologetic grin dashed into the room.

Elizabeth's mouth flattened into a narrow white line as her glance slid to Julian. As the highest ranking gentleman in the room, etiquette required she take his arm and allow him to escort her to the dining room. Mischief bubbled up in him and he returned her frown with a knowing smirk. Her antipathy tonight couldn't hurt him more than her twenty years of silence.

With a lift of her chin she sailed to Killiane's side. Given the disdain still stiffening the viscount's lips, the two could share a charming evening of mutual misery.

Julian strolled toward his niece. "Lady Teresa?"

"Yes, my lord?"

"'My lord' is so formal, considering our relationship." Not to mention the specters the title brought to mind. "I would welcome being your uncle in truth as well as in name."

"I should like that. Uncle."

"I realize I am not exactly an eligible young man, but may I escort you to…" His words died away as he followed the line of Killiane's narrow-eyed stare to Miss Vance.

Reginald Fleming waited with proffered elbow and challenging stare to usher the governess to the dining room. Revulsion and…fear?…churned in her eyes, but she lifted her chin and pasted an impassive expression on her face.

"Uncle?" queried Teresa.

"Ah…" He yanked his attention from Miss Vance to Teresa. "Yes, dinner. My apologies."

A sly grin tweaked one corner of his niece's mouth and washed the lingering shadows from her eyes as she tugged on Julian's arm. Not toward the dining room but in the opposite direction. Toward her governess. "Perhaps you can be…the mysterious older gentleman. Uncle, do you know my cousin Reggie Fleming?"

"My lord. Rather cold here, isn't it?" Fleming bowed with a flourish. His overly bright eyes, faint slur and potent breath bespoke a fondness for liquid warmth. "What brings you to Northamptonshire this winter?"

"Business."

Teresa released Julian's arm and positioned herself between her cousin and Miss Vance. "You made a grand entrance, Reggie."

"I arrived late just to annoy Niall." *Or to swallow a few last drops of brandy,* Julian thought.

"A shame you don't put your efforts to more constructive purposes." Teresa grabbed his arm and led him in the direction of her mother. "Imagine what you could accomplish."

"And destroy my reputation with respectability?"

Their playful banter faded as they moved away, leaving Julian alone with Miss Vance. At least tonight he could be assured she wouldn't search his belongings while he dined.

A frown drew down the corners of her mouth as she stared after her charge.

"Come now, Miss Vance." He extended his arm. "You seemed to enjoy my company on our previous…encounters. Surely a dinner doesn't warrant such a fierce scowl."

"I seem to remember our previous…encounters somewhat differently." She rose from her seat and reached for him, the shawl slipping off her shoulder.

He lifted a lacy edge and slid it back in place. "Your handiwork?"

"My mother's." She rested her palm on his arm, her slender, well-formed fingers curling around his sleeve. The chill in her hand permeated the fabric and raised prickles of awareness on his skin.

Together they approached the dining room. Chairs ringed a long table shimmering with crystal and silver. Without awaiting his sister's instructions, Julian led Miss Vance to an empty seat and held it for her. Her back brushed against his hand as she sat, the wool warm against his skin. Then he claimed the chair beside her for himself. Right next to his sister.

"With your permission, Lizzie?"

"If you insist, Chambelston." She used his title, not his name.

"Of course. Why would I wish to forego your gracious company?"

"So you can conclude your business with Benedict and be on your way." And here he'd thought the presence of others would minimize the snide remarks he would have to endure.

"No doubt your husband anticipates many more such evenings of unpleasantness, but I thought I should reserve this one for myself."

Elizabeth's chin rose again. "I believe father got his just reward when he ended up with you as his heir."

"Your sentiments no longer surprise me." Nor did they particularly concern him—unless his father had shared them.

Wedged between Lord Chambelston and the detestable Reginald Fleming, Leah shifted on her seat and swallowed her discomfiture with a forkful of fish. Unfortunately both lodged in her throat, seemingly determined to destroy her dinner as surely as Lady Sotherton's sniping. For a woman so concerned with appearances, if not authenticity, she should realize the staff could overhear every taunt. Gossip would supplement the meal below stairs tonight as those servants present during her fit of pique shared the details with their colleagues.

Leah's father would have used the opportunity to point her to the appropriate axiom, perhaps one of Johnson's witticisms or that verse from Proverbs—the one about a dry morsel and quiet being better than a feast and strife. She grabbed a goblet and tried to wash the fish from her throat and the reminders of her parents' faith from her mind.

What would they think of her…supplementary income? Of her lies and disloyalty and downright treason? She stole a glance down the table where Lord Sotherton—her employer—engaged his mother in meaningless repartee that had the dowager chortling with amusement.

"My grandmother seems in rare good spirits tonight," Viscount Killiane said to the old woman's companion.

"I'm glad to see it. She had another episode this morning." Despite the bleak darkness of Miss Godwin's dress, her sable hair hinted of former beauty just as the gold locket at her neck suggested a former love. "I thought we should send for the doctor, but her ladyship quite insisted against such a course. I worry for her."

And for herself? As a mere companion, Miss Godwin's future depended on the dowager's longevity. The poor woman occupied a position even more precarious than Leah's. And doubtlessly more wearisome, given the dowager's normally difficult nature.

Mr. Fleming inclined his head toward Leah, a smirk curling on his mouth. A scar, only partially hidden by the ebony curls, bisected his forehead above his left brow. When she'd last seen the mark, it had been raw, red. Bleeding. "And how have you been, my dear Miss Vance?"

Her stomach knotted around her dinner. Memories of that horrible day engulfed her mind. The summer heat. The smothering helplessness. The poker she'd used to save herself from his assault. She shoved the images away, determined not to let him see her agitation. "My life seems to have taken a sudden turn for the worse again." In more ways than one.

His chuckle gusted wine-soaked breath across her face. "You are frowning mightily at your meal, Miss Vance. Does the fish displease you?"

"Truly, sir, I am not so ungrateful as to scorn any fare this winter, no matter how humble."

"Huzzah, Miss Vance!" From across the table, the dowager's exclamation pierced all other conversation and brought it to a halt. "In my day young people showed the proper respect for what was provided."

Awkward silence hung over the guests for several interminable moments while all attention focused on Leah. In no one's imagination was she a *young* person anymore. She stifled a sigh, waiting until the polite hum of tedious conversation resumed.

Truly, despite the quality and quantity of the fare, Leah much preferred the company when she ate her usual meal alone, without her disapproving employer, the leering Reginald Fleming or Lord Chambelston.

Infuriating. Irritating. Intriguing.

"Tell me, Miss Vance, how do you amuse yourself when you have a few minutes of your own?" The soft rumble of his masculine baritone snared Leah's awareness and drew her gaze.

"I'm much too serious to concern myself with entertainment, my lord."

"But surely you must have some…interests." Lord Chambelston's fine blue coat stretched across broad shoulders that alluded to his previous livelihood. The gilt buttons winked in the candlelight with a gleam that rivaled the sardonic glint in his eyes. "Do you sketch?"

"Badly."

"Perhaps then you embroider?"

"Dreadfully."

"Surely doing something poorly doesn't negate the enjoyment of the activity. I like to sing, but others tell me I should save my musical endeavors for those occasions when no one else is near enough to hear."

"A pity you aren't musical." Viscount Killiane leaned forward in his chair. "Miss Vance is an accomplished pianist."

"Unfortunately we tended to use the space on frigates for water and gunpowder, not large musical instruments, so I can't make the same claim." Chambelston tilted his head and studied Leah until heat crept into her cheeks. "I hope I have an opportunity to hear you sometime."

Lady Sotherton tapped Killiane's arm. "Miss Vance will be entertaining us after dinner."

Oh, would she? Leah's fingers tightened around the handle of her fork.

Lord Chambelston edged closer until she detected the subtle spice of his scent over the aromas of her dinner. "Don't let Elizabeth's presumption spoil the things you enjoy." His whisper stirred the hair by her cheek, and delicious warmth radiated from the shoulder that brushed hers.

Leah lifted her chin. "How do you know I enjoy the piano?"

"Because unlike sketching or stitching, you apparently do it well."

Julian sat with Killiane and his brother-in-law, and forced himself to listen to their deadly dull political discussion. Not an easy task when his attention kept drifting to his niece and the merriment she shared with Fleming and his friend. Befuddlement had replaced Warren's taciturn reserve as he anchored his stare on Lady Teresa. Under his untidy dark locks, his ears glowed redder every time she chanced to glance his direction.

Over where she embroidered with the dowager, Elizabeth had also noticed the young man's interest and aimed fierce frowns his direction. From the other corner of the room Miss Vance accompanied the dowager's companion—Miss Godwin, wasn't it?—on the piano on a suitably slow and proper air.

"Chambelston?" Killiane called Julian's attention back to their debate about taxes and appropriations. "What do you think?"

"Ah…I'm not sure this is the right time."

Another burst of laughter reverberated from Teresa's group. Elizabeth's lips narrowed to a concerned slit. She tucked her work away and rose from her chair with a swish of impatient skirts. "Teresa, why don't you and Miss Vance play the piece I heard you practicing earlier."

"But Mother, I've only recently begun…" The mirth seeped from Teresa's eyes and lips, and color rushed to her cheeks. "Yes, Mother."

She shuffled to the piano and exchanged nods with Miss Godwin, who ambled to a seat beside the dowager. Miss Vance slid over to make room and offered Teresa a taut smile of encouragement.

A few whispers passed between the women, one even eliciting a giggle from Teresa. Then they launched into the piece together. Even Julian's musically ignorant ears appreciated the difficulty of the work.

And recognized Teresa's difficulty with it. Each mistake brought another wince to her lips, another shadow to her eyes. Miss Vance adjusted her playing to the younger woman's skill. After one particularly egregious blunder, Fleming rose from his chair and approached the piano. He tapped Teresa on the shoulder and the music stopped.

"Excuse me, cousin. Mr. Warren had a question about a local site. Perhaps you could assist him while I take over for you here? I practiced this piece in the not too distant past. So complex. Took me weeks of work."

Relief eased over Teresa's face as she relinquished her place to him. Fleming inched closer to Miss Vance, who stared at the music, tension stiffening across her shawl-clad shoulders. With a curt nod, she began again. Fleming played with enthusiasm, if not exactly accuracy. He reached for a lower note on the keyboard, crowding close enough his arm brushed hers.

Miss Vance's fingers stumbled, the flub obvious enough to interrupt even Sotherton's lengthy discourse about the duties on spirits. She leaped from the seat, her face flushed with her agitation as she looked to Elizabeth. "As Mr. Fleming said, a difficult piece. I fear I've developed a headache, my lady. With your permission, I shall retire."

Elizabeth deigned to glance her way and even offered a nod. "Good night, Miss Vance."

Head bowed, Miss Vance scurried from the salon. But for her obvious distress, Julian might have feared she intended another examination of his belongings. No, her agitation seemed genuine, and he doubted he'd encounter her in his chamber this night. A pity, that—on both counts.

Despite her dishonest activities, he liked her. After nearly two years of pursuit by women whose only goal was to trap him—or any other man endowed with similar income and position—in matrimony, he'd developed an unexpected respect for those who'd made contingency plans.

He studied Fleming, who continued to entertain at the piano. What had happened between him and Miss Vance that caused her distress?

"Lord Chambelston?" The butler stepped into the room with a silver tray. "A message arrived for you."

Julian snatched the note, frowning as he recognized his housekeeper's handwriting. He broke the seal and perused her entreaty. Maman needed him. Now.

Once he'd been responsible for the lives of nigh a thousand men under his command. Why did he find it so difficult to balance the conflicting obligations of finding justice for his father with providing comfort for his mother?

He'd have to get his instructions to Miss Vance tonight. Perhaps Teresa would deliver a message later. She seemed wont to believe a budding romance existed between her uncle and governess.

"Bad news, Chambelston?" Elizabeth's brows arched above her icy blue eyes.

"I must leave at first light tomorrow."

"I hardly consider that bad news."

No, she'd be delighted to see him go. The sting of her rejection jabbed at his heart. "Then perhaps you will find the rest worthy of your disappointment. I'm afraid my business here is not yet concluded so I'll be returning as soon as possible."

Chapter Four

Julian paused on the sagging stoop of a modest house. Behind him the sounds of London—lumbering carts, barking dogs, bellowing men—echoed down narrow streets and between close-set buildings. A year ago his brother had asked him to visit here, but Julian had resisted. Today, he had no choice.

He knocked.

He wished he could do more—needed to do more—to answer the questions about his father's death, but he could hardly infiltrate the insurgent group himself. Not when his father had assisted the more rational members in their grievances. Unfortunately Julian knew—and trusted—few others capable of completing such an assignment.

For the first time since his father's death, he realized how very alone he was.

The door swung open to reveal an unremarkable man of middling years.

"Lawrence Harrison?"

The man's unexpectedly keen eyes narrowed, then the crow's feet at the corners deepened with his smile. "My lord, how good of you to call. Won't you come in?"

"Thank you." Julian stepped over the threshold and removed his hat. Inside the house the hubbub of countless children dwarfed the noises of London.

"Mr. DeChambelle!" One of the whirling forms paused long enough to attach himself to Julian's leg. The boy shoved a scrap of brown paper with a crudely inked star into Julian's hand. "See what I drew?"

"The children have been enacting the story of the wise men for Twelfth Night. Sorry, lad. This is Mr. DeChambelle's brother, Lord Chambelston." Harrison peeled the child away and gestured to the oldest boy. "Andrew, take them to your mother."

Julian passed the childish picture to Harrison while Andrew herded the hoard into the next room.

"I was sorry to hear about your father." Harrison tucked the paper in the pages of a chair-side Bible.

"Thank you. He will be much missed."

"I never met him, but your brother always spoke highly of him. How is Kit?"

"Well, the last we heard."

A fleeting smile touched Harrison's face. "He wrote us some months back to inform us he'd resumed his university studies."

As many younger sons, Kit had been destined for service in the church, but dropped out of his classes at Oxford to… join the war effort. "A great irony, that he will become a clergyman after all."

"But this time because he feels God calling him and not simply because it's expected of him." Harrison hesitated, his gaze searching Julian's face. "I presume you didn't seek me out to discuss your brother."

"Can we go somewhere and talk?"

Harrison grabbed his coat and hat from a peg and led Julian out the door. A year ago Harrison had had the thinning hair and thickening middle common to a man of his years.

But in this winter of want he slung his frayed coat over a much leaner frame. Julian's mind skipped back to the mass of children in the other room. Had Harrison forgone a few meals to see his children fed? To what lengths would a man go to protect those he loved?

And could the same be said for a woman?

His feet, and pulse, stuttered. Why did thoughts of Miss Vance creep unbidden into his mind again and again? Because he wanted to believe something altruistic—not selfish or malicious—motivated her actions?

Even now she should be planning how to accomplish his instructions. That is, if she were simply a naive governess sucked into a bad situation and not a traitor to her king and country.

The two men walked in silence along the road until they reached the river's edge. The stink of the Thames, only partially subdued by the winter wind, tickled Julian's senses with reminders of his past. Ships moored along her shore. The same gusts that whipped his cloak also tossed the ships' rigging and moaned amongst their furrowed sails. He lingered. Watched. Remembered.

Two decades ago when his thirteen-year-old self—a gangly youth all knees and elbows and anxiety—had boarded his first ship, he'd never guessed he would someday miss that life. The months of endless watches. The hours of boredom. The minutes of thrilling terror.

The camaraderie.

"My lord?" Harrison interrupted his reverie.

Julian drew himself back to the present, to the problems that seemed so incredibly complex compared to the simplicity of youth. "I'm seeking someone to work for me. I'll pay you, and well."

"Jobs that pay well at such a time as this are usually dangerous or illegal."

"Not illegal."

"How dangerous?"

"I'm not certain." Though someone had credited one murder to the radicals already. "And it requires travel."

"Dangerous and requires travel." Harrison's brown brow arched over amused blue eyes. "Sounds as if you're conscripting me for the navy."

"Not that much travel. Only as far as Northamptonshire. I don't know what you did for our government during the war—"

"And you never shall, my lord."

"And that is precisely why I wish to hire you. I believe you have some…special talents I lack." Julian's brother had shared precious few details of what he'd done during the war, only that he'd worked as a spy. With Lawrence Harrison. Imagining the oh-so-mundane Harrison in dangerous, clandestine work almost lifted Julian's lips into a smile. The man was perfect for the part—unremarkable in every way. "You know what happened at Spa Fields?"

"The riot?"

"I recently learned the incident may not have formed spontaneously."

Harrison blew a low whistle through his teeth. "You think there is a conspiracy to foment unrest? That is a serious charge."

"Aye, treason," Julian agreed quietly. A half-respectable tavern perched along the street. Julian waved at its facade. "I have a long day yet ahead of me. Let's continue this discussion over a meal. I'll pay, of course."

Harrison followed Julian into a dim interior that smelled of grease and hard labor. But the fire radiated warmth and the harsh wind didn't buffet them with cold. The day was yet young enough the taproom held few people. Once they'd settled themselves in a quiet corner, Julian retrieved the anonymous note from his pocket and slid it across the table.

Harrison pulled off his gloves and examined the page. His brows drew together as he perused the words. "When did you receive this?"

"The morning of my father's funeral."

"Have you enemies? It could be a deception."

A serving girl brought them bowls of watery stew. "I considered that. But I had to inquire further, so I traveled to Northamptonshire." Julian fished through the broth for an elusive vegetable or cut of beef.

"I thought Lady Sotherton was estranged from the rest of her family. Have you reconciled?" Despite the meal's poor quality, Harrison gulped his food hungrily all the same.

"Sadly, no. I spoke with her husband—the Home Office undersecretary—and he claims my father did indeed have a relationship with some of the petitioners."

"So we can't rule out the allegations of murder without more information." Harrison set down his spoon and examined the note again, his lips pursed with concentration. "The parchment is of high quality and the phrasing suggests the writer studied rhetoric. The lines are fine, implying a new or freshly sharpened quill. But some of the letters fluctuate, suggesting your anonymous author is a person of means and education who tried to disguise his handwriting."

"I see I was right about your special talents."

"So what else happened in Northamptonshire?"

"I discovered a member of my brother-in-law's staff searching my room." Julian hesitated, his thoughts harkening to those moments in his bedchamber when he'd first encountered Miss Vance. "She claims she receives remuneration for her activities."

"Selling government information gleaned from Sotherton? Did you inform your brother-in-law?"

"Not yet. I came to see you instead."

"If she is telling the truth about her compensation, that indicates planning. And funding."

"And collaboration with either a hostile power or revolutionaries within our own country. If what I surmise is true, there will be further unrest."

"The current hardships add impetus to their cause. Men with hungry bellies are easily led. Such as I." Harrison eyed his empty bowl as he refolded the note and returned it to Julian.

"My original objective was to determine the letter's veracity—and if true, bring my father's killers to justice. But it seems I chanced upon something greater than my poor troubles."

"Tell me about the informant."

Julian hesitated, strangely reluctant to reveal her identity. "My niece's governess, Miss Vance."

"The governess?" Harrison's widening eyes revealed his first surprise of the day. "Been with the family for long?"

"Eight years."

"So she could have begun her enterprise during the war, selling Sotherton's secrets to the French."

Nausea roiled the broth in Julian's belly. He pictured Miss Vance's frayed coat and vintage gown. "If she did, she hasn't spent her ill-gotten gains on her attire."

"A smart woman wouldn't."

And she was that. "She seems quite close to her charge." And yet she was betraying the Sothertons for a fee. Surely the woman who had claimed her cynicism stemmed from a French shell wouldn't have conspired with England's enemies. "However, I don't know if she'll remain with the family after my niece's comeout in the spring."

"Eight years is long enough to form significant connec-

tions in the neighborhood. Someone knows her well enough
to realize she'd be receptive to betraying Lord Sotherton."

The serving girl collected the empty bowls. Julian placed
a few coins on the table and earned a gap-toothed smile. "I
suspect my sister is a demanding employer."

"So demanding a woman would betray her country to settle her grudge?"

Julian rose from his seat, his thoughts turning back to Miss
Vance's comment about evil and the disparity of power. "She
seems to feel injustice keenly."

"So she might believe her actions justified."

"I meant such an idealistic nature would be unlikely to
have sided with the Corsican tyrant during the war."

Harrison pulled on his gloves, the side of one finger visible through a rent in the fabric. "You seem wont to defend
her, my lord. What are you going to do about her?"

"I've hired her to pass on my messages to her compatriots. I left her instructions to inform them of my suspicions
regarding their involvement in my father's death."

"That could be dangerous to you, my lord."

"Then I'd have my answer."

"If her sympathies lie with the radicals, your offer of remuneration might not be enough to buy her loyalty. I don't
suppose you left any bogus messages in your chamber before you left."

"To test her credibility?" The wind whipped against him
as he exited the building. Julian turned up the collar of his
cloak. Once before he'd entrusted a subordinate with a con-
fidential communication, only to find himself deceived. He
would do well to remember that. "I'll do that when I return
to Rowan Abbey. Perhaps a letter suggesting the government intends to crack down on the growing unrest and will
be sending troops to Wellingborough will garner their attention. Will you accept the position?"

"Only a foolish man would decline an opportunity to feed his family this winter." A gaunt horse lumbered past them. The wagon behind skidded on the dingy, packed snow, eliciting a bellow from its driver. "I'll travel to Northamptonshire and join the local group of radicals. However, my lord, as an outsider, I probably can't penetrate far enough into the leadership to glean much of their plans."

"True, but you have better prospects than any other. I can hire someone from Bow Street to conduct inquiries in London about the Spa Fields riots."

"I'll get you the right man. He is very good—but not cheap."

"I'm prepared to pay what I must."

Harrison stared at a pigeon roosting on a rooftop for several moments. "My lord, you do realize you have placed this governess in a precarious position? Should her contacts learn of her duplicity, I doubt they will be as obliging as you."

Julian shoved his hands into his pocket. The crackle of the anonymous note tossed his mind back to the simple nativity star Harrison's youngest had drawn with childish scrawl. Misgivings mingled with determination. "She placed herself in danger when she began this game. I doubt the government would have been more forgiving than the mob had the magistrate caught her first." Or his sister Elizabeth. "Should I inform Sotherton of my discovery and our stratagem?"

"Let's see what your governess achieves for us."

"And offer Miss Vance a chance to redeem herself?"

"We are all in need of redemption, captain."

Julian startled to hear his old title—not the one he'd inherited so unexpectedly, but the one he'd studied for, worked for, earned. He stared at a nearby ship whose masts disappeared into the London fog. Perhaps even he had a bit of the revolutionary coursing through his veins. "It seems I'll be visiting my sister for an extended stay. She won't be pleased."

"Reconciliation is every bit as necessary as redemption." Harrison directed Julian's attention from the ship to a tenement in the distance. "Our quarters are simple and the fare is modest, but you are welcome if you are staying in London."

By the looks of Harrison, their meals tended to the meager. "I spent years of my life at sea. I'm not so fastidious as you might imagine. Unfortunately I must journey immediately to Somerset. My housekeeper writes my mother is not well. I shall return to Northamptonshire as soon as feasible." Julian retrieved a purse from inside his coat and passed it to the other man. "Buy whatever you need for the task—including any provisions your family will require during your absence."

Leah stared across the rolling fields of sun-glazed snow. The bare branches of leafless trees framed the footpath as she hiked to the entrance of a large estate. A high stone fence enclosed the grounds and ivy covered the manor's walls, as if they hid from the world, ashamed. She glanced over her shoulder. Assured none save a few thin, shaggy cattle observed her movements, she marched to the gatehouse.

The gatekeeper came out and fitted a key in the lock. "Another Sunday visit, eh, Miss Vance?" He pushed open the foreboding iron gates that shut out unexpected visitors. And shut in any residents bent on escape.

"Yes, thank you." She slipped through the opening, fighting a wince as the lock clicked behind her.

Eerie quiet reverberated across the lawns as Leah trudged to the house. Despite the lofty status of the residents, most of their families limited contact to paying the exorbitant fees. Few carriage wheels had left their impressions in the snow, probably only the occasional delivery dray. But as she drew closer to the house, Leah caught the unearthly moans, punctuated by the occasional screams, of mental distress. Sunlight winked on discreet bars that lined the windows.

Breath tightening in her chest, she climbed the steps and rang the bell. The door swung open to reveal the unsmiling matron in a dress as white as the grounds.

"A bad night, Miss Vance."

"But she is better now?"

"As much as we can expect."

As if any of them had expectations for Phoebe. Leah lingered on the stoop, then forced her feet across the threshold. The heavy oak door slammed in place, the sliding of the bolt echoing like a thunderclap through the empty entrance hall. The familiar sense of panic squeezed around her stomach.

Unlike a typical home, no personal touches warmed the interior. No rugs blanketed the floors. No sideboard sported a vase presented to some long-forgotten ancestor. No flowers filled the air with perfume. Only cold utilitarian sterility filled the rooms.

"Alice will take you to your sister's chamber." The matron gestured to an orderly who marched up the staircase, shoes tapping against a flight of bare risers.

Leah removed her hat and gloves, then willed reluctant feet to follow.

Down a hallway the orderly paused by a door and retrieved her keys. "We had to administer a double dose of laudanum last night. Your sister was most agitated—tried to kill herself. Took three of us to get the laudanum into her." Alice pushed open the door.

Leah stepped into a room that reeked of sweat and urine. Despair washed over her. Phoebe lay still and deathlike on the mattress that comprised the room's only furnishing. Filth dulled the shorn blond locks that had once been her glory. "Why hasn't she at least been bathed?" Phoebe's care cost enough coin.

"We have to wait until she regains her senses. She could drown in her current state."

Leah stared through the bars that prevented escape via the window, feeling as trapped as her sister. The sun glared against the snow-swathed grounds so brightly as to cause her eyes to sting. And yet the thought persisted. Did Phoebe, in her more lucid moments, seek to flee her mental and physical prison, even by death?

"If you need anything, or if you decide to leave before your usual time, ring for me." Alice passed Leah a small silver bell.

Leah sat on the mattress beside her sister's motionless form and closed her ears to the sound of the lock imprisoning her in the cold, barren chamber. Why the need for locks for an insensate woman? "Phoebe?" She shook a thin shoulder. Phoebe's head rolled to the side, her cold cheek coming to rest against the back of Leah's hand. But for the gentle rise and fall of Phoebe's breathing, she could have been dead. Leah raised one of her sister's wrists and examined the skin for welts or bruises. Relief welled within her at the sight of the unblemished skin. While she disapproved of the matron's enthusiasm for laudanum, at least here the orderlies eschewed binding unruly patients.

Leah retrieved a comb from her reticule and set to work unsnarling the tangled nest of Phoebe's hair. The golden strands gleamed with memories despite their dirty condition. If only Leah had thought to have Alice bring a warm, wet cloth to wipe the dried sweat and grime from the porcelain skin.

Guilt welled in her, spilling out at the corners of Leah's eyes. Clever David had been their parents' pride and lovely Phoebe their joy. For years Leah had resented her role as the plain, overlooked middle child, had envied David his quick wit and Phoebe her beauty.

What kind of malicious God would spare her while taking everyone else?

* * *

"That the house?" Caroline pointed out the window as the carriage pulled up before Rowan Abbey.

Julian glanced past his youngest sister to the forbidding pile of redbricks. The many-paned windows sparkled in the sunshine, an ironic counterpoint to the anything-but-sunny welcome he expected inside. "Yes, that's the house." Unfortunately.

He could already imagine Elizabeth's reaction. If only he could have left Caro with Felicity…but Maman needed respite. Grief and exhaustion had drained her body and mind—not that Caro could understand. No, she demanded the same care and attention from her only parent. He had to separate them, for Maman's sake. For now.

On the facing seat the maid interrupted her nap long enough to glance at Sotherton's manor house. Anna wiped her nose with her sleeve, making him yearn for the days when Nanny had been young enough to travel.

The coachman reined the horses to a halt, and a footman came to assist Caro with the carriage step. The sun had melted the top layer of snow, turning it treacherously icy for one with Caro's precarious balance. Julian gripped her arm and waved the maid to take the other side. The trio ambled to the entrance where the butler opened the door.

"Good afternoon, Hawkesworth." Julian passed him their coats.

"I'll tell his lordship you have returned."

"Thank you. I must speak to my eldest sister first. Where is Lady Sotherton?"

"The blue drawing room."

"I'll show myself in. And Hawkesworth, please inform the housekeeper to have a room prepared next to mine for my youngest sister. Lady Caroline will be here for a short stay."

Not even the excessively impassive butler held his surprise

in check. His gaze darted to Caroline, then with supreme control, he recovered his composure. "I'll have Mrs. Anderson make the gold bedchamber ready, my lord."

Julian led the increasingly wary Caro by the hand to the blue drawing room where his oldest sister concentrated on her needlework. "Ah, Lizzie. Did you miss me?"

Elizabeth raised her chin. "So you returned."

"As promised." He offered a brief bow and an infuriating smile.

"Benedict and Killiane leave for London on the morrow."

"Then I will meet with him forthwith." Julian's business no longer involved Sotherton anyway—although he'd have to provide his brother-in-law with a convenient excuse for his continued stay. His jaw tightened as he swept Caro forward. "Elizabeth, I'd like you to meet Caroline. Your youngest sister."

The warmth of the room brought a rosy glow to Caro's cheeks that, with her diminutive size, made her appear so much like a porcelain doll. She glanced at Julian through her oddly uptilted eyes. Julian smiled and gestured, and she dipped into a pretty curtsey.

Elizabeth locked her perpetual frown on her face "What is she doing here?"

"Caro has come for…a short visit."

"How short?"

"Several days." Julian wrapped an arm around Caro's shoulders. "Perhaps several weeks, depending on how long my business lasts and how well Maman fares."

"Bad enough you seem to have taken up residence in my house—"

"Lord Sotherton's house—and with his permission."

"But now you are inviting guests."

"Caroline is not a guest. She is your family."

Elizabeth rang the bell for a servant. "I understand there are establishments for her kind."

Under his arm, Caro trembled. Julian hauled her closer.

"My lady?" An older woman with a cap covering her graying hair entered the salon.

"Mrs. Anderson, please show our guest—"

"Lady Caroline. Her name is Lady Caroline." Julian folded his arm across his chest and fixed a defiant stare on his older sister.

"—to her bedchamber."

"Very good, my lady." The housekeeper dropped into a curtsey.

Julian transferred Caro's hand to the maid's grasp. "You and Anna go with Mrs. Anderson."

Doubt and confusion and caution darkened Caro's blue eyes. "Jules."

"Go on." Julian touched her cheek. "I'll be along after I take care of some business."

"Come, my lady." The housekeeper grabbed Caro's other hand.

Caro glanced back one time at Julian before she exited the room.

Elizabeth's frown etched new lines around her tight mouth. "She seems quiet enough. I suppose she won't be too much bother so long as her nursemaid restrains her."

"Caro is not an animal that must be caged. She's a human being, and a far kinder one than many I know."

Elizabeth clamped her lips together. Reconciliation never seemed so far away.

Leah smoothed the rag over Phoebe's brow. Alice had been none too pleased with the request. But a reminder of the fee Leah paid, along with a suggestion that perhaps the matter could be taken up with Alice's employer, had convinced the grumbling orderly to bring a cloth and a pan of tepid water.

Footsteps rapped against the hallway floor, then the door clicked open. Alec strode into the room and settled onto the mattress beside her, lowering a large strong hand to her shoulder. His grim green eyes stared at Phoebe, his cheeks tight with emotion.

Leah tossed the rag into the basin. "Last night she tried to…"

"I know. I heard." He drew Leah close and tucked her head under his chin.

She rested her face against the rough wool, letting some of the anxiety and fatigue bleed out of her for several blissful moments. The outline of the pistol under her cousin's coat—left over from his army days—pressed against her cheek.

Presently, Alec released her and rose. "We should go. You can't do any more today."

"But it will be another week before I can return."

"And hopefully Phoebe will be more responsive to visitors. Besides, if we leave now, you'll arrive back at the Abbey before dark." Alec jingled the bell.

Leah brushed her knuckles along her sister's cheek, the cold skin soft and smooth to her touch. Her impotence weighed heavily on her heart.

The orderly reappeared, unlocked the door and escorted them to the entrance hall where the matron met them at the door. "Miss Vance?" She waited, hand outstretched.

Leah opened her reticule and extracted the requisite coins. Only a few remained—not enough to cover Phoebe's care another week. The great expense of her sister's extended illness had depleted their father's legacy by last year. Leah had continued to provide for Phoebe these past few months by furnishing Alec's…friends with the contents of Lord Sotherton's correspondence.

But what to do now? Lord Chambelston had provided only instructions—no payment—before his hasty and mysterious departure.

"I heard Chambelston left the county." Alec seemingly read her mind as he escorted her along the drive.

"Thursday morning."

"Will he be returning?"

"Assuredly."

The gatekeeper let them out with a cheery wave. Leah breathed more easily outside the estate's confining atmosphere.

Alec fell into step beside her. "Tell me about Lord Sotherton's other guests."

"Viscount Killiane and his brother, Mr. Fleming." Fortunately, with the departure of both Mr. Warren and Chambelston, Lady Sotherton hadn't needed to press Leah and Miss Godwin into attending dinner again. "Viscount Killiane will be leaving with Sotherton for London tomorrow."

"It's my understanding that while Killiane is a frequent visitor, Fleming hasn't called on his family in some time."

"Three years." Thirty wouldn't have been long enough.

"I can understand why Killiane would visit his uncle, what with their mutual interest in politics. But what is Fleming's business?"

"Pleasure, I suppose." His, and no one else's. "So far as I know, it's his only occupation."

"That makes no sense. If the man is a fribble, what would he be doing in Northamptonshire in the middle of winter? He'll find no entertainment here."

"Perhaps he needed a retreat from his creditors? For certain, he and Lord Killiane seem to be at daggers' drawn."

"So two men who can't stand each other decide to travel from Ireland to Northamptonshire to spend the remainder of their holiday together?"

A fair point. So why had Reginald Fleming come? To torment his brother?

To torment her?

The houses and barns of tiny Norford loomed before them with a crossroads in the center of the hamlet where she and Alec would part. The road to their right led south toward his lodgings in Heckton, while the other direction headed westward to her duties at Rowan Abbey. Her residence, but never her home.

"Did you learn the reason for Chambelston's visit?" The fringe of mahogany hair peeking out from Alec's hat brim gleamed with fire in the sun and lit a twinge of guilt in Leah. But other than agree to Lord Chambelston's proposal, she hadn't actually done anything yet. Nothing that could cause Alec harm.

"He believes certain factions of your group murdered his father."

Alec's face stilled. "The late Lord Chambelston? Why would we kill him? He was an ally of our cause."

Leah stopped so abruptly Alec stumbled on his bad leg and nearly went sprawling into the snow. "An ally?"

"Of sorts. He offered to assist us in presenting our grievances to government."

"Then who would want the man dead?"

"The son who inherited his title and fortune?"

An image of Lord Chambelston's eyes—the blue muted with grief—flashed through Leah's mind. "I think not."

Alec's brows arched as he studied her face. Could he read her cooperation with—and fascination with—the new earl? Heat crept over her cheeks.

Who stood to gain if the cause failed…and would be willing to murder an earl to achieve that goal? "Alec, be careful. If the government believes your group responsible for Lord Chambelston's death…"

"They will interpret every demand as a declaration of war and respond accordingly." Alec's vivid green eyes regarded her steadily for several long seconds. "You must be careful, cousin. The county...the country...is in turmoil. Things could quickly become dangerous."

Chapter Five

Julian escaped Lord Sotherton's study after a brief consultation with his brother-in-law. He climbed the stairs—thoughts focused on where he would stash his carefully crafted note—and nearly knocked over a redheaded maid polishing the woodwork.

"Pardon me."

The maid blinked, as if she'd never been addressed by a member of the household. Knowing his sister, she probably hadn't.

Julian strode into his bedchamber and scanned the furnishings. Where would Miss Vance look should she prove disloyal? Perhaps the armoire? He slid open a drawer and tucked the note amongst his linen shirts, trying not to imagine her searching his belongings. And hoping against hope she wouldn't betray him.

Now to check on Caroline. He exited to the hall and tapped on the door next to his bedchamber. Silence. "Caroline?" He knocked again.

Unease stirred low in his stomach. He twisted the knob and let himself into the room. A cheerful fire blazed on the hearth, its light glowing on the golden walls. A quick survey of the room revealed only Caro's nursemaid dozing in a chair, but no Caro.

"Anna!"

She blinked sleepy eyes, then bolted out of the chair. "I—I'm sorry, my lord."

"Where is Lady Caroline?"

"Lady Caroline?" She glanced toward lonesome toys in the corner and blanched. "She… I—I—"

"You lost her?" Julian marched out of the room, the groveling maid pleading forgiveness in his wake. He gestured down the hallway. "You look there."

"Yes, my lord." She curtsied and backed away, then turned and ran.

With a sigh, Julian retraced his steps to the still-polishing maid. "Excuse me."

She lifted a wary gaze to his. "My lord?"

"I seem to have…misplaced my sister, Lady Caroline. She is small, with brown hair and blue eyes. I was rather hoping you might have seen her." Surely Caro wouldn't have wandered to another floor, not when stairs gave her such difficulty.

The suspicion on the maid's face softened. "I saw Mrs. Anderson bring her here, but I didn't notice her leaving. She is…" The maid hesitated, as if searching for a gentle word to describe Caro's condition.

"Yes."

"I'll locate Mrs. Anderson. Perhaps she knows where your sister is." The maid collected her rag and disappeared to find the housekeeper.

Julian checked his own bedchamber, just in case Caro had wandered there in search of him. No one. He returned to the hall.

"Caro!" he called to the face peeking from behind a door across the hallway.

"Jules!" She rushed to embrace him.

He glanced past her to a gaping doorway. "What were you doing?"

"Look for you."

"You found me." He started to wrap his arms around her, but she pulled away.

"See?" She held up a hand and uncurled her fingers to reveal the gleam of gold.

"What do you have here?"

"Pretty gold."

"Yes, very pretty. May I?" He picked up the item, a gold locket and chain. "Can you show me where you got this?"

Caro grabbed his hand and pulled him toward the room. Assuming he wasn't violating a woman's privacy—Elizabeth had mentioned no female guests in residence—Julian followed her into a masculine-looking chamber of dark paneling and rich green fabrics. Opposite the four-poster bed, a paper-strewn desk was home to a half-filled brandy decanter and glasses. An odd location to find such a feminine bauble. His sister paused on the rug, her head tilted and her bemused gaze on him as she waited.

"Where did you find this, Caro?"

She pointed to the armoire.

Julian slid open the drawer and peered at a cache of other feminine trinkets. He settled the locket against a bit of green ribbon. Sentimental reminders of a lost love? Hopefully their owner—Killiane? his brother?—wouldn't notice they'd been disturbed. "Come, Caro." Julian guided her to the hallway and pulled the door shut behind them just as the maid returned with the housekeeper.

"Ah, Mrs. Anderson. Thank you for coming. As you can see, my quest met with success."

"I'm delighted you found her, my lord."

"Yes, it is a relief to us all."

But no doubt especially for Anna, the nursemaid who raced to join them, her face red and her breaths rapid and raspy. "For shame, my lady! Running off like that!"

Julian bit back his annoyance for his sister's sake. "Come, Caro." He wrapped an arm around her shoulders and drew her toward the gold bedchamber. Once he had shut the door behind the three of them, he rounded on the nursemaid. "Don't you ever again berate my sister for your negligence."

Anna's gaze dropped to the floor. "Yes, my lord."

"Now, we shall speak no more of this." Unless Anna proved inadequate to the task. He leaned forward and kissed the top of Caro's head. "I have to go for a while, but I'll return in time for dinner."

"Dinner." Caro's face broke into a smile. "What for dinner?"

"I don't know yet. Perhaps we can convince Cook to provide you a special treat. You stay with Anna." Julian let himself out of the room.

Dinner. Another obstacle. Undoubtedly Lizzie would reject the notion of Caro eating with the family.

He paused beside the maid who had returned to her polishing duties. "Do you know where I might find Lady Teresa?"

"I believe she often reads in the blue salon on Sunday afternoons."

"Thank you. I shall check there." He paused, turned and looked at the maid again. "And thank you...?"

"Molly, my lord."

"Thank you, Molly, for your assistance with my sister."

"I had a sister myself thus, but she died quite young—only eight." A sad sort of smile tugged on the maid's face. "We all loved her the same and felt her loss keenly."

Julian tried to remember Caro at eight, but he'd spent most of that year—the year of Trafalgar—at sea. "I'm sorry. When was this?"

"Four years ago."

A younger sister, then. Like his.

"My sister found enjoyment in simple pleasures."

"Yes, Lady Caroline has much to teach the malcontents." Including him. And Elizabeth, if she were only willing to surrender her resentment.

The maid's expression closed again, returning their relationship to its proper distance. "Is there anything else you require, my lord?"

"Ah, no. Thank you." He withdrew and traipsed to the blue salon.

"Uncle Julian!" Teresa smiled as he entered. "Did you just return?"

"About an hour ago." How would this relative accept the news of Caro's arrival? "I brought a guest with me. Your aunt Caroline."

"How delightful! Caroline is your...youngest sister?"

"Yes. Felicity is between your mother and me." As had been Gregory, whose untimely death had propelled Julian from ordinary sea captain to a land-owning aristocrat. "Our youngest brother Kit lives in America, and Caroline is our baby sister—not much older than you, in fact." In years, anyway.

"I should like to meet her." The blue cushion of the window seat echoed the same hue in Teresa's eyes.

"She is in the chamber next to mine—the gold bedchamber, I believe Hawkesworth called it. I left her there with her maid. Caroline is..." Not like other people.

Understanding softened Teresa's brilliant gaze. "I've heard." That she seemed indifferent could only issue from her governess's influence. He didn't doubt Miss Vance's sense of justice and compassion for the weak and oppressed—even if he disapproved of how she manifested those convictions.

"I, ah, thought perhaps I would ask Miss Vance if she

would evaluate Caroline." An unwelcome thrill simmered through him at the prospect of seeing Teresa's governess again. "You wouldn't know where I could find her?"

"She has Sundays off, of course. I think she goes to visit a friend. Or maybe a relative."

Friend or relative—or companion in arms against the government? "Do you know where?"

A sly smile stole across Teresa's mouth. "I can't say for certain, but I believe she usually walks in an easterly direction. She should be returning presently if you'd like to intercept her."

"Then perhaps I shall ride that direction. Would you care to join me?"

"Thank you, but I already agreed to ride tomorrow with my cousin Reggie. I think I shall visit my Aunt Caroline. It's long past the time I should have made her acquaintance." Teresa set down her book and rose from the seat. She walked to the doorway with him.

"I'm certain Caro will enjoy your company." He gave her a bow and marched away. Once at the stable, Julian ordered the groom to saddle Sotherton's bay.

"I'm sorry, my lord. Mr. Fleming took him out some while back. Perhaps the black gelding…?"

"That will be fine." Julian yanked his gloves over his fingers. When the groom had readied the horse, he rode off to find Miss Vance. And her mysterious friend.

The sun's glare had warmed the top layer of snow to slush, and as Leah trudged along the path, water squished inside her boots and soaked her stockings. The cold radiated from her toes upward, until the chills rippled along her spine and reminded her she needed her boots resoled. With what funds?

She considered the few coins remaining in her reticule, and the weight of her responsibilities sat heavily on her shoulders.

A few birds flitted among the branches of the rough-barked trees along the path, and she watched their flight with envy. If only she could mount the sky and escape.

In the distance a beautiful bay—Sotherton's stallion, she was certain—raced across the snow-covered field, its well-mounted rider dressed in black. His tall hat and fashionable cloak marked him as a gentleman. Lord Chambelston, perhaps, returned to finish his quest—or to spy on her? Anticipation stirred in her belly. Leah squinted, but the low afternoon sun hid the rider's face in shadows.

She glanced over her shoulder, but Alec, like the small hamlet where they'd parted, had vanished in the distance. Her cousin's last words echoed in her mind and circled her heart with icy dread as the horse and rider drew closer. The blood froze in her veins as she identified that scornful smile.

Not Lord Chambelston.

To be certain, she'd rather meet a roving band of rioters than this so-called gentleman.

"Good afternoon, Miss Vance." Reginald Fleming steered the horse to block her path. "Are you having a pleasant stroll?"

"Until now." She tried to continue forward, but he refused to let her pass. "Excuse me."

"Oh, no. I fear I can't do that. Didn't your companion warn you the path is dangerous for a woman alone?"

Her heart pounded in her chest. "My companion?"

"Shame on him, leaving you to fend for yourself." He nudged the horse closer, forcing her to retreat into deeper snow. "And here you give the appearance of such a paragon. What would my virtuous aunt say about your wanton ways? Surely she would not approve of keeping her daughter in the care of such a woman."

A frisson of fear joined the cold rippling down Leah's spine. What price would Fleming demand for his silence?

And how much more expensive should he ever discover the destination of her Sunday walks? *Phoebe*.

Too much.

Fleming leaned from the horse. His arm snaked forward as he reached for her wrist. *No!* Leah yanked away, leaving her glove in his grasp. Her momentum propelled her backwards against a tree trunk and knocked the wind from her chest. A bare branch scraped her cheek as she struggled to regain her equilibrium.

Too late. Fleming seized the advantage of her momentary paralysis.

His fingers circled her forearm. He hauled her closer, close enough she could see the mad pleasure that lit his eyes at her unease, could smell the wine that polluted his breath, could feel the excited heat of his power over her. His hat tumbled to the ground, revealing the scar on his forehead. Unfortunately she would find no convenient poker this time.

The temperamental horse lurched and snorted and stomped on her foot, pinning her in place. Pain shot through her leg.

A leer of lewd pleasure twisted Fleming's lips. "A pity it's so cold. Perhaps we can find a more sheltered place—a place where we could finish what we started three years ago."

"No!" Never, never, *never*. Leah jerked but he tightened his grip.

"Oh, you will regret—"

She lowered her shoulder and thrust it into the horse's side. The stallion's ears plunged back as it staggered and thrashed. Fleming lost his hold on her hand in his attempt to control the animal. Leah snatched the opportunity and—ignoring the agony in her foot—fled to the other side of the tree.

Fleming lashed the horse's haunches and charged toward her, crop raised above his head. She ducked under a branch, steeling herself against the imminent blow.

Air whooshed above her, then a crack reverberated across

the landscape, that of leather on flesh, followed by a roar. But not hers. A stripe of red slashed the length of Fleming's cheek. He wiped his sleeve across his face, dropping his crop as he whirled to face this new threat. "Who do you— Chambelston!" He fought to control the high-strung horse.

"Fleming." Chambelston's low growl rolled across the suddenly still landscape. A tic throbbed along the tense line of his square jaw as he once more swished his riding crop against his shoulder. The bay stallion flinched and pranced again, footfalls muffled by the packed snow.

"What are you doing here, *my lord?*" Fleming hauled on the bay's reins, his eyes glittering challenge and promised retribution.

"My business is not yet concluded. And I believe you have an urgent commitment. Elsewhere."

Fleming aimed another—threatening—stare at Leah. "As you say, my lord, a pressing commitment elsewhere. Miss Vance, your servant. I didn't realize your next companion would arrive so precipitously." He wheeled the horse around and cantered off in the direction of the hamlet where Leah— and Alec—had recently passed, his uncovered locks bouncing in the breeze.

What if he should encounter her cousin? And learn his identity?

"If I may be so bold as to escort you home, Miss Vance?"

Slowly Leah turned to look at Chambelston, high above her on an ebony horse, crop still upraised like an avenging angel's sword. Several days' absence only made him more imposing, and her pulse quickened with her reaction. His dark cloak billowed out behind him, and his hat threw all but his frown in shadows. And yet, though she couldn't see his eyes, she felt their careful regard, studying her, weighing her.

Much as she appreciated his timely intervention, she feared

his uncanny perception. "Thank you. But don't let me divert you from your business."

"You are my only business today."

"Me?" Had he a suspicion of Fleming's plans and followed him? Or had he sought out her in particular?

"You have a job to do for me."

"Oh, yes, of course."

Lord Chambelston hesitated for interminable seconds, then swung down from his seat on the horse. The cloak swirled around him as he moved unnervingly nearer. "You are bleeding." Golden flecks of compassion glittered in the eyes of brilliant blue. He tugged off his glove and stroked her cheek, his bare fingers soft against her skin. Not even the sting of the scrape protected her from the disquiet of his gentle concern.

"'Tis only a scratch." Heart pounding, she brushed his touch away.

"Come. It grows late." He held out a hand to her.

Ignoring his offer of assistance, she stepped forward. Pain shot up the length of her leg and her knee buckled, plunging her toward the snow.

Chambelston swooped down and caught her before she reached the ground. His arm wreathed her shoulders as he held her erect. "You are injured."

Warmth invaded Leah's heart, and the tang of wool and leather teased her senses. "The horse trod on my foot. I shall be fit enough presently."

He cast a skeptical eye toward the low-hanging sun. "Not soon enough, I'll warrant." He hefted her onto the horse, his hands strong and dependable around her waist. Safe.

And so very unlike Fleming.

Leah struggled to find her balance, unaccustomed to the awkwardness of sitting sideways on a man's saddle. The movement shifted her skirt and revealed a slash in her boot where the bay's iron shoe had sliced the brittle leather. New soles would be of little use to her old boots now.

A splotch of gray against the trampled snow drew Leah's attention. "My glove!"

"I've got it." Chambelston retrieved the article and passed it to her. His palm brushed hers and propelled a fresh torrent of emotions swirling through her. Then he gathered the reins and led the horse along the path at a sedate walk that allowed her to keep her seat.

"So, this job. What would you have me do?"

"I made inquiries while in London. The right money to the right people… I think I'm closer to finding out what really happened at the riot." He stared ahead at the horizon, his square jaw rigid.

She thought back to the anonymous note in his pocket. "The riot where your father was injured?"

He gave a single, curt nod. "I want you to inform your friends."

"I'll see to it tonight when we return." Leah hesitated, then decided sharing Alec's news harmed no one—and might even help her cousin and his confederates if it triggered Chambelston's sympathy. "I heard—overheard, that is—two people talking about your father." One being her.

He tilted his head and studied her from under the brim of his hat. "Oh?"

"They claimed your father supported the people."

"You are suggesting my father allied with the rebels?"

"No, only that he empathized with the people's suffering— that he acted as an intermediary between the government and those with grievances. I deduced he was much admired."

Silence descended over them for several minutes. "Thank you for those kind words."

Did he believe her? She parsed his words and tones for any sarcastic edge, but found none. "You're welcome."

"My niece told me you typically spend your Sundays away from Rowan Abbey, Miss Vance."

Suspicions prickled along the nape of her neck at this abrupt change in subject. "I visit a friend."

"Anyone I should know about?"

"Only if you have an interest in invalid females." The horse faltered through a dip in the path. Leah grabbed for the animal's mane to prevent herself from sliding out of the saddle. "My friend is much too ill to concern herself with politics."

Chambelston's grip tightened on the reins, the drifted snow reaching nigh to his knees. "I'm sorry to hear of your friend's distress. Has she suffered long with this affliction?" He climbed out of the deep drift and tapped the snow from his boots.

"Ten years. But surely you don't wish to hear any more." And she most especially did not wish to discuss more. Should any discover proper governess Leah Vance had a sister with an unsound mind… "I can think of few subjects more tedious than a stranger's ailments."

"Unless, of course, I am similarly plagued and desire information on effective remedies."

"I doubt you would benefit from her treatment." Although locking him in a cell and rendering him senseless with laudanum might profit Leah. And perhaps Alec. "Besides, with your superior resources, I'm certain you'd find a better situation than the ones available to her."

"Do I detect resentment, Miss Vance?"

Oh, yes. But it would never do to antagonize this man. "I'm sorry. Blame the fatigue—and fear. I try to help as best I can, but…"

"But a governess has limited means. I'm sorry your friend doesn't have the wherewithal for the very best of care, Miss Vance. I do have superior resources, as you call them—but they do not shelter me from all hardships. I must confess I had another reason to seek you out today. I asked my niece where I might find you because I have need of your expertise."

Or because he didn't trust her? "You find yourself in need of an embroidery stitch after all?"

A chuckle bubbled in his throat and mitigated some of the tension that swirled around him. "Not exactly. I brought my youngest sister with me. Perhaps you have…heard about her?"

Leah searched her memory for any tidbits of gossip about Lady Sotherton's family. Wasn't there one who was…not normal? "I believe so."

"I brought a nurse to care for her, but I question whether we have done Caroline justice in her education. I suspect she might be capable of learning more than we have credited her. You have some experience with teaching young ladies. I thought perhaps you would observe her and give me your opinion."

Surely Chambelston's family had already consulted the best doctors and teachers. "I doubt I can offer more than anyone else, but I would be willing to meet your sister."

"I'd be grateful for anything you can recommend. Teresa plans to ride tomorrow with her cousin. Perhaps I could bring my sister then."

"She's going riding with Fleming?" Leah glanced over her shoulder, but her nemesis had disappeared from view. Had he discovered Alec? As she faced forward, she caught Chambelston's frown.

"You seem troubled at the notion, Miss Vance. Has Fleming importuned upon you on other occasions when you traveled beyond Rowan Abbey?"

The stone fence denoting the easternmost boundary of Sotherton lands edged the path. What new torments would Reginald Fleming plot upon his return? "Not recently." Not during the three years he'd stayed away.

"Fleming spoke of another in your company."

"My invalid sis—friend's cousin also called upon her. We were going in the same direction, so he escorted me part of the way."

"A man who visits his invalid cousin? Are you certain he went to see his kinswoman and not her guest?"

"Don't be ridiculous." She aimed her stern-governess expression at him, the one she had used long ago when an attention-starved Teresa resorted to disobedience to secure notice. Alas, such machinations had only widened the chasm between mother and daughter. "He is only a local man, made poor by war and adversity."

"I yield to your superior knowledge about men in general and this one in particular."

"I'm not so ignorant as to the ways of men as you believe. I once had a brother."

His gaze sobered and the derision twisting his lips softened. "You speak in past tense, Miss Vance." He patted the horse's neck, his hand disturbingly close to where she threaded her fingers through the animal's mane.

"He died during the war."

That French shell she'd mentioned. Julian stared across the rolling miles of white, like an endless sea of snow all around him. Sympathy and understanding washed through him and fed a spark of hope that someone so personally impacted by the war wouldn't have sold state secrets to the enemy. "You have my condolences. I lost a brother myself but two years past."

"And then your father recently."

"Yes." A gust of wind tugged at his hat. "But Gregory's death was a surprise. He was only five years my senior. I suppose to a degree we all expect to outlive our parents someday even if that day oft comes too soon."

"Was your brother killed during the war?"

"No. Perhaps that contributed to my shock. I spent twenty years in the navy, most during wartime. And I survived—only to watch my brother die of disease. How degrading, to see his once vigorous form waste away. I own I would rather endure a quick death via combat."

"He was firstborn—the heir before you. Were you ever jealous of him?"

"Like Fleming and Killiane, you mean?" He glanced over his shoulder to see if the younger man had returned to pursue them, but saw only their own long shadows that marked the end of the day. "Shamefully, yes. My parents sent me away at thirteen while Gregory remained behind to get his education and take his place as heir. Like most men I compared my lot to Gregory's and concluded I had the more difficult road."

"Perhaps you did." The breeze tossed escaping tendrils against her face. The askew bonnet and disorderly hair softened the usual severity of her appearance and the uncertainty in her expression relaxed the sternness of her manner. "Thirteen is very young to leave home—especially to go to war."

"I am only now appreciating all Gregory did for the Chambelston tenants—thankless work, acknowledged by few. My work contained danger, yes, but excitement and admiration also. Every young man craves excitement and purpose and dragons to slay." A smile slipped out as he remembered a childhood of searching for buried treasure and chasing imaginary pirates. "Consider Mr. Fleming. Unlike me, his parents didn't provide him with an occupation. Idleness breeds mischief."

"Or in Mr. Fleming's case, malice."

Once again Julian recalled her words about evil and power, this time in light of Fleming's violence against her today and his earlier provocation at the piano. A long-standing problem for Miss Vance? "Would you like me to speak to Sotherton?"

"No!"

And a word to his sister would probably exacerbate the issue. Another twinge of sympathy pricked his conscience. If Miss Vance had been his sister—an uncomfortable thought—no man would have dared vent his spite on her. And yet her plight was typical for a woman of her situation. "Was your brother in the army?"

"No, the navy." The new softness about her extended to her mouth, which curved in a faint smile of remembrance. That charming dimple reappeared on her cheek, and Julian vowed to see it emerge again, and often. "David was four years my senior. He pulled my hair, teased me mercilessly and saw I took the blame for his misdeeds. He was everything an older brother should be—clever, courageous and oh-so-handsome in his midshipman's uniform. My parents had such hopes for him."

And then it all came to an end. Julian had seen the same tragedy again and again, in bloody battle after bloody battle. How different her life might have been if her brother had lived. Perhaps he would have earned enough prize money to provide her a modest income—at least, enough to save her from an impecunious governess's fate. "Do you have sisters?"

Her eyes darkened, brown swallowing the green. "I had one. She suffered a grievous injury."

"I'm sorry. When was this?"

"Ten years ago."

Shortly before she became Teresa's governess. Was there a connection between the two events? "Younger or older?"

"Younger."

"Ah, so you were an overlooked middle child—like me?"

"I cannot imagine you allowing yourself to be overlooked by anyone."

"If that is your polite way of suggesting I executed wicked deeds to attract attention, you are probably right." During the difficult period of his parents' marriage, even the DeChambelle children had felt the strain—and he had acted accordingly. And then his parents had sent him off to the navy. Perhaps those dark days explained the change in Elizabeth from the merry sister of his earlier memories. "I fear I shared all your brother's hair-pulling, sister-teasing faults with none of his virtues."

Miss Vance eyed him dubiously from under her bonnet, a frown drawing her brows together above her narrow slice of nose. "I'll grant you bedevil me even more than he, but I question your assertion that a man who rose to your rank possesses neither intelligence nor daring."

The path wound through a grove of snow-encrusted hawthorns, their berries glittering in the last rays of daylight. "I notice you didn't include an assessment of my appearance in comparison to your brother's."

Their gazes met. Locked. Held for interminable moments while the horse stumbled and tossed Miss Vance to the side—like the shift in his world. Julian clutched her arm to steady her, adding a physical dimension to the connection. Despite the afternoon's deepening cold, warmth washed through him.

She maintained her stare for several more seconds, her eyes wide with uncertainty, longing, fear. "Thank you, but I have—"

A shot shattered the stillness and tore branches from a nearby bush.

Chapter Six

Leah's fingers tightened around the horse's mane. Too late. The animal lurched, jerked and reared. Perched sideways on a man's saddle, Leah's precarious balance failed and she surrendered to gravity. At least the snow cushioned her fall. Mostly.

"Whoa!" Above her Chambelston hauled on the flailing horse's reins. He glanced over his shoulder, and Leah realized that not only did he seek to protect her from the thrashing hooves, he'd also maneuvered the animal between her and the origin of the gunshot.

Despite her fear—and pain radiating from her newly sprained knee—warmth kindled inside her at his gallantry, then mingled with her concern for him. Words bubbled in her throat, a rusty plea for help, protection. But would anyone—the One—hear her or heed her? Using her arms as leverage, she pushed herself up to see if she could identify who had fired the gunshot.

"Stay down until I say!" Chambelston scrambled into the saddle Leah had unwillingly vacated.

Down? Where she might be trampled—again? The horse reeled, and Leah obediently dropped back onto the ground. Snow sprayed against her cheeks and stuck to her eyelashes. She tensed as nerve-racking seconds ticked by. No second shot. Had their assailant reloaded? Or had the entire episode been an accident, a wild shot from an overzealous hunter?

Chambelston dragged on the reins until the animal's agitation diminished to a mere tossing of its head. "Now!" He leant over, one hand stretched down to her.

Leah popped up and clutched his arm, holding onto its steel strength as he pulled her onto the horse. He settled her in front of him, all the while still using his own body as a bulwark against further attacks. Then he urged the horse into a gallop. The skittish animal needed little encouragement to make haste. Leah shivered—from their near escape, the horse's speed, the cold or her proximity to one Lord Chambelston?

His arm still circled her, pressing her against the fine wool of his coat so that every breath infused her senses with him.

She struggled to gain a little space, a little poise. "Did you see who fired the shot?"

"No. My only concern was a swift retreat. And your safety." His deep voice rumbled in his chest and vibrated against her ear. "The first rule of battle is to avoid a fight unless you know you are the better armed."

"But it may have only been a hunter—"

"On Sotherton's lands? At dusk?"

"A poacher, then. A tenant trying to feed his family this winter."

"He would be a very inefficient one in that case. My dear Miss Vance, that shot was fired from a pistol, not a rifle." And Chambelston, a man who'd spent years at war, would know the difference, of course. "Besides, I doubt even a blind poacher could mistake us for a rabbit."

Leah's turmoil and fear began to modulate into a new, more disturbing worry. Who would shoot at them? Fleming? Or had some of Alec's compatriots guessed at her perfidy? The cold began to creep through her coat to her heart.

Unless the shot was meant for Chambelston. Could he be right that his father had been murdered?

"Your friends?" His voice echoed her thoughts.

"Or perhaps your enemies." Relief speared through her as she spied Rowan Abbey through the deepening gloom. Candles gleamed a welcome glow through the windows. "Besides, as I told you, the radicals are not my friends."

"Ah, yes. Your only friends are invalid females and their exemplary relatives." Chambelston steered the horse toward the stable. "Do all your visits end with such excitement?"

"Not until I met you."

"As soon as the groom takes the horse, I'll assist you to the house."

The groom! Wetherel would have known about Leah's absence and Chambelston's ride. Had he become suspicious after seeing them together last week? Suspicious enough to fire a warning? Their arrival together on the same horse would feed speculations.

Chambelston drew the horse to a halt beside the building and swung down from the saddle. He was reaching for Leah as the groom came out of the stable. "Ah, there you are. As you can see, Miss Vance suffered a fall on her outing today. Fortunately I encountered her on my ride and was able to assist her."

Wetherel eyed the gelding's lathered state, a frown drawing down his mouth. "I hope Miss Vance will recover."

"I'm certain she'll be fine with the proper rest." Chambelston gathered her in his arms and lifted her off the horse.

Leah fought the urge to protest. She wanted to walk—flee even. But what with both her foot and her knee, she feared such an attempt would make even more of a spectacle than the sight of their esteemed visitor carrying the governess to the house.

Pressed against his chest—one arm around her back and

the other below her knees—Leah kept her gaze focused outward, afraid he would intercept so much as a glance should she chance to look up. If he noticed her awkward silence and taut muscles, he graciously refrained from commenting. Her skirt cascaded over his arm to reveal the slice in her boot. The foot inside continued to throb. Tomorrow she would sport an ugly bruise. Or worse.

"Upstairs?" he asked once they had reached the narrow staircase that wound through the rear of the manor.

"Yes." The dark passageway magnified the even rasps of his breaths and added another layer of uncomfortable intimacy to her predicament. Fortunately they didn't encounter any of the servants, not even the prescient Molly and her uncanny ability to find Leah at the most inopportune times.

At the top of the stairs Leah tapped on Chambelston's shoulder. "Thank you, my lord. I can manage from here."

He lowered her feet to the bare plank floor—but kept his arm around her shoulders. At least the pain in her knee had mitigated to a twinge. "You should be careful with that foot until you know if any bones were broken. I'll explain to Teresa."

She shuffled to the closed door of her humble chamber. "Thank you for all your assistance today." Especially for the rescue from Fleming. She waited for him to leave.

He didn't. "Aren't you going to invite me into your chamber? It seems only fair. Besides, we wouldn't want you to further injure your foot." That sardonic smile flashed in murky darkness.

"I believe you enjoyed teasing your sisters all those years ago."

"And pulling their hair." He tipped back her bonnet and gave a stray strand of her hair a tweak. She stared into his eyes, her heart accelerating.

Footsteps tapped against the floor. Leah jerked back and bumped her head against the door of her own room.

"Ah, Molly," Chambelston greeted the maid who strode toward them. He knew her by name? "Miss Vance suffered a serious fall today. Would you bring her a tray so she doesn't have to navigate the stairs?"

"Of course, my lord." Molly gave him a curtsey and Leah a smile.

"And Miss Vance, I'll bring my sister Caroline to see you in the schoolroom tomorrow. Good night." He whirled and strode to the steps, leaving Leah full of disquiet and questions.

Just why did an earl know his sister's maid by name? Uncommon consideration, romantic interest, or…additional reconnaissance?

Julian paused in the doorway of the schoolroom. Morning sunshine filled the chamber with cheerful brightness. A flood of memories cascaded over him as he examined the tidy battalion of books that marched across shelves, the neat arrangement of papers that garbed the desktop, the childish sketches of local landscapes that adorned the walls. How long had it been since the schoolroom at Chambelston House had heard children's laughter?

Not since the death of his brother Gregory's son in the same epidemic that had taken Julian's older brother.

Responsibility once again gnawed at him. He would have to marry, produce children—if only to provide reassurance and a promise of stability to the people on his estate, those whose lives and livelihoods depended on him and his family.

At the desk Teresa and her governess sat with heads bent over a book. Suddenly his niece glanced up and caught him lingering in the doorway. "Uncle Julian! Oh, and you've brought Aunt Caroline. How delightful."

Miss Vance rose from her chair—slowly, her movements

stiff and jerky. She had her hair pinned back in her usual straight, severe style. And yet he imagined a new softness in the wide hazel eyes that met his. Held.

Caro tugged on his hand.

"I hope we're not interrupting." He guided his younger sister into the room.

"Only in the best way. Miss Vance is valiantly trying to correct my atrocious French. A hopeless cause, I tell you." Teresa swept forward and circled an arm around Caro's shoulders, drawing her from Julian to her governess. "Miss Vance, this is my Aunt Caroline."

"How do you do, Lady Caroline? Do you like stories? I thought perhaps we could read together this morning." A smile touched Miss Vance's lips and triggered the dimple in her cheek, transforming her face from plain to…something else. Julian's breath caught in his chest.

Caro glanced uncertainly over her shoulder at Julian. Strange situations and new people always made his sister apprehensive. "It will be all right. Anna will bring your luncheon here later."

"Then go home?"

"Not today—but soon." Maybe. Julian surveyed Miss Vance over the top of Caro's head. "How is your foot today?"

"Bruised and a bit swollen, but nothing broken, I think."

"That's good. I'm sorry to disrupt your day."

"Well, I'm glad you did." Teresa tilted her head at a jaunty angle. "I'm hopeless at French—I haven't the ear for it. I only consented to learn the language so that in the event I ever meet Napoleon, I can tell him what I think."

"And because your mother insisted." Fondness laced Miss Vance's words. "Although should you ever have occasion to speak to the little tyrant, no doubt he will find your accent his most severe punishment."

"You see?" Teresa looked at Julian with a smug nod. "Hopeless."

Julian let a smile escape. "My mother was raised in France."

Teresa's eyes grew wistful. "I know. I wish…"

"We'll make it happen." He didn't know how he would convince Elizabeth to let Maman meet her oldest grandchild, but he would. Teresa needed her family. And so did Maman.

"I imagine you have excellent conversational skills in French, Uncle Julian."

"Not exactly. My brother Kit—Christopher, that is—is the linguist. I excelled at mathematics. And teasing my sisters. That's the reason our parents sent him to the university and me to the navy."

"Perhaps you should stay, then." A mischievous grin curved the corner of Teresa's mouth. The matchmaking minx. "I'm sure Miss Vance would teach you French. And perhaps read to you also."

If only he could read Miss Vance—her motives for her actions, her potential for betrayal. Would she yet deceive him? More and more he hoped not, believed not. Her real, and returned, affection for her charge suggested one who cared deeply for others. An image formed in his mind of a governess frantic to save an impoverished and invalid friend—enough to commit treason even? Was her crime borne of desperation rather than greed? "I'll be out for a while, but I shall return this afternoon." He intended to investigate the local pub. Not that he expected to learn much, but one should at least know the lay of the land. And since Miss Vance had informed the radicals of his presence in the neighborhood, he'd let them have a look. "Will you be staying?"

"Only for another hour or so. I'm to ride with Reggie this afternoon."

A frown wiped away Miss Vance's dimple. "Don't ride too far."

So she disapproved. Of a certainty the man had behaved dreadfully toward her, but surely she didn't believe Fleming would abuse his cousin, did she?

Would he?

Leah held up another picture card for Lady Caroline. "What is this?"

"Dog."

"Very good." She looked into the uptilted eyes whose lids had started to droop. "And what does a dog say?"

"Woof." Caroline touched the sketch—Teresa's work, of course. Not Leah's. "Like Henry."

"Is Henry your dog at home?"

Lady Caroline nodded, sadness mingling with exhaustion in the wide blue eyes. "Miss him."

"And I'm sure he misses you just as much." Leah gave the girl's narrow shoulders a squeeze.

Memories washed through her mind and yielded an unhappiness that matched Lady Caroline's. Two decades ago, Leah had shared similar afternoons with her younger sister Phoebe. And afterward with a young Teresa.

Loneliness settled in her soul as she contemplated the future. And from here, where?

The door squeaked open and Leah shoved the melancholy images away. "Molly—" She stopped as she identified the handsome face and broad shoulders that entered the room.

"Jules!" Lady Caroline leaped from the chair and flew to her brother.

Leah's heart began to pound at an accelerated rate despite her stern admonishments to herself. How ridiculous to develop a tendre for a man so far beyond her reach. And at her age, no less. A man who held her life—and her sister's—in his hands. Pride straightened her spine lest he perceive her folly. "Can we help you, my lord?"

"I came to see how Caro fares." Chambelston wrapped an arm around his sister.

Leah fought back the momentary spurt of jealousy at Lady Caroline's good fortune. At least she—unlike Lady Caroline or her sister Phoebe—had the ability to provide for her own needs, no matter how onerous she found the task. Or rather, the employers. "I enjoy Lady Caroline's company."

"But is she too much extra work for you? That is…" He glanced around the room, a frown tugging at his mouth. "I don't see Anna."

"I sent her to manage Lady Caroline's wardrobe." Leah folded her hands and stared at him from over her fingers. "Anna is… That is, I think perhaps her talents would be better served as Lady Caroline's maid than as her nurse."

"Yes, I've become aware of her shortcomings." Sorrow darkened his eyes. "Our nurse in Somerset is too old to travel such distances now. Indeed, my mother is Caro's primary caretaker."

His mother? The Countess of Chambelston?

A bit of his grief lifted from his face. "I see you are shocked at the notion of a mother caring for her own offspring."

"Well, I must consider that if too many mothers followed her example, women like me would find themselves without means."

"I think there will always be enough women like my sister that your future is secure."

Secure. Would she ever know true security?

Chambelston drew his sister back to the picture-strewn table where Leah and Lady Caroline had been working before his interruption. "What have the two of you been doing?"

"Your sister has been learning the alphabet."

He blinked, those long dark lashes sweeping against his cheek. "The alphabet?"

Leah lifted a picture card and showed it to Lady Caroline. "Tell your brother what this animal is."

"Lion!"

"Very good! And what sound do lions make?"

The girl discharged a credible roar, her blue eyes alight with amusement. Even Chambelston emitted a chuckle.

"Exactly." Leah picked up a card with a letter. "And what is this?"

"C!"

"And what sound does C make?"

"KKK. Like Caro."

Leah patted the back of her hand. "Perfect."

"This is wonderful, Caro." Lord Chambelston tilted his head, a lock of gilded hair coming to rest across his brow as he looked from his sister to Leah. "But do you really think—"

Leah forestalled the rest of his question with a raised hand. "Perhaps you would like to look at pictures with your sister for a moment?"

He arched a brow at this command but obediently asked Lady Caroline about the next picture while Leah painfully crossed the room and rang the bell. She hovered there in the corner, watching the interaction between brother and sister, once more feeling the outsider.

The door glided open again. "Yes, Miss Vance? Oh, my lord!" Molly dropped into a curtsey, eyes downcast.

Leah patted the maid's shoulder. "Molly, would you help Lady Caroline see to her, um, personal needs?"

"Of course, Miss Vance. If my lady will come with me?" Molly offered the girl an understanding smile as she took her arm and led her to a door at the far side of the schoolroom.

Leah waited until it shut behind them. "Yes, I think Lady Caro could learn to read."

"Read?" Hope mingled with skepticism in his eyes. "Miss Vance, when I asked if there was anything you could do for my sister... I love Caro dearly, but she can barely feed herself. She needs assistance with the simplest tasks—such as even now." He glanced meaningfully at the door where Lady Caroline had vanished with Molly.

"All those tasks involve her hands. Reading would engage her mind."

"But she has the mind of a child of five years or so."

"And many children of that age do read. Perhaps not Shakespeare, but they can recognize basic words. Consider, my lord, Lady Caroline can identify pictures and letters. Why not simple words?"

"I...don't know what to say." The blue in his eyes smoldered with...approbation? Even admiration?

As the silence stretched, tension tightened around her lungs. "I doubt Lady Caroline will ever be able to write so much as her name, but I see no reason why she couldn't learn to read it." Leah pushed the words through her constricted throat.

"When I asked you to assess Caro, I never expected... That is, like everyone else, I underestimated her." He cupped Leah's cheek, his palm warm and hard and strong against her skin. "Thank you, Miss Vance. Thank you for letting me see my sister in a new light."

A door squeaked and footsteps tapped against the floor. Leah jerked back, her face still burning from Chambelston's touch, as Molly and Lady Caroline returned. "I...ah..." She pulled her gaze from that mesmerizing stare and focused on anything other than the larger-than-life man in the room— the desk, the window, the wall, the clock.

The clock.

Lady Caroline had returned to her brother's side, happily

identifying pictures and even a few letters on the cards scattered across the desk.

Leah sidled closer to the maid. "Has Lady Teresa returned from her ride?"

"Not that I've heard." Molly's mouth flattened, her lips fading to white as she glanced from the clock to the window where the waning afternoon warned of coming darkness. "She went with Mr. Fleming, didn't she?"

The two women shared a look that sent shock reeling through Leah. Molly, too?

"I'll ask Mrs. Anderson." The maid slipped out of the room.

Leah ambled to the desk where Chambelston still patiently plied his sister with questions. Her stomach churned with anxiety. And the proximity to the man in her schoolroom.

The one who looked up at her approach and smiled. "Miss Vance, may I talk to you about a position?"

"A position? I thought you already…employed me."

"This is for a more traditional role. And perhaps more enduring. Caro enjoys your company, and you see potential in her no one else has. My niece is of an age where her need for a governess is coming to an end, and you will need a new situation. Would you consider a position in my household?"

A shard of disappointment sliced through her before she could stifle it. How silly, how ridiculous the longings of a lonely spinster. Instead she focused on what his offer meant for her future. Money—possibly more than customarily provided to an ordinary governess. Enough to cover Phoebe's expenses? "Caring for your sister?"

"At our family seat in Somerset."

The ray of optimism crashed against the shores of reality. Given the rift between Chambelston and Lady Sotherton, how often would the family travel to Northamptonshire? How could she visit Phoebe from so great a distance? "I—"

"Miss Vance?" Molly stepped into the schoolroom. "No one in the household has seen Lady Teresa since this morning. Would you like me to check with Wetherel?"

Leah glanced at the snow-covered gardens beyond the window, feeling the chill grow within her.

"I'll go." The gentle baritone rumbled along Leah's spine. "If she hasn't returned, I'll mount a search," Chambelston said.

"I'll come with you."

The tawny brows arched. "Miss Vance, may I remind you that by your own admission, you aren't a proficient rider."

"But I know the countryside."

"So do Sotherton's grooms, I imagine."

Unfortunately he was right. Leah would slow him down. But she couldn't let him go without her. What if Teresa had been thrown from her horse or shot at like Leah…or worse? Leah let her eyes fall shut for several long seconds. Images flashed through her mind, a combination of horrific memories and terrible imaginings. Bile raced to her throat at the dreadful possibilities. She couldn't let Teresa be found without a woman present. "My lord, please…"

"Very well, get your things. You'd probably just follow anyway and then if you got lost, we'd have three missing people from the household." He gave his sister a smile and a hug. "Molly can stay with Caro if that is agreeable."

Despite the concern shadowing the maid's eyes, she smiled. "I should enjoy that, my lord, but I must confirm that with Mrs. Anderson."

"I'll speak to her when I get my coat." Chambelston pivoted and marched to the corridor.

Leah hobbled into her small chamber next to the schoolroom and glanced at her simple gown. Hardly a riding habit, but it would have to do. She shoved her feet into her battered boots, wincing as the stiff leather squeezed her bruised, swollen foot. She rammed her tattered bonnet over her hair, wrapped a scarf around her neck and grabbed her coat and gloves. Worry and hurry made her movements clumsy, and she was still struggling to find her coat sleeve as she limped into the hallway.

An assisting hand on her collar halted her. Her stomach tensed even before she turned and looked into blue, blue eyes. So close. Much too close. He had already retrieved his cloak, and she spied a brace of pistols tucked in his waistband. Did he also expect trouble?

"Ready?"

She nodded and led him down the narrow stairs that led to a door near the stable. The sun sat low on the horizon, warning of coming cold and darkness. Not even the stable's warmth and sweet smells of hay and horses alleviated the horrible knot around Leah's ribs.

Wetherel's eyes widened at the sight of the two of them in the stable again.

Chambelston stepped forward. "Have Lady Teresa and Fleming returned from their ride?"

"No, my lord. Not yet."

"Did they take a groom with them?"

"Lady Teresa assured me she didn't need one to accompany her, seeing how she had her cousin."

As if Fleming would be of assistance in a crisis. And indeed he would mostly likely be the cause of it.

"Saddle horses for Miss Vance and me—and for the grooms. We'll search for them."

Wetherel nodded and shouted orders to the stable boys. A swarm of activity ensued.

"Do you know where they intended to ride?"

"They were heading east when they departed, my lord."

East. Toward the location where only yesterday Leah had encountered Fleming, Chambelston and a gunshot.

"Very well, we shall begin in that direction." Chambelston led Leah outside and lifted her onto a calm sorrel mare, his hands strong and solid under her foot. "An excellent choice of horse for you." He mounted the black with an easy, masculine grace and then barked orders to the grooms to fan out on either side of them. His voice boomed with authority over the snowy landscape, offering Leah a glimpse of the commanding captain he'd once been.

Leah threaded the reins through her fingers and concentrated all her attention on maintaining her seat as they set off at a sprightly cantor. She peeked at the ground, so far below and disappearing so rapidly behind. No, better to keep her eyes focused on the darkening horizon. The chilly air gusted against her cheeks and tugged at her bonnet. They crested a knoll when one of the grooms exclaimed, "My lord, there!"

The groom on the far left pointed to a riderless bay trotting toward them. Lord Sotherton's prize stallion. The group pushed their horses to even greater speed. Leah's stomach fell as if it had tumbled from the horse when she spied the figures milling around a prostrate form. Cudgels rose and fell while a lone rider circled the group, weaving in and out of the trees, her frantic pleas carried on the wind.

Teresa.

Brave, foolish girl. Leah's pride mixed with terrible fear.

Chambelston whipped out a pistol and raised it in the air. The shot reverberated over the rolling fields like the one Leah had heard only the day before. The attackers paused, then scattered in all directions, most heading to cover in the nearby trees.

Teresa vaulted from her horse and crouched next to the unconscious man on the ground as the five from the Abbey— three grooms, a governess and one English earl—drew near.

"See to Teresa!" Chambelston shouted as he wheeled his horse and pursued one of the fleeing assailants.

Leah pulled the mare to a halt and clambered out of the saddle. Her legs trembled and her foot ached as she trudged through the snow and knelt at Teresa's side. The girl's hat had disappeared during the fray. Locks of dark hair drooped from her chignon and wisped around her wide, frightened eyes.

"Are you injured?" Leah tugged on her arm, noting the rent in the fabric of the fine riding coat.

"Not me." Teresa's hands shook as she pressed a handkerchief against her cousin's temple near to the spot where Leah's poker had left its mark three years ago. Bright red blood infected the white linen and the supple dun of her gloves. "But Reggie…"

Leah's gaze traveled over Fleming's abused body. In addition to the gash on his head the angry shadows of forming bruises stained his eyes and cheeks. His hat had long vanished, and the tattered remnants of his coat waved in the breeze. She tugged a glove off his hand, noting the swelling already stretching the red skin. Despite her loathing of the man, a fragment of sympathy lodged in her heart.

Approaching footsteps tossed snow against Leah's skirt. She glanced up as Chambelston squatted beside them. "Did you catch any?"

"They all got away. Knew just where to hide."

Which meant they were local. Some of Alec's…friends?

Leah pulled her gaze from the mesmerizing pools of blue and glanced around. Only then did she realize how close they were to the place where someone had fired a shot only yesterday. At her.

Chapter Seven

Julian studied Fleming's swollen, broken body where he lay amid snow trampled by boots and spotted with blood. The slash across his cheek—administered by Julian only yesterday—had disappeared under dozens of angry welts. A warning or an interrupted murder? "How is he?"

Miss Vance's troubled gaze met his. Did the same questions whir through her mind—or did she know the answers? "He needs a doctor, and soon."

"I sent two of the grooms back to retrieve a sleigh." Julian ripped his stare from the unruly tendrils defying her normal tidiness and focused on his niece. "Teresa, did you recognize any of your attackers? Were they from nearby?"

"I don't know." Teresa's chignon slipped a bit farther as she tilted her head to peer up at him. Her cousin's blood sullied the trim of her riding habit and the fingers of her gloves. Anger and pride warred in Julian. No fainting spell or hysteria for his niece. She had kept her head during the assault, indeed her bravery bordered on foolishness. "That is, they spoke like local men, but they'd blackened their faces with soot, of course."

"That should make them remarkable. We'll ask around.

Someone will have noticed a man covering his face with soot."

Miss Vance tapped his arm. "It's Plough Monday, my lord."

"What day?"

"Plough Monday. Do you not celebrate the day in Somerset?"

"I can't say I'm familiar with the term." But then, Julian had spent most of his life at sea, not in England at all.

"On the first Monday after Twelfth Night, it is customary for the farm workers here to cover their faces with soot. They decorate their ploughs and pull them from house to house asking for money."

"Must be a local custom. I've never seen any such procession."

"It provides farm workers with a few extra coins during the depths of winter."

"How convenient that of all days of the year, Fleming would be attacked on a day when half the men in the district have blackened faces." What a perfect opportunity to commit mayhem.

"Perhaps someone will remember a gang of painted plough boys without a plough."

"But why Fleming, a mere visitor to these parts?" Ugly thoughts invaded Julian's mind. A visitor, yes, but one who had attacked a local woman only yesterday. A local woman with a connection to the violent rabble who had fatally injured his father? He looked to Teresa again. "Do you remember the size of this mob? I counted five."

She pursed her lips. "That is probably correct, but it seemed like more."

No doubt. "Did they have any weapons? A pistol perhaps? A knife?"

"Not that I saw. Only the cudgels."

In other words, they were perfectly inconspicuous.

"My lord!"

Julian whipped his head up as the two grooms reappeared with the sleigh. They drew the horses to a stop near Fleming. "We'll have to lift him. Grab his feet," he instructed one of the grooms. Julian positioned himself behind the prone man's head.

The groom clamped his arms around Fleming's boots. "Ready, my lord."

"Lift!"

The two of them hoisted the wounded man onto the upholstered seat. A moan escaped Fleming's lips once and his eyelids flickered, then he fell back into his swoon. Teresa followed them to the side of the sleigh.

Julian covered her hand with his. "Would you prefer to ride with your cousin?"

The blue of Teresa's eyes hardened to crystal and her skin tightened over her cheeks. "I would be more useful on horseback if they return."

"They won't." Julian hoped. He led her toward Wetherel, who held her horse.

She accepted the reins, then paused when Julian would have assisted her into the saddle. "I'm glad you arrived when you did, Uncle Julian."

"The credit belongs to your governess. Miss Vance worried when you didn't return home in a timely manner."

A smile flickered on her mouth despite the shadows that lingered in her eyes. "Then I'm pleased she persuaded you to join the search."

He hoisted her onto the horse, then sidled closer to Miss Vance. The breeze ruffled the collar of her coat. Fleming had harassed her at the piano and assaulted her on the path. And more? She had good reason—perhaps even more than he knew—to detest the man and wish him ill rather than well. "Someone needs to ride in the sleigh with Fleming and monitor his injuries."

"And as the least experienced rider, I'm the preferred candidate." Resignation darkened the hazel eyes to brown.

"I realize this is difficult for you. Fleming doesn't deserve your kindness." He smoothed a finger along a cheek pinkened by the cold. "Just don't take advantage of his swoon to complete his attackers' mission."

As he'd hoped, the dimple momentarily flashed before she straightened her shoulders. "I'm surprisingly resistant to such urges. Consider, my lord, you know a secret dangerous to my well-being—and I haven't yet murdered you in your bed to prevent you from publicizing it."

"For which I am vastly grateful." He wrapped his hands around her waist, lifted her into the sleigh and waited while she arranged a blanket over Fleming's motionless form. "How far to the nearest doctor?"

"Assuming he isn't out with another patient, you'll find him several miles to the north in the village."

Past the copse where the assailants had disappeared. Julian considered the assembled group. With the miscreants possibly yet lurking in the vicinity, he couldn't send a single man alone into the area. "Wetherel, take a man with you and fetch the doctor. And take this also. Just in case Fleming's friends return." He extracted the second, still-loaded, pistol.

"But my lord, you may have need of it."

"I have another." Julian thrust the weapon into the man's hand.

"Already discharged, sir."

"But they won't know which is which. You are riding toward them while we are riding away. You have the greater need."

A silent look passed on the long gaze the groom leveled at

him. "Thank you, my lord." He gestured to one of the other men who mounted Miss Vance's horse, and the two rode away.

Leah lifted the edge of Teresa's handkerchief and examined the wound on Fleming's head. At least the bleeding had subsided to a trickle. The fiend would probably survive. She returned the cloth to his forehead, applying pressure to this bloody injury so near to the jagged edges of his three-year-old scar. The one she'd drawn with a poker.

"Whoa!" The driver gave a shout and the sleigh skidded to a halt before the grand entrance to Rowan Abbey.

Long established boxwoods directed visitors toward the door that now swung open. Lights blazed from the windows in expectation of their return. Stable boys rushed forward to take the horses while footmen—and even Hawkesworth the butler—scrambled from the house to carry the injured man. Lady Sotherton swept into the fray, her frown drawn more tightly than usual as she studied her nephew.

Leah backed into a corner of the sleigh while men seized Fleming and lifted him out of the vehicle. "Watch his head."

The butler gave a crisp nod. "I'll see to him, Miss Vance."

Lady Sotherton retreated a step as the servants carried Fleming past, then she looked to her daughter. Her eyes, normally so cold and hard, widened as her gaze swept over the disheveled hair and blood-spattered coat. "Teresa? Are you… are you injured?"

"I'm unharmed." Teresa dismounted from her horse, then sagged against her mother.

Leah scrambled to exit the sleigh, but a hand on her shoulder forestalled her.

"Give them a moment together." Chambelston's deep voice rumbled in her ear and his warm breath wafted against her cheek.

"I…" Leah watched in wonder as mother and daughter

clung to each other. Conflicting emotions collided within her—happiness for Teresa's sake, and yet, a redoubled sense of exclusion—as the two moved to the house.

"She still needs you."

"Not really. Not for much longer."

"And she'll always love you."

"But it's her mother she most wants." As it should be. Still…Leah pulled her gaze from the women disappearing into the manor and stared at her hands. With Fleming's blood staining the threads, her gloves were well and truly ruined now. Absently she tugged them off her fingers and dropped them onto the upholstery.

Chambelston's hand, still resting heavily on her shoulder, gave her a squeeze. "Come. You need to get inside, too."

Except for the groom waiting to drive the sleigh away, they were alone, all the others having retreated to the house. "Yes, thank you."

Chambelston held forth his hand. The dark fabric of his greatcoat disappeared into the deepening gloom of twilight, but the lights from the house glimmered on his face. After a flicker of hesitation she placed her palm against the leather and let him assist her out of the conveyance. "Where are your gloves?"

"I…" In what way could she explain her revulsion to all things related to Reginald Fleming?

As the groom urged the horse into motion, Chambelston tugged the leather from his fingers, then wrapped his hand—big, strong, warm—around hers. His thumbs stroked the sensitive skin of her wrists right above her frantically beating pulse. "Your skin is like ice. I hope you haven't succumbed to frostbite."

How could she think of cold when his actions filled her with warmth? Nightfall spawned shadows. And intimacy. The quiet closed around them as the horses retreated to their stable. She should move away—run, even—lest she create more heartache for herself.

Instead she raised her gaze to his face.

His eyes gleamed with unfamiliar intensity and…yearning? Time slowed. Stopped. Tension coiled low inside her as he lifted her hands—both of them—and pressed them to his cheeks on either side of his face. Warm skin and rough stubble tingled against her touch. "Leah." He whispered her name, the name only her cousin had used in…how long?…and lowered his face. His lips brushed hers. Soft. Seeking.

The breeze tossed silken strands of his hair against the sensitive skin of her knuckles, a whisper-light caress. A spark of delight ignited in her heart and radiated through her, a sweet burning ache in her chest. The power of her loneliness and longing flared through her, melting the strength from her bones.

And then he withdrew. Only inches, yet far enough to let the rush of common sense and regret return.

Leah lowered her hands and retreated a step on shaky knees. Foolish, foolish woman with no more sense than a silly girl. How could she ever allow herself to suppose that one of her position, of her past and with her insane sister could aspire to a match with a wealthy lord? "We should go in the house before we are missed." Or seen.

He stretched forth his arm—as if to tempt her to imprudence once again—and then as if he too realized the absurdity of their actions, he let his hand fall to his side. With a nod of his head, he fell into step beside her. "Miss Vance, it was unpardonable of me to put your reputation at risk like that. Still, I beg your forgiveness."

"Of course." The dull throb in her foot paled beside the intense agony in her heart.

"Good. For the world, I wouldn't have you think me the kind of man who takes advantage of unprotected females."

Lord Chambelston had offered her a position, but she could never serve on his staff. Even if she hadn't had Phoebe to concern her, she could never live in his household and subject herself to the agony of seeing him day after day. Not after these sweet, reckless moments.

Once inside the entrance hall Chambelston passed his coat to the hovering butler. "I trust the men have Fleming safely settled in his chamber?"

"Indeed, my lord."

"Good." Chambelston stared thoughtfully at the servant. "Hawkesworth, do you know of any unusual activity involving Mr. Fleming? Have any been inquiring about him of late? Or did he receive any messages recently?"

"No, my lord."

"Thank you. The doctor should be here presently. Notify me when he arrives."

Hawkesworth withdrew while Chambelston escorted Leah across the entrance hall.

At the bottom of the staircase she paused and labored to imbue her words with a lightness that revealed none of the heaviness inside her head and heart. "Thank you for all your assistance today. What with Lord Sotherton and Viscount Killiane's departure for London, I don't know what we would have done without you."

"My niece is fortunate to have you in her life. And perhaps my sister has at last located some of her misplaced humanity. A pity it took such an atrocity."

"Better now than never, I suppose." With a final nod, Leah scaled the stairs to the schoolroom above.

What did it mean? She brushed a finger against her lips, as if she yet felt Chambelston's touch. A momentary lapse… or something more? The better she understood the man, the less she thought him capable of trifling with the affections of an impoverished governess. After all, he hadn't used his power over her when he'd had the opportunity, nor seen her fired or charged for her crimes. Why would he put her position in jeopardy for whim?

Painful memories assailed her with familiar doubts. Once before she'd placed her hopes in a man's attachment, only to find his ardor wane when faced with the reality of her situation, her sister. The jaws of responsibility snapped around her again, imprisoning her in her nebulous existence. No doubt with the weight of an earldom on his shoulders, Lord Chambelston would find such connections—to her, to Phoebe—equally intolerable.

Unless he didn't know until after the vows had been spoken.

So many advantages—for her. Funds for Phoebe's care. Safety for Alec. Even security for herself. But could she be so callous as to take advantage of his regard for her own gain?

Leah paused in the schoolroom entrance and watched the maid playing with Lady Caroline. The two held hands and twirled, then dropped to the floor in a flourish of giggles. Sorrow tightened around Leah's chest as memories of a young Teresa bombarded her mind. Her life here was coming to a close. Where would she go?

Molly glanced up, her anxious gaze flickering over Leah. "Miss Vance?"

"We found Lady Teresa. She is fine." Leah strolled to the other side of the room to join the two women. She extended a hand and helped Lady Caroline to her feet. The light of the laughter in her eyes reflected on the soft blue of her gown.

"I'm so glad." The concern eased from the Molly's mouth. "Anna?"

Leah turned to see the maid in the doorway.

"I've come to take Lady Caroline to her dinner."

"Dinner." The girl's smile broadened and she obligingly left with her maid.

"No doubt Mrs. Anderson requires me." Molly paced toward the door, then stopped and turned. "What of Mr. Fleming?"

"A gang of men attacked and severely beat him. He was still unconscious when we returned. Wetherel went to fetch the doctor."

"But they left Lady Teresa unharmed?"

"Other than being understandably distressed, yes."

Pain shadowed the maid's eyes and rested on her still features. "Mr. Fleming obscenely used women he didn't consider his equal. Perhaps he ill-treated the wrong man's sister or wife. Still, I will pray for his recovery."

"And do you believe God will hear your prayers?" He had ignored enough of Leah's—and if Molly had fallen victim to Fleming, at least one of hers had also gone unheeded. Leah no longer bothered the Almighty with her petitions.

"God always hears our prayers, Miss Vance. But sometimes he has another plan, a greater vision for our future than we can see with our limited focus on the here and now."

Try as she might, Leah had never perceived any great purpose in her sister's suffering. "And what great design did your God have in mind when He allowed you to be abused by the likes of Fleming?" The unkind words and bitterness poured forth before Leah could block them as she had for so many years.

"Perhaps, Miss Vance, God allowed my ordeal so I could minister to you." With quiet dignity, the maid exited.

Leah stared at the closed door for several long moments, emotions whirling with a mix of contempt and contrition. Despite the hardships, Molly had a serenity Leah lacked.

Because…?

Her gaze dropped to the desk where she'd sat for so many hours and days and years with Teresa. Teresa, who even now probably shared dinner with her mother and other members of the family, except for her incapacitated cousin.

Who had attacked Fleming? Local men, if they came on foot and knew how to disappear like wraiths into the trees. But why?

Leah slid into the chair and withdrew a sheet of paper. After a moment's hesitation she also retrieved her invisible ink and its antidote—just to be safe. Then she composed a note to Alec. Once she had completed the words—both visible and not—she sealed the letter and departed for the stable.

Somehow she would find a way to leave the manor on the morrow.

Julian tapped on the schoolroom door. His heart pounded a louder tattoo in his chest as he debated what he would say, what excuse he would make. Should he apologize? He didn't feel particularly remorseful for kissing Miss Vance—Leah—in the yard where all and sundry could see them. Indeed, he felt…enthralled. Even optimistic. And like doing it again. The murky future extending before him crystalized into splendid possibilities.

The silent seconds stretched. He glanced over his shoulder, aware that should any of the staff find him skulking in the hallway like an infatuated schoolboy, he would irreversibly damage Leah's reputation.

Had she retired for the night already? He knocked on the door one more time, waited, then turned to leave. Only to spy her stealing around a corner.

Her eyes widened the moment she detected him. "My—my lord. Did you need something?" Surprise? Or guilt?

Pink roses bloomed on her cheeks from embarrassment at his presence…or exposure to the cold night air. His gaze traveled the length of her humble gown, pausing at the piece of straw still stuck to her hem. Not a typical schoolroom accessory.

He desperately wanted to believe it lingered from their legitimate sojourn to the stable that afternoon—before their madcap ride to Teresa's rescue, her return via the sleigh, their kiss in the courtyard. Alas, he'd never been one to gamble against the odds, and he wouldn't start now. Not when his future, perhaps even his heart, was at risk.

Julian could deduce only one reason she had visited the stables at this time of night, why a woman with an injured foot would ignore the pain to scale the stairs and traipse through the corridors. Dreams—real, for all that they were yet indistinct—blew away like grass in the wind. Mere illusions without substance. "I came to ensure you suffered no ill effects from this afternoon." The lie came easily. The anger even more so.

"No. No. I'm fine, as you can see." Her large, expressive eyes glimmered in the glow of a distant sconce.

"In all the…excitement, I forgot to ask if you had delivered the message."

"About your inquiries into your father's death? Yes, I took it to the stable last night."

Last night. If only she'd said tonight. "And do you know if your mysterious contact received it?"

"I believe so. I'll check in the morning."

A whiff of lavender teased his senses with false promises. He fought back the urge to gather her in his arms and demand answers. Perhaps there was an explanation. Perhaps he was too sensitive and suspicious, too susceptible to cynicism. "Good, then." He backed away, intent on retreat.

"Has Dr. Grant come?"

"Ah, yes. He seemed more concerned about some of the critical blows to Fleming's person than the wound on his head. The doctor fears he could well be bleeding internally."

"Is there anything to be done?"

"Only wait." And wait is all Julian could likewise do—wait to see if Harrison's endeavors uncovered Miss Vance's dependability. Or disloyalty. "He awakened finally, though he seems very weak and confused. He is suffering rather acutely—the miscreants broke several of his ribs and the bone in his forearm—so the doctor gave him a sedative. The maid Molly is going to stay with him during the night."

"Molly! You can't ask that of her."

"She volunteered. Is there some reason she isn't competent for the task?"

"Oh, no. Of course not. Molly is supremely capable. It's only…"

Julian waited, but she didn't elaborate. "The magistrate will come tomorrow to speak to Teresa." And Fleming, if the man regained consciousness.

"The magistrate?"

"A crime was committed, Miss Vance." He stared into the wide hazel eyes. Did Miss Vance fear for her confidants? Unfortunately Julian doubted either his niece or her cousin could provide the necessary details to identify the villains. "He'll want to question Teresa. Fleming also, if he is up to it."

"Oh, yes, of course."

Julian offered her a brief bow, then with heavy feet, and heavier heart, he left to find solitude. He had nearly reached his bedchamber when a footman intercepted him.

"My lord?"

"Yes?"

"This message arrived for you moments ago."

Maman again? Pulse pounding, he accepted the missive and dismissed the servant with subdued thanks. In the seclusion of his room, he broke the seal.

Not Maman. Worse, really. Harrison wanted a meeting to discuss their next actions. As Julian read the words a second time, the last vestiges of his regard for Miss Vance vanished. The radicals had begun to make moves on Wellingborough. Someone, it seemed, had discovered the bogus report in his bedchamber and shared its contents.

He tossed the note on the fire and watched it burn—like the dreams he'd injudiciously entertained—to ashes.

Chapter Eight

The expressive song of a piano drew Julian to the music room where Miss Vance perched on the stool, her fingers marching across the keys in absolute precision. And yet, for all her meticulousness, she imbued the music with both passion and poignancy.

He leaned against the doorframe and let the melancholy harmonies mitigate his anger. An ivory ribbon twined through the simple knot of her brown hair, a contrast of light and dark rather like the woman herself.

She stopped, as if suddenly aware of another presence, and turned her head. Vague, unfocused eyes gazed upon him.

"I'm sorry. I interrupted." He started to retreat.

"No, don't go." The dreamy mien cleared from her gaze, replaced with a smile that stretched all the way to the dimple on her cheek.

He fought his reaction with reminders of her duplicity as he joined her at the piano. "I haven't heard you play since that dinner."

"I haven't. I, ah, I've found much to occupy me of late."

Or reasons to avoid Fleming? He gestured toward the pages on the music rest. "What are you playing?"

"Mozart's *Piano Sonata in C Minor*." She lifted her hands

from the keys and folded them on her lap. "How is Mr. Fleming this morning?"

"The doctor just left. He believes the worst may be past."

"The dowager will be relieved."

But not Miss Vance? "Fleming is still somewhat confused, but that could be an effect of the laudanum the doctor administered for his pain." Or a blow to his head from which he might never recover all his faculties.

"Did he tell you anything of the mob that attacked Lady Teresa and him?"

"Very little. The magistrate will be arriving later. I realize you didn't get a good look at Fleming's assailants, but by chance, would you have any conjectures as to their identity? You've been working with a group of local radicals."

"I've been passing messages along, not joining mobs or bludgeoning gentlemen."

"Tell me the identity of those who receive your messages."

Wariness shuttered her gaze and removed his last qualms. "I told you, I don't know. But I don't believe local men attacked Teresa."

"Such would be hardly a worse crime than those they've already committed." A bitter vision of his father's broken body lodged in Julian's mind. "If they resent the aristocracy, why would Teresa's presence be a deterrent?"

"Her father is a powerful official and confidant of the Regent himself."

"Many youth of France went to the guillotine with their parents."

"Surely you do not find the situation here in any way similar?"

"I suspect you have some sympathy for the rabble rousers, Miss Vance, but surely you can see they must be stopped."

The muscles along her jaw tightened as she lifted her chin.

"I pity all people with empty bellies—but not enough to endanger Teresa."

No, in all her transgressing, Miss Vance had thus far carefully avoided involving her charge. Julian acknowledged it would have been uncharacteristic of her to plan an assault when she knew Teresa would be present. "Very well, I concede your loyalty to Teresa."

She inclined her head, but her eyes still glittered with affront. "Is the maid Molly still with Fleming?"

"No, she went to get some rest. One of the footmen—William, I think—is tending to his needs today."

The conversation languished into silence. Truly, what was one expected to say to the woman he'd kissed, only to see her betray him mere moments later? What kind of woman would exchange her chance to snare an earl—a wealthy earl, no less—for a few coins? The intensity of the loss roused his rage again and tightened around his throat. At least he hadn't offered his heart to one so undeserving. He retreated a step to expand the space between them. "I've distracted you from your pleasure long enough." He bowed and exited.

More distance. More anger. Less pain.

The early afternoon sunshine pushed into the schoolroom where Teresa parted the curtains to peer out at the drive. "The magistrate has arrived. What will I say to him?"

Leah pulled the thread through the fabric before she glanced up from her creation, a collar with unfinished—and uninspired—embroidery. "The truth, of course."

"What if I get something wrong?"

"You've suffered a distressing experience, and it's natural for the aftermath to leave you disquieted. Mr. Mason is not here to trap you—just to prevent the men who hurt your cousin from harming anyone else."

"My lady." Mrs. Anderson tapped on the door. "The magistrate is here."

Teresa concentrated a full barrage of wide, pleading eyes at Leah. "Come with me."

"What could I possibly contribute to the magistrate's inquiry?"

"You were there."

"Not for all of it, or even much of it."

"My lady?" Mrs. Anderson rapped again.

"Please, Miss Vance, you needn't say much, or anything at all—but I would feel ever so much more composed with you at my side."

Leah glanced at the clock. Perhaps if she performed this service, her charge would cooperate with Leah's later endeavors. She set aside her tedious work and rose from the chair. "Very well, I'll come with you, if only so you will answer Mrs. Anderson's inquiry rather than leave the poor woman knocking on the door any longer."

Moments later Leah followed Lady Teresa into the drawing room. At least her foot no longer throbbed with every step—good news if she intended to take that hike to meet Alec later. Lady Sotherton swept forward, clasped her daughter's hand and drew her toward a man of slight stature and extensive girth. "Mr. Mason, I'm certain you remember my daughter Teresa."

"Lady Teresa." The magistrate offered her a lumbering bow. The spectacles perched on his nose imparted a more scholarly than scary appearance. "You have become such a beautiful young lady. I regret seeing you under these circumstances."

"Thank you." Teresa shuffled forward and perched on the edge of the settee. Her mother selected a nearby chair while Leah flanked her on the other side.

"I see you brought your governess." Chambelston flicked

back the tails on his coat and resumed his seat. The stark white of his carefully tied cravat matched the formality of his expression. The blue of his gaze—so appealing and attentive when he had kissed her only last night—narrowed. Despite his carefully crafted nonchalance, Leah detected the reappearance of his cynicism, just like during those awkward moments in the music room. And yet, below the palpable chill, she glimpsed traces of…vulnerability? Confusion swirled in her mind, her heart.

"I—I asked Miss Vance if she would… That is, is it not all right if she remains?"

"Of course Miss Vance should be here if it will make you more comfortable." The magistrate offered a kindly smile. "I apologize for asking you these questions, Lady Teresa, but we need some answers."

"I understand."

"Your uncle informs me that you and your cousin were attacked while riding yesterday."

"Yes." Teresa clasped her hands in her lap.

"Tell me about the attack. Where were you?"

"Reggie and I had been riding for a couple hours. There is a manor some miles away he wanted to see, near Norford."

Icy unease rippled along Leah's back. The asylum?

"Did your cousin have an acquaintance at this house?"

"No, we only rode past, then we started home. We raced a bit—just in a spirit of fun because Reggie had the faster horse. And—and then we came upon the grove of trees near Ricks Run. Men rushed out from behind the trees and seized the bridle of Reggie's horse. Reggie pulled out his pistol, but his horse reared and the shot went wild."

Fleming had a pistol? Leah glanced at Chambelston in time to catch the contemplative blue eyes focused on her.

"Can you tell me how many men there were, my lady?"

"Uncle Julian suggested five yesterday. To tell the truth, I didn't count. There was nothing distinctive about their dress, and with their faces blackened, I couldn't distinguish among them."

"Ah, yes, Plough Monday." Mr. Mason templed his fingers and leaned back in the chair. "What did the miscreants do next?"

"They dragged Reggie from his horse. He yelled at me to ride away, then I saw him hit the ground." Teresa's throat bobbed as she swallowed. Leah edged closer and patted the girl's clenched hands. "Th-the men circled around him and began to beat him with their clubs."

"Take your time, my lady."

Teresa nodded. "I screamed. I don't know whether I was more angry or afraid, but I shouted at them to stop. I swung my crop at one—"

"Next time you should take Reggie's advice," Lady Sotherton scolded. "You could have been killed."

The magistrate tapped a stubby finger against his chins. "This man—did you hit him? Could he be sporting a welt today, perhaps on his face or arm?"

"I—I don't know. He jerked my crop from my hand. I kept pleading with them to stop, but they refused to listen to me. And then Uncle Julian and Miss Vance arrived moments later." Moments that had seemed forever, no doubt.

"You have lived in this district all your life, Teresa." Chambelston sauntered to a desk and poured a glass of water which he passed to his niece. "Did you notice anything distinctive about the men's voices—anything that might identify them? Did they speak like local men?"

Teresa sipped her drink before she answered. "They didn't say much—mostly shouting and such. Or perhaps I was too frightened to notice. I—I wish I could be of more help."

Leah squeezed her shoulder, felt the tremble that vibrated through her. "Are we finished, Mr. Mason?"

Lord Chambelston's broad shoulders stiffened, and the muscles around his mouth tightened. So Leah hadn't imagined his reserve. Did he regret his impetuosity of the previous night? Did he object to her interference? Or only to *her?* How like a man to blame the woman for what happened.

The magistrate offered a sympathetic smile. "Thank you for all your help, my lady. I'm sorry you had to recall so traumatic an event."

"I wish I had more to offer." Teresa surged to her feet. Ever polite, both men rose.

Chambelston touched her arm. "Teresa, you and your cousin were gone for several hours yesterday. During all that time, did he say or do anything you find remarkable in hindsight? Anything that might provide us a clue as to who would have done this?"

"No, nothing. In fact, he mostly asked about Miss Vance."

"Me?" Leah felt Chambelston's heavy regard, but she refused to turn, refused to look. At least Fleming would be indisposed for a while. But afterward? Her throat burned as she considered what delicious scandal he might share.

Teresa's impish smile flashed for the first time since her ordeal yesterday. "I think he rather fancies you, Miss Vance."

As the cat fancied the mouse—for torture and a tasty treat.

"We all admire Miss Vance, of course." Lady Sotherton hastened to add, as if to assure everyone her nephew suffered no undue—personal—interest in a mere governess.

Mr. Mason presented the women with a parting bow. "My lady, if any other details occur to you, you have only to send for me and I will come immediately."

"I will."

Leah trailed Teresa up the staircase. She needed to leave if she was to meet Alec at the appointed time, but what excuse could she provide to escape the manor? The two women reached the schoolroom with Leah's mind still whirling with possibilities.

"Please tell me you won't make me practice French today, Miss Vance." Teresa cradled her head in her hands. "I haven't the concentration for it. My head already aches."

"As a matter of fact I do have an errand I need to accomplish."

"A meeting with an older, mysterious gentleman perhaps? I noticed the way my uncle Julian watched you during the meeting."

A thrill of feminine pleasure charged through Leah despite her better sense—and her own observations about Chambelston's demeanor today. "He was probably exasperated with me for not insisting a groom go with you. I doubt those hooligans would have tackled two men."

"If the district is so dangerous, perhaps you should take an escort for your errand."

"Any thief would realize I haven't the coin to make such exertions worthwhile."

"You think the men intended to steal Reggie's money?"

No. "It's a possibility." Leah grabbed her coat from a peg. "Give Uncle Julian my regards."

"*If* I happen to see him, I'll deliver your message."

Leah shoved her arms into her coat sleeves and, ignoring Teresa's smirk, left to find her cousin.

Julian led the magistrate to Fleming's chamber. The injured man's labored breathing filled the air with raspy wheezing. Heavy green drapes swathed the windows, casting the room in shadows and intensifying the odors of blood and sweat and drugs.

The footman jumped from a bedside chair. "My lord?"

"William, isn't it?"

"Yes, my lord."

"The magistrate is here to ask Mr. Fleming some questions."

Fleming twisted his head toward them, then winced. His eyes flickered in their bruised sockets, then fell shut again. "Chambel…" His reedy voice drifted off.

"I'm sorry, my lord." The footman swallowed, causing his Adam's apple to bob above his cravat. "Mr. Fleming was in such pain, I gave him another dose of laudanum like Dr. Grant instructed. If I'd known you would be coming to speak to him, I'd have waited a few more minutes. I'm afraid his thoughts are rather muddled."

"No one will criticize you for showing compassion." Julian gestured the magistrate to take the footman's vacated chair and hauled another to the bedside for himself. "Why don't you go to the kitchen and ask Cook to get you something to eat? The magistrate and I will see to Fleming for a few moments."

"Thank you, my lord." The footman beat a hasty retreat.

"Fleming?" Julian exchanged a look with Mr. Mason. "Fleming? Can you hear us?"

"Hurts."

"Yes, of course." The magistrate studied the purple welts on Fleming's face, the unnatural angle of his nose, the splint on his arm. "Do you remember why it hurts?"

"Niall…letter."

Mason's gaze flickered to Julian.

"His brother, Viscount Killiane, is with Lord Sotherton in London." Julian leaned closer to the bed, trying to get Fleming's glazed eyes to focus on him. "Yes, we've sent word of the assault. Do you remember—"

"Not Niall." Fleming jerked his head violently to the side. "Chambelston."

"I'm here, Fleming. We want to discover who attacked you. Can you tell the magistrate?"

But the wounded man's eyes drifted shut in their swollen, purple sockets.

"Poor fellow." Mason shook his head. "I'm afraid we'll get no answers today."

"Yes, the injuries and laudanum have rendered him incoherent." Julian pounded his fist against his knee in frustration. "Perhaps he'll be more lucid tomorrow."

"I pray so. Send for me when he regains his senses." Mason focused one last pitying look at Fleming. "Mr. Fleming, I wish you a speedy recovery."

A gust sent dollops of snow falling as branches danced in the wind. Leah eyed the tree's thick trunk warily, suddenly cognizant of Teresa's contention that the attackers hid in the forest. A shame Leah hadn't suggested the library for this rendezvous.

Fortunately Alec was right where she had instructed him to meet her.

He greeted her with a grin. "How did you escape the dragon's lair on a Tuesday?" The afternoon breeze tossed Alec's hair across his forehead.

Leah joined him under the leafless oak. "Lady Teresa helped." Because the romantic girl suspected a tryst between her governess and uncle. Leah didn't disclose that little detail to her cousin. She couldn't predict Alec's reaction should he learn of Chambelston's flirtation. Especially that kiss.

Alec took Leah's arm and led her deeper into the grove of trees. "Now what was so terrible you couldn't wait until tomorrow to speak of it?"

"I want to know who is responsible for yesterday's outrage."

"By outrage, you mean the attack on Sotherton's nephew?"

A chill passed along her spine at this confirmation of her suspicions. "So you know about it? This is a dangerous game your people play, Alec. They've been accused of murdering a peer. An assault such as this will only add credence to the rumors."

Alec pinched the bridge of his nose, his expression pained. "Leah, Fleming's presence in the district at this time, and his flogging—by all accounts, a well-deserved fate—are happenstance."

"Then his beating had nothing to do with your group?"

"Fleming wasn't involved in our cause. According to you—and others in the district—he was a ne'er-do-well reprobate who probably provoked the wrong man to violence."

"He was." And more. "But the aristocracy won't care. They'll see the assault as one of their own being attacked by radical revolutionaries—in the presence of a lady, no less. They involved the daughter of a powerful man in their feud, and I fear it has escalated the tensions."

"Lady Teresa wasn't injured, was she?"

"Not physically. But there are other ways to harm a person." Ways that caused scars on one's heart and soul. "She didn't deserve to be a spectator to their violence."

Alec's moss green eyes stared levelly at her for several unnerving moments. "You are very attached to Lady Teresa, Leah. Perhaps too much so. Have you given further consideration to what you will do when your employment ends? I worry for you."

Leah ignored his counsel rather than respond to his question. "Then perhaps you understand how I feel about the risks you take with your neck. I feel this will end badly. Alec, do you really believe what you do will make a difference?"

"I don't know. I only know I must try."

The afternoon sun glared against the snow as Julian set off on Sotherton's prize bay. At least he needn't compete with

Fleming for use of the horse over the next few days. Maybe never, if Fleming didn't recover from his injuries.

Was Miss Vance a party to the attack, vengeance for Fleming's mistreatment? She had connections to radicals who'd already demonstrated a tendency toward violence—but surely she would never have involved Teresa. His mind skipped back twenty-four hours, to Miss Vance's concern when her charge had failed to return. Perhaps Fleming's attack had nothing to do with the radicals. But then, why Miss Vance's late outing to the stable last night?

He steered the horse along the road, toward the grove of oak and hawthorn specified in Harrison's note. The breeze carried the ring of a blacksmith's anvil from the distant village. All seemed serene, peaceful. Deceptively so? Yesterday Fleming's black-faced attackers had disappeared into a wood similar to this one.

Julian glanced over his shoulder, then started when he noticed a man scuttling out from between the trees. Rags hung on his form, and the stump of an arm peeked through a mangled sleeve. Below the floppy brim of an ancient hat, a patch covered one eye. Sadly, an all-too-familiar sight in the years since the war's end.

The man limped closer. "A penny for a man wounded in the king's service, my lord?"

Julian reached inside his coat. If vagrants had made camp in these woods, he and Harrison would have to adjust their plans… "Harrison?"

The beggar grinned. "If I says aye, does that mean I don't get me penny?"

"But how do you…?" Julian stared at the severed arm.

"The art of illusion, my lord."

Julian knew too much about illusion, and disillusionment, today.

"Come." Harrison gestured to the wood with his visible

good arm. "I've already investigated the area. We'll be safe from discovery here."

"Are you certain?" Julian eyed the well-trampled path that led deeper into the trees.

"My handiwork. Less suspicious than a pair of tracks in the snow."

Julian climbed down from the horse and looped the reins around his hand. He ducked under a low-hanging branch as he followed Harrison deeper into the shadows. "What did you learn?"

"First, my contact in London hasn't yet uncovered any witnesses who claim the radicals intended your father harm. Nor have I heard anything here—which isn't particularly surprising. It takes a long time to thoroughly infiltrate such a group, my lord—weeks, months, even years. I pray our country won't suffer strife for so long a period."

"And Wellingborough?"

"The radicals have stationed sentries along the road to watch for any advancing troops." Harrison paused in a small clearing. "Before you blame your governess, I remind you that many people in Sotherton's household have access to your chamber."

But how many knew of his interest in the current unrest—and would investigate his personal effects? "Is there anything else?" The stallion shifted and shook his head. Julian absently patted the horse's neck to quiet the skittish beast.

"The attack on Sotherton's nephew yesterday? I have reason to believe those responsible are part of the radicals. I spent some time with one of them after the others retired last night. Nothing loosens a man's tongue like lots of ale, a willing listener and a triumph to brag about."

"I shall have to keep that in mind for the future. What did this man say?"

"They'd been ordered to stop Fleming."

"Stopping him could mean his tendency to woo the women of the district with his fist."

"Except I've never met a man who would claim to have been 'ordered' to join a melee like that." Harrison scooped up a handful of snow and crushed it into a ball. "Besides, they knew where and when to find Fleming."

"So someone informed them of Fleming's plans to ride that day." Hawkesworth had reported no unusual messages—but then, Miss Vance had managed to deliver hers outside regular channels. Was there another spy in the Sotherton household? Or the same one?

"How is Fleming?"

"The magistrate tried to ask him about the attack, but we gleaned little from him."

"I'll see if I can learn any more." Harrison gave Julian a last nod, then disappeared deeper into the trees.

Julian waited several seconds, then tugged on the bay's reins.

Voices drifted to the clearing from beyond the trees, the distance too great for him to distinguish timbre or words. He flipped the stallion's reins over a branch and crept through the trees until he had an unobstructed view of the road. And its occupants.

A couple approached, the woman's arm laced through her companion's elbow. An unknown man—but escorting a most familiar female.

Leah Vance.

Julian froze, as much from shock and disappointment as from a desire to remain concealed. The last of his admiration for her melted like snow in sunshine. They continued past him, oblivious to his presence, then paused when they reached the crossroads a quarter mile hence. At last the man raised his hand and touched her cheek in a painfully personal gesture. Then they parted, the man striding one direction while Miss Vance continued toward Rowan Abbey.

Julian observed her from his station for several more minutes before he ducked back between the trees and retrieved the impatient horse. He led the animal to the road, mounted and guided it away from Rowan Abbey, intent on approaching the house from a different direction. He'd rather not meet Miss Vance in his current mood. The horse pranced and stomped, and rather than hold it back any longer, Julian gave the stallion his head. The animal raced away to enjoy his freedom. The road disappeared in a blur, and yet, Julian's anger endured. If only he could outrun his disappointment. His pain.

After a mile or so he steered the stallion in a loop back to the mansion. A stable boy rushed over to take the bay's reins. "Looks like you had a good run, my lord."

The horse had, anyway. Julian's fury still simmered. "He's a fine animal." Julian vaulted out of the saddle and left the stallion with the boy.

"My lord!" a harried Hawkesworth greeted on his entrance. "We are so thankful for your return. Her ladyship is most distressed."

Julian paused, hand on the top button of his greatcoat. "Where is she?"

"Mr. Fleming's bedchamber. You'd best hurry, my lord."

Despite the warmth of the house, a chill prickled along his arms. Had Fleming succumbed to his injuries after all? "What has happened?"

"I'm afraid he lies near death, my lord."

Poor Elizabeth. Julian nodded his thanks and marched to the stairs.

Chapter Nine

Leah slipped into the manor near the narrow back stair-case, removed her coat and rolled it into a ball. She crept up the steps, the garment tucked under her arm. With luck and caution, she'd reach the schoolroom with none but Teresa the wiser that she'd even left. As she drew closer to the landing, shouts exploded from the hallway and reverberated against the walls.

Such a commotion could only portend bad news. The elderly dowager? Or Fleming?

Oomph. Her head ricocheted off the hard skull of another. As pain shot through her temple, she forced her eyes to focus on the blurry form in front of her.

"Oh, Miss Vance. I'm so sorry." A maid—not Molly—navigated around Leah to continue her headlong rush to the bottom of the stairs.

Leah grabbed her arm and halted her flight. "What is it?"

"Mr. Fleming. William found him near death in his bed."

Her stomach tightened as an emotion akin to equal parts dread and delight surged through her. "When?"

"Just moments ago. Please, Miss. I must send Wetherel for the doctor."

"Of course." Leah started to ascend. "Wait," she exclaimed.

The maid paused, turned.

"Take this." She tossed her coat around the girl's shoulders. "It's cold out."

"You're very kind, Miss Vance." The maid dashed down the stairs. Seconds later the slam of the door echoed through the narrow confines.

Ignoring the throbbing in her skull, Leah climbed the remaining stairs to the floor where the Sothertons and their guests slept. A dithering assortment of maids and footmen gathered round the doorway to Fleming's chamber. She tapped a parlor maid on the shoulder, and the servant deferentially sidled to the left to let Leah pass.

The room reeked of the same wastes and wretchedness as Phoebe's prison. Leah joined Lady Sotherton, Miss Godwin and even the dowager at their vigil beside Fleming's bed. But for the barely visible rise and fall of the sheet, his unconscious form lay prostrate and unmoving. The candle's glow highlighted the purple bruises that covered his face and neck and provided colorful contrast to his otherwise pallid skin.

Leah tamped down the burgeoning memories. How many times during the past three years had she wished for just such an outcome? But not one that involved Teresa. Would the girl blame herself for her inability to halt the attack? For agreeing to the ride or for not insisting on a groom? For the first time in many a year, Leah tendered a plea to the so-distant Almighty.

The dowager's fist tightened around the handle of her cane, yet she swayed all the same. "The doctor is on his way, Reggie." Fleming's knavish treatment of women may have earned him the well-deserved thrashing, but he was still the dowager's grandchild, second son of her only daughter. Even Leah felt a niggling of sympathy.

Miss Godwin clasped the old woman's arm. "Come, my lady. Let me take you to your room, lest you overtax yourself. The others can remain with him until the doctor arrives."

"No!" The old woman punctuated the word with a thump of her cane that made the candleholder rattle against the bedside table. "I will not abandon my grandson."

"As you wish, my lady." The companion fidgeted with her necklace.

Leah retreated a step lest the dowager's cane strike her already injured foot—then froze as she became aware of a presence behind her. *His* presence. Chambelston marched into their midst with the calm and command of an admiral. His dark greatcoat covered all but his cravat and boots. Disarrayed strands of tawny hair wisped around his face as if he'd just disembarked from his ship.

"Of course you must stay if it brings you comfort, my lady." He seized a chair from its berth by the window and deposited it next to the bed. "But Miss Godwin is right to be concerned for you."

The dowager carefully lowered herself onto the seat with a brief nod of thanks, her watery gaze fixed on her grandson.

Chambelston glanced at Leah. His gaze hardened with... scorn?...then slid away. Several hours absence had made his heart grow harder. "Where is Teresa?"

"She was in the schoolroom when I last saw her." Some three hours ago.

"Go stay with her. And collect my sister on your way, so she isn't exposed to this, either."

Did he mean his younger sister? A hysterical giggle bubbled in Leah's throat at the notion of hauling Lady Sotherton away. Or at Chambelston's sudden hostility? She muffled her response with a subservient curtsy and backed away.

Julian leaned over and pressed his ear to Fleming's chest. "He breathes yet." But for how much longer? He'd seen enough death and dying—too much—to identify a hopeless case. In all likelihood, Fleming would be gone before the doctor arrived. He swiveled to face Miss Godwin. "The doctor?"

"Jane ran to find Wetherel about ten minutes ago. He should have left by now. Provided he finds the doctor home…" She twisted a gold chain around trembling fingers. "Poor Mr. Fleming. I heard he was much improved since last night."

"He was awake but confused this morning when the magistrate tried to question him." That he now seemed so much the worse… What could even a doctor do for him if, as the doctor had indicated yesterday, Fleming bled inside?

Elizabeth edged more closely to him. "Did he remember anything of yesterday's attack—anything to help the magistrate identify the criminals?"

"No, he spoke only of his brother. I told him you'd sent a message."

"Thank you." Her gaze locked on his. The depths of blue churned with distress and an unexpected remorse that called to mind Harrison's advice about reconciliation. "Julian, I…"

"Yes, I know. See to your staff, dear sister." He said the endearment without hesitation or sarcasm as he gestured to the hallway where frightened servants yet lingered. "Keep them occupied. They need your assurance at a moment like this."

"You must have been a terrific officer, Julian—and I'm glad you were here during this difficult time." She stiffened her shoulders, swept out of the room and began issuing commands with all the confidence of a field marshal.

Julian sought a chair for Miss Godwin and positioned it near the dowager. Fleming's grandmother wilted on her seat, her face as devoid of color as the dying man's sheets. Julian patted her locked hands, as concerned for her as for Fleming. "Let me ring for some tea for you, my lady."

Miss Godwin had poured her employer a second cup by the time Hawkesworth escorted Dr. Grant into the room.

The doctor offered the assembled family members a curt

nod as he strode to his patient. He checked Fleming's pulse
and eyes, then glanced at the bedside table.

"Fleming!" Grant shook him. "Fleming!"

Fleming's head lolled to one side, but his eyes remained
closed to the world.

Nausea stormed through Julian's gut. He bolted to the bed
and joined the doctor, but Fleming failed to revive.

After several moments Grant stepped back and shook his
head. He trudged over to the dowager. "I'm so sorry, my
lady. He is gone."

The dowager clutched a hand to her chest and swayed, face
pale. Miss Godwin jumped from her chair and wrapped an
arm of support around the elderly woman. "There, my lady.
At least he passed peacefully in his sleep."

"Perhaps you would like a few minutes with him, my lady."
The doctor caught Julian's gaze and jerked his head toward
the door. "My lord, a word if I might?"

"Of course." Julian followed him to the corridor and pulled
the door shut firmly behind him as Elizabeth approached.

"I told Mrs. Anderson to prepare—" She stopped as she
studied their faces. "Reggie? He's not…?"

"Unfortunately so, my lady." The doctor glanced grimly
between Julian and his sister. "I'm afraid you'll have to send
for the magistrate."

"The magistrate again?"

Julian stepped forward and touched Elizabeth's arm. "Mr.
Fleming succumbed to his injuries. The men who attacked
him are now guilty of murder."

"Not exactly, my lord." The doctor folded his arms across
his chest. "Mr. Fleming died from an excessive consumption of laudanum."

Julian stared at Fleming's forever-silenced form. Only one
day after a brutal assault, the man now lay dead. Coincidence—

or had the miscreants Julian and the grooms thwarted yesterday found another means to their end?

His father had been killed in an accident that might have been no accident. And now Fleming had succumbed to a second murder attempt in as many days. His father had essayed to alleviate the people's suffering. Fleming had never exhibited any altruistic inclinations. If Fleming thought of others at all, it was only to ascertain how he might best use them for his own purposes and pleasures. And yet, Julian sensed an elusive link between the two murders. What was the relationship—other than the connection each had to him?

"Mr. Mason, my lord," Hawkesworth announced from the doorway.

"How good of you to come so quickly." Julian gestured to a chair near the leaded-glass window. "Doctor Grant is attending the Dowager Countess Sotherton at present, but he will be with us presently to advise us of his suspicions about Fleming's death."

"Poor woman." The magistrate lowered his substantial girth onto the seat's green upholstery. The delicate furniture creaked ominously. "To see her grandson laid low, and under such appalling circumstances. Losing a child is the worst blow of all."

"Have you children?"

"Two boys. We had a daughter, but she succumbed to the fever three winters ago." Mason's gruff voice cracked.

"I'm sorry for your loss." Julian stared at his hands, thoughts caught up in recollections of Maman's pain at Gregory's death. She had lost Elizabeth to rancor years earlier, but perhaps now that he'd found the fissure in his sister's bitterness, Elizabeth would yet reconcile with her family.

Footsteps tapped against the parquet, and a shadow passed across the doorway as the doctor joined them.

"Ah, Doctor. How is her ladyship?" Mason ripped his stare from the body on the bed.

"Understandably distressed, of course. I administered a sedative, and Miss Godwin is with her now."

"Lord Chambelston reports you find Fleming's demise suspicious."

"Absolutely." The doctor retrieved a small brown bottle from the desk and passed it to the magistrate. "I left a full container of laudanum last night, in case Mr. Fleming experienced pain from yesterday's trauma. And yet today I find the bottle nearly empty."

"So you believe an excessive dose of laudanum killed Fleming rather than the beating he sustained?"

"When I arrived this afternoon, Fleming demonstrated all the signs of acute opiate poisoning. His pupils were mere pinpricks, and his respiration only a fraction of its normal rate."

"Could the poisoning have been accidental? Perhaps the footman administered a bit too much. Or perhaps another member of the staff gave Fleming a second dosage right after he'd already consumed a measure of the medicine."

"No. For one thing, a twofold amount might be dangerous, but most likely not deadly—particularly if discovered in time. But for another, it wouldn't account for the substantial amount of laudanum missing from the bottle."

Mr. Mason deposited the bottle on a table beside the bed and wiped his hands against his coat. "We need a list of everyone who entered this room today."

A floorboard squeaked as Julian crossed the room to pull the cord. "The footman William spent most of the day with Fleming and administered laudanum on at least one occasion this morning. Doctor, how would Fleming ingest such an exceedingly large amount?"

"An excellent line of inquiry, my lord." The doctor nodded. "Possibly in a meal, most likely in a drink."

"Then we should also question the cook to see what food and drinks she prepared for Fleming today." Of course Fleming had never seemed particularly abstemious on the occasions when Julian had had dealings with him. An easy task, perhaps, convincing him to swallow a bit of brandy? "Doctor, can you estimate when Fleming consumed the excess laudanum?"

"Recently. Probably within an hour of his death. That much laudanum would have killed him very quickly."

Only moments before Julian's return from his meeting with Harrison.

Hawkesworth marched into the room. "My lord?"

"Would you please send up William? And tell Cook we would like to speak to her in the drawing room presently."

"Of course, my lord." The butler backed away and pulled the door shut again.

Julian folded his arms over his chest and stared at Fleming's lifeless body. "Wouldn't Fleming question the taste?"

"Perhaps not if he had ingested a small amount shortly before the poisoning. He might have been confused enough not to notice the change."

Or perhaps his fondness for drink overpowered his palate.

"My lord?" The footman shuffled into the room, his gaze darting from one man to the next.

"William." Julian gestured to the portly man beside him. "Have you met the local magistrate, Mr. Mason?"

"I never had need of a magistrate, my lord."

"Of course we wouldn't expect anyone in Lord Sotherton's employ to be guilty of criminal behavior." Mason tucked a hand into his coat. Julian stifled a snort at the irony. If the magistrate only knew. "We have a few simple questions for you about Mr. Fleming."

"I'll do my best to answer them, sir."

"I know you will. Now then, tell us about this afternoon. I am given to understand you tended Fleming?"

"Yes, sir. The maid Molly stayed with him through the night. Then Lady Sotherton sent her to rest and tasked me with caring for her nephew."

"And did you at any time dispense laudanum to your patient?"

"Yes, whenever Mr. Fleming complained of terrible pain."

"How many times?"

The footman wiped his palms against his breeches. "Well, Molly showed me how much to give him, so I offered him some more right before you and Lord Chambelston came to talk to him. If I'd known you were coming—"

"I understand."

"Thank you, sir. And then I gave him a bit more tonight. Did I do something wrong?"

The doctor patted the young man's arm. "No, a few drops two or three times today should have been fine. When did you last administer the laudanum?"

"Perhaps half an hour before I discovered him...found him..."

"Insensible?"

"Yes. Mr. Fleming said he felt pain from his wounds. I gave him the medicine and waited for him to calm. Then I left to prepare for dinner. Hawkesworth is most particular about our appearance during mealtimes, especially when we have distinguished guests here." William's eyes flickered toward Julian before reverting to the doctor.

"And how did you come to discover Mr. Fleming tonight?"

"I returned to check on him one last time before attending to my other duties." William's voice rose in pitch. He swallowed once, twice and continued. "I—I found him near death."

Julian dropped his voice to a low, soothing volume. "Tell me, William. Where did you keep the laudanum bottle?"

"On the table next to the bed, of course."

"Thank you, William. We appreciate all your assistance. You may return to those other duties."

"Yes, my lord." William bobbed his head and backed out of the room.

"If we are to believe young William, anyone could have entered here and dispensed a lethal dose of laudanum."

"If that is indeed how Fleming died." The magistrate leaned closer to Fleming's lifeless body. "When I saw Fleming this morning, he was weak and confused. He had ingested laudanum, so we know he would have shown signs of it being in his system—and he suffered grievous injuries only yesterday that we feared might kill him. Doctor, you are absolutely certain excess laudanum caused his death and not his injuries?"

The doctor pulled back the covers and opened Fleming's shirt. "Do you see these bruises?"

Julian edged closer.

A snap split the silence as his shoe landed on…something. He retrieved the broken item and studied it in the light.

"My lord?" Mason peered at the pieces in his hand.

"I believe it fell from the bed when Dr. Grant shifted the blanket." Julian dropped the three fragments on the coverlet. The pale ivory gleamed against the deep green. A woman's hair comb. He arranged the pieces in their original shape, marveling at the detailed craftsmanship in the carved designs. Above the fine white teeth, a treble clef sign curled in the comb's spine. A memory flitted through the recesses of his mind, then disappeared back into the shadows.

The magistrate traced the musical notation with his stubby finger while Julian retrieved a candle and held it nearer. "Who has been caring for Fleming?"

"The footman today. One of the maids last night." Julian had seen such work before, many times over.

"This doesn't look like a maid's ornament."

"Unless she had a beau in the navy." Or...a brother?

"My lord?"

"Life on a ship often offers little stimulation beyond work and battle. Entertainment is limited, so bored sailors frequently fashion such creations for wives and sweethearts during long voyages. I would guess this one was formed from whale ivory." Julian flipped the delicate comb over.

His breath caught in his throat as he stared at the name engraved on the back.

Leah Vance.

Leah lifted another picture card from the stack and showed the face to Lady Caroline. "Do you remember this letter?"

The girl glanced at the paper, then shifted her gaze to the corner of the room where Teresa studied.

"Are you tired, Lady Caroline?" Leah snatched a slim book from the stack on the table. "Perhaps you would enjoy a story instead?"

"Draw."

"If you like." Leah removed the book and situated a sheet of paper on the table. She dipped a quill in the inkwell and passed the implement to her guest.

"Pretty." Lady Caroline shook the plume. Specks of ink peppered her hands and cheeks, and probably Leah's, as well. At least her dress was dark.

"What should we draw? A puppy maybe?" Leah guided the girl's hand lest another spray of ink splatter over them.

"Miss Vance?" Molly tapped on the door, then pushed it open. "Lord Chambelston and Mr. Mason requested your presence in the drawing room."

"Mine?" Not Teresa's?

"I'll stay with Lady Caroline."

"Thank you. She would like to draw pictures. You might want to get an apron for her clothes." No telling where the ink might land next.

"I see." Molly pointed to her cheek. "Ah, Miss Vance, you have a bit of ink…"

Leah scrubbed at her cheek as she traipsed down the stairs. Whispers followed her through the hallway. Whatever could the magistrate want with her? She had nothing to offer beyond what Teresa had already shared. She paused at the drawing-room entrance. Voices drifted through the door, then the heavy oak swung open. Cook marched past, her lips locked in a white line and tension taut on all her chins. Leah stared at the amply endowed matron's retreating back.

"Miss Vance?" The magistrate gestured to a settee. "Won't you join us?"

Did she have a choice? "Ah, yes." Leah recalled her mission, if not her composure. She shuffled to the settee and dropped onto the upholstery, feeling much like the accused in the witness box.

"Lord Chambelston and I have a few questions for you."

Despite her better judgment, Leah's gaze flitted to the man positioned next to the fireplace, one casual arm propped against the mantle. Notwithstanding his proximity to the fire, ice still hardened his eyes, and his unsmiling mouth admitted no thaw of attitude. "I—I'm not certain I can be of any assistance. Lord Chambelston was with me yesterday when we located Lady Teresa and Mr. Fleming. I fear I have nothing to add beyond his account."

"We'll discuss that presently." Mr. Mason lowered himself onto a nearby chair and folded his hands over his abundant middle. "Right now we want to discover what happened this afternoon. Miss Vance, were you in Mr. Fleming's chamber at any point today?"

"Briefly. I heard a commotion, so I ran, ah, down the stairs. I found a gathering of family members and servants assembled in Mr. Fleming's room." Leah allowed herself to relax slightly. "Mr. Fleming appeared near death."

"Did you approach Mr. Fleming when you noticed his distress?"

"No, Lord Chambelston arrived straightaway. He tasked me with the care of his younger sister. Lady Caroline's chamber is across the hallway, and he didn't want her to witness Mr. Fleming's condition. I ushered her to the schoolroom, and I remained there with her and Lady Teresa until you summoned me here moments ago."

"And you weren't in Fleming's room at any other time today? Or perhaps yesterday?"

Suspicions flitted across her mind. Why the speculation about her presence with Fleming? "I had no reason to be." And she wasn't likely to pay him a friendly social call.

"All I need is a simple yes or no, Miss Vance."

Unease began to stir in her stomach. "No."

"That's most interesting because we found something we believe to be yours."

"Mine? But…I didn't lose anything."

"It has your name on it, Miss Vance." Lord Chambelston ambled toward her, his towering form looming even farther above her than usual. He uncurled his fist to reveal a spiny white object.

The tips of Leah's fingers brushed his palm as she accepted his offering. Not one item, but several. Her puzzlement transformed to pleasure as she arrayed the pieces on her skirt. "My comb!" Her brother's smile flashed once again across her mind. He'd carved musical notations into the whale ivory and presented her the gift on his last visit, before…

"Can you tell us how it came to be in Reginald Fleming's chamber?"

"Fleming's chamber? I—I wouldn't know. It's been missing for years." Surely her comb couldn't have remained in the house all this time. A maid would have discovered it while cleaning—and with Leah's name engraved on the back, someone would have returned the article to her.

"Years? How many years?"

"Three." Since that fateful day when Reginald Fleming had trapped her in his chamber. Revulsion swirled around her stomach and surged to her throat. The images and impressions etched into her soul once again flashed across her mind. The humiliation of his hands on her. The terror that slowed her responses. The panic when her well-aimed blow laid him on the carpet. She forced the bile back with determination and pragmatism. Not the same chamber. Obviously Fleming had had her comb in his possession for the past three years. Where had he kept it? And why bring it back to Northamptonshire— other than to torment her further? "Where did you find this?"

"It fell out of Fleming's bed."

His bed. But… Her gaze jumped from one man to the other, reading cynicism and contempt on their features. They suspected the worst of her. And why wouldn't they, given Fleming's proclivities? The same helplessness she'd felt that day three years ago washed over her again. Fleming would have his revenge on her, even from the grave. That she'd ultimately saved herself from his advances wouldn't cleanse the stain from her reputation.

Leah dropped her stare to the pieces of the comb in her hand—David's last gift to her before he'd marched out of this life and into the hereafter. She'd wept when she had realized she'd lost it. Now at last it was returned to her—broken. Like her family, her dreams, her life.

She was dissembling. Julian had seen Miss Vance before when caught in a misdeed—particularly that night when he'd discovered her searching *his* bedchamber. Had she entered Fleming's in similar circumstances? What better time to rifle the man's belongings than when he was unconscious.

The pale smoothness of the comb gleamed against the dark fabric of her skirt, similar to the way the ivory ribbon contrasted with her brown tresses. He focused his thoughts back to their meeting in the music room this morning. Same dark gown, same modest knot of hair with the same simple ribbon threaded through it. No, she hadn't worn the comb this morning, nor could he recall seeing it in her hair at any time. So why the feeling of familiarity when he'd first held the piece?

She stroked a finger across the smooth surface of the ivory, eyes downcast. "How did it break?"

"I stepped on it." Julian retreated to his chair.

Her chin jerked up. "You what?" A dark smudge stained her cheek on the site of her occasional dimple. A bruise?

"Accidentally. It fell to the floor when the doctor moved Fleming's sheets."

The magistrate tapped his knee. "Miss Vance, can anyone verify your comb has been out of your possession all this time? Did you tell anyone? Report it lost at the time?"

Wariness and vulnerability, even fear, flickered in the wide hazel eyes. "No, of course not. Why would I concern anyone else? It's of only sentimental value."

"Then perhaps you would share the circumstances of how an item of sentimental value went missing three years ago."

"I—I had gone for a walk. And when I got back to my room, I noticed it missing. I looked for it later, but never found it. Perhaps Mr. Fleming discovered it during his visit here."

"So despite the snow covering the ground, he stumbled across an item missing for three years. And then he tucked it between his sheets?" Mr. Mason brows rose dubiously.

Miss Vance's fist curled around the shattered pieces, but she offered no further explanations or excuses.

"Young women frequently share such sentimental items with men as an expression of their affection."

"I never gave Mr. Fleming any indication of a-an attachment!"

A rather telling reaction. Julian leaned back in the chair and folded his arms. "Then what is your theory to explain how it came to be in the man's bedchamber, Miss Vance? We know it wasn't in his bed last night when the footmen carried him there."

"Surely, I don't know and I can't speculate. I was never in his chamber until those minutes before his death. Indeed I didn't even know which chamber he occupied until yesterday."

And yet she had managed to discover Julian's chamber within hours of his arrival here.

Mr. Mason drummed his fingers against his knee. "Yesterday, Lady Teresa suggested Mr. Fleming spoke much about you, Miss Vance. Did he ever express such an interest to you, in either word or deed? Perhaps offering gifts or seeking your opinions or requesting your time?"

"I…" She stared at the rigid clasp of her hands. "Mr. Fleming accosted me Sunday while I was returning from a visit with a friend. Lord Chambelston arrived and intervened."

"And where did this…dispute take place?"

"Just this side of Norford."

The magistrate glanced at him, brows raised. Julian nodded. "Yes, that event happened as Miss Vance says." Ugly suspicions crowded his thoughts. Fleming's harassment when he caught her alone Sunday afternoon. Her reaction to Fleming at dinner and later at the piano.

The magistrate rose from his chair and paced to the fireplace. "Miss Vance, we have reason to believe Mr. Fleming was murdered. Today."

"Murdered…*today?*"

"A couple hours ago. Three at the most."

"But the attack was yesterday." She uncurled her fingers and stared at the comb, as if to draw strength from its presence. A smudge identical to that on her cheek darkened her palm, like Lady Macbeth's spot that wouldn't wash away. Was Leah Vance also an accessory to murder?

No, she couldn't have poisoned Fleming. Not with her own hands, if Dr. Grant had presented them with an accurate timeline of the events. But whoever planted the comb—whoever intended to see her thusly accused—didn't know of her venture off the estate this afternoon.

Julian waited for her to offer the name of the man who could provide her defense, but she held her silence like she had guarded so many other secrets. Who was the man that she would protect him so? Julian leaned forward and braced his elbows on his knees. "You see why we have a problem, Miss Vance. While we endeavored to discover the identity of the strangers who thrashed Fleming during his ride yesterday, someone in this household poisoned him in his bed today."

Chapter Ten

Leah slogged up the stairs to the schoolroom, the magistrate's final instructions to remain at the house still reverberating in her ears. As if she had anywhere to go even if she wanted to escape. She had no money, only a few worn clothes and two similarly indigent relatives. If the magistrate questioned her further, the truths about three years ago would eventually come out—truths she didn't want to face, didn't want to remember. Worse, truths that would end her employment *and* suggest a reason she might want Fleming dead.

She twisted the knob of the schoolroom door and trudged into the room. The scratching of quill on paper whispered from the table where Lady Caroline and Molly still drew pictures. Teresa glanced up from the desk where she yet sat. Nothing and everything had changed in the few brief minutes of Leah's absence.

Teresa closed her book. "What did the magistrate want, Miss Vance?"

A murder suspect, it appeared. "He's still investigating the circumstances surrounding Mr. Fleming's death." Would Chambelston divulge what he knew about Leah's association with the radicals? She seemed destined to hang despite agreeing to betray her cousin and his friends.

"Poor Reggie! I can't believe he is gone. I should have tried harder to stop those villains!" Teresa's distress darkened the heavy black crescents under her eyes. "If only I had done more—"

"Stop!"

A hitch of her breath conveyed Lady Caroline's apprehension at Leah's sharp tones.

Leah swept across the room to Teresa's side and dropped her voice in volume, if not intensity. "You are *not* to blame for being unable to rescue your cousin against the strength of five men."

"But if I had done as Reggie instructed and ridden back for help—"

"Doubtlessly he would have died alone out there at their hands before any assistance arrived." Leah covered Teresa's cold, trembling hand with one of her own. "You did the best you could under horrifying circumstances. You distracted at least one of his attackers, possibly forestalling them long enough your cousin yet lived when help arrived."

"And it was all for nothing. My best wasn't good enough." Bitterness edged Teresa's voice and clouded her eyes. "Reggie died anyway."

Leah peeked over her shoulder and met Molly's uneasy gaze. "Perhaps you should escort Lady Caroline to her chamber. No doubt she could use a light repast."

Molly nodded and slid the girl's chair away from the table. "Come, Lady Caroline. We'll ask Anna to get you some food."

Caroline obligingly accompanied the maid.

Leah waited until the door shut behind them before sharing the remaining—worse—news with Teresa. "What you did wasn't for nothing. The magistrate doesn't believe your cousin died from the blows he sustained yesterday."

Teresa blinked, her blue eyes a blend of self-recrimination and confusion. "But then…"

"Poison."

"Poison! But—but how? When?"

Leah considered the magistrate's last words before he had dismissed her with instructions not to leave Rowan Abbey. "This afternoon, I believe." Whatever poison the assassin had administered, he had done it in sufficient dosage to kill Fleming in a very short time.

"Who would want to kill Reggie?"

Probably any number of women. Leah's stare fell on the chair Molly had vacated only moments ago. How many others had Fleming abused during his visits over the years? Add in any male servants who might be infatuated with one of them or susceptible to a financial inducement, and suddenly everyone in the household—with the exception of Lady Caroline and possibly the dowager—became a suspect.

But the magistrate had focused on Leah—because of a hair comb lost years ago.

"Teresa, this morning you told Mr. Mason your cousin expressed an interest in me. What did he wish to know?" Fortunately Lady Sotherton had halted the magistrate's further inquiry. Did she know of Fleming's misdeeds? Or did she fear her nephew had developed a serious interest for a most unsuitable—that was, unendowed—female? Whatever the reasons, Leah was truly grateful Teresa hadn't provided the magistrate with additional grounds to believe her a murderer.

"Oh, just little things. Where you hail from. Where you go on your day off." Teresa's guileless blue gaze shimmered with the remnants of her grief. "I suspect you fascinated him."

Leah started to protest, then paused. Perhaps Teresa's sunny naïveté was to Leah's advantage. After all, a woman hoping for a marriage proposal from a man above her station would hardly want to see him dead.

* * *

"Can you tell me what we are searching for, my lord?" Mr. Mason paused in the center of a Persian rug and surveyed Fleming's chamber.

"Not exactly." But Julian would know it when he saw it. "I thought we might find a few clues into Fleming's interests and activities."

"And from there, a list of people who might wish him ill."

"Yes." Julian slid open the drawer where Caroline had... explored a few short days ago and held a candle aloft. The green ribbon still curled in its spot, but the gold locket nestling beside the silk had disappeared. "Come look at this."

Mason sidled over to stand next to Julian. "My lord?"

"Several days ago I had occasion to see the contents here, and I noticed several items of a feminine nature."

The magistrate lifted an end of the ribbon. "As I mentioned to Miss Vance, young men frequently collect such tokens from women who hold their affection."

"So I considered. However, there was another article— a gold locket—which has disappeared. Such a piece would sell for a fair amount." Or it would in London. But in rural Northamptonshire?

"You think the murderer stole the piece?"

"Or perhaps a member of the staff while Fleming was riding yesterday. But someone has an item that recently belonged to Fleming."

"And it would behoove us to talk to that person. I'll make inquiries in the villages. Such an article would be noticed." The magistrate moved to the desk and rifled through a stack of papers.

Julian investigated the remaining drawers of the armoire, and discovered...nothing. At least the magistrate hadn't asked how he came to know about Fleming's cache of feminine trinkets. He pushed the last one shut and joined Mason at the desk. "Are you having better success than I?"

"That depends. Do you like horse racing?"

"Not especially. It isn't a common form of entertainment on a ship."

"Understandable." The magistrate chuckled and passed Julian a paper of statistics with notes scribbled in the margins. "Fleming seemed to enjoy it, however. Do you suppose he owes money?"

"Possibly." Likely, even. Julian moved the page to the light and stared at Fleming's script, a memory niggling in his mind.

"Enough that someone would want to kill him? Except that wouldn't explain how his enemy got into Lord Sotherton's house."

"He'd only need to find someone on the staff whose assistance could be purchased." Like Miss Vance. Acid churned in Julian's belly. Did anyone else in the house know of her dual loyalties? Perhaps even the same person who would deposit a comb—a comb with her name engraved into the ivory—in Fleming's bed?

"Still, why kill a person who owes you money? You'd never get it back. Better to demand the funds from his brother. Doesn't Viscount Killiane have an interest in politics? A man with those ambitions would be susceptible to blackmail. He might wish to rid himself of an embarrassing relative standing in his way."

"The same could be said for Lord Sotherton. If we start requiring decency and decorum from the relatives of our political class, half the members of Parliament will be at risk of blackmail."

Mason chuckled. "This morning you said Killiane had been informed of the troubles here. Have you received a reply?"

"I don't know." Julian tossed the paper onto the desk next

to an empty decanter. The method the murderer used to in-
still the poison into Fleming's system? "Come, we should ask
Lady Sotherton. But not in this room." He grabbed the candle
and led the magistrate out of the bedchamber.

"I'm afraid now you'll be sending Fleming's family even
worse news." Mason followed Julian down the stairs and
into the drawing room. "But hopefully, we can provide them
with some comfort in this time of great distress if we identify the murderer."

Julian gave the bell pull a yank. So many possibilities—
and the magistrate seemed focused on only one.

"My lord?" The butler paused in the doorway, a salver
outstretched.

"Ah, Hawkesworth, would you see if Lady Sotherton is
able to join us?"

"At once, my lord. And if your lordship pleases, I've com-
piled the list of names you requested."

"You are a wonder, Hawkesworth." Julian seized the paper
off the tray, flipped it open and skimmed the names in the
butler's neat script.

"Anything useful?" Mason dropped onto a chair.

"Not particularly." Upwards of a dozen people had passed
through Fleming's chamber, from the dowager and her companion down to the footman and lowly chambermaids. Miss
Vance's name was significant only by its absence. But then,
Julian knew she hadn't even been in the house this afternoon.
So why the prevarications? Why not simply provide them with
her excuse? Unless she couldn't disclose her friend's name.

Mason withdrew a handkerchief from his coat and mopped
the perspiration from his shiny brow. "Hiking those stairs
drains a man's energy."

"And we've kept you unconscionably past the dinner hour."

"I do look famished, don't I?" The magistrate placed his
hands on his rotund belly and chuckled. Then his face so-

bered as Elizabeth appeared in the doorway. He jumped to his feet again. "My lady, may I offer you my condolences on the death of your nephew?"

"Good evening, Mr. Mason." Tension exaggerated the lines around her mouth and the dark wreaths under her eyes that even the muted light of night couldn't hide. "My brother is right. We have monopolized much of your time tonight."

"I'm only doing my duty, my lady. I want to see this business handled correctly. How is the Dowager Countess Sotherton?"

"Sleeping now." Elizabeth's skirts swayed as she strolled into the room. "Thank you for your concern and attention, Mr. Mason. May I offer you a light repast?"

"Answers are all I need."

"I'll tell you everything I know, of course. Please, do sit." She sank onto the settee.

"Thank you, my lady." The magistrate resumed his seat. "Have you heard from Mr. Fleming's brother or Lord Sotherton?"

"A note arrived from Benedict earlier this evening. Of course, he hasn't yet learned of today's tragic events. Benedict wrote that Killiane decided to call on his friend Mr. Warren."

"Then he is not presently with Lord Sotherton?"

"He'll join Benedict in London in time for Parliament's opening. I don't know what we'll do about a service for dear Reggie, what with the new session of Parliament beginning later this week and his mother so far away."

"I remember when Mr. Fleming's mother lived in the district. What a dear, sweet lady who will be absolutely heartbroken. And you must be exhausted yourself, my lady. I'll try to keep my inquiries brief. Mr. Fleming died from a lethal dosage of laudanum."

"Perhaps his pain was acute and in his delirium, he accidently consumed overmuch."

Julian selected the chair on the other side of the marble fireplace. "I highly doubt Mr. Fleming died by his own hand—either deliberately or inadvertently. The doctor discovered the laudanum bottle on the desk, not next to the bed where your footman claims to have left it. When I observed Fleming earlier today, he hadn't the strength to rise from the bed, let alone hike across the room and back."

Elizabeth's pale features turned a ghastly shade of green. "Are you suggesting William…?"

"Or someone else. William claims he administered the usual dosage, put the laudanum next to the bed and then left Mr. Fleming alone some minutes while he prepared for dinner. The butler corroborates his story about leaving Mr. Fleming's chamber. Your cook says she didn't send up any food or drink at that time. However, Mr. Fleming had a brandy decanter and glasses in his room. Perhaps not coincidently, we discovered the laudanum bottle on the same desk as the empty brandy decanter."

"Then who might have killed Reggie?" Elizabeth's restless hands fidgeted on her lap.

"Assuming William and Hawkesworth speak the truth, anyone could have slipped into Mr. Fleming's room during those minutes when he was alone."

Mason shifted, causing the chair's frame to squeak. "We did make one peculiar discovery in Mr. Fleming's bedchamber."

Despite his proximity to the fire, a chill rippled down Julian's back. At destroying the remnants of a woman's reputation? "As yet, we don't know how it relates to his death."

Elizabeth's gaze flickered to Julian before returning to the magistrate. "A discovery?"

"A hair comb belonging to Miss Vance—a rather personal item to be lost in so private a place as the man's bedchamber. She has identified the item in question as hers, but I find her explanations for how it arrived in Mr. Fleming's possession decidedly implausible. My lady, did anything concern you about Mr. Fleming's relationship with Miss Vance? Did you notice anything unusual on that score? Has she ever seemed particularly friendly toward your nephew? Or perhaps markedly hostile?"

Elizabeth's familiar frown reappeared, deepening the lines around her mouth. "I can't recall any specific incidents. But then, I don't recall Miss Vance wearing a hair comb at any time."

In the interest of reconciliation, Julian refrained from an acerbic question about how well his sister knew any of her staff, beyond their ability to perform their duties diligently and without undue stress on her. "Elizabeth, do you remember Mr. Fleming's last visit?"

"Why, yes. It was…three years ago, I believe."

Three years. The same length of time Miss Vance declared her comb missing. Confirmation of Julian's suspicions? "Did anything unusual happen during his time here? Anything that seemed to make him concerned or offended or even especially pleased?"

"He injured his head while he was here. He tripped on the rug and fell against the fireplace mantle. I remember because I offered to send for Dr. Grant, but he declined."

"In what room did this happen?"

"His bedchamber, I believe."

"The same one he occupied on this visit?"

Elizabeth pursed her lips. "I would have to ask Mrs. Anderson, but I doubt so. Neither you nor Killiane were present at that time."

Sadness twined around his heart as suspicions lodged in his mind. "Is it possible Miss Vance did indeed lose her comb three years ago and Mr. Fleming had it in his possession all this time?"

"Why would Reggie keep an item of Miss Vance's?"

"Perhaps he had formed a tendre for her. Teresa did say he spoke much of her yesterday."

"Impossible. Reggie can do—could have done—so much better."

"Miss Vance was the daughter of a clergyman and sister of a fellow officer. There is no shame in an alliance with her."

Elizabeth's eyes narrowed. "You know a surprising amount of Miss Vance's background for such a recent acquaintance, Julian."

Undoubtedly more than his sister who'd employed the woman these past eight years. "You don't think I would entrust Caro to a woman of low character, do you?" And yet, he had surrendered his sister's care to a woman of proven disloyalty. He could have forgiven her devotion to her cause if only she hadn't lied to him by omission.

"I don't question Miss Vance's virtue, only her appropriateness for Reggie. Her father was an impecunious vicar. Reggie knew he needed to marry well. More likely the attachment traveled the other direction—a lonely woman hoping for more than life as a governess. Perhaps she tried to exploit the relationship for gain."

And yet, Fleming was the one with a reputation for exploitation. "Then she chose a flawed target since, as you say, Fleming needed to marry well."

"It's a motive for murder."

"A spurned female of several years past? A very weak motive."

Mr. Mason folded his arms across his chest. "Perhaps we should invite Miss Vance back to give us a more detailed accounting of her whereabouts at the time of Mr. Fleming's murder."

Julian knew full well where Miss Vance had spent the afternoon. Not where his sister supposed her to be, he'd warrant.

But since his own desire to see if she would name her associate meshed with the magistrate's need to charge someone with Fleming's murder, he pulled the cord to summon the butler.

Elizabeth settled folded hands on her lap. "Did you find nothing else of note when you searched Reggie's belongings? No other indications as to who would do such a terrible thing?"

"Is it possible your nephew owes someone money?" Julian instructed Hawkesworth to fetch Miss Vance, then returned to the cheerful fire blazing on the hearth. "Could he have lost a sum of money on wagers or bad investments?"

"I don't know what his financial situation is—was. I believe his brother provided him with an acceptable allowance."

How many others of Fleming's ilk found their allowances less than adequate for their expenses and entertainments? And couldn't a relative with a rapacious appetite for money and mischief also be a motive for murder?

"My lord?" Miss Vance's feet tapped against the floor as she inched into the room. She'd secured her mother's shawl around her shoulders. For warmth or for courage? The ivory complemented the ribbon of the same hue and softened her features. Then she caught sight of her employer on the settee. Her lashes dipped to cover the sudden flash of vulnerability as she dropped into a curtsey. "My lady."

"Come in, Miss Vance." Elizabeth's frosty tones were colder than January. "Mr. Mason has a few additional questions to ask of you."

Her gaze flickered to Julian, the candle's subdued glow revealing pools of fearful brown. He hardened his heart with reminders of her duplicity. Not a single event—possibly misconstrued or wrongly ascribed—but a series of incidents that pointed to serious deceit. Her unexplained visit to the stable the night of Fleming's attack. The information in his chamber that found its way to the radical group. Today's meeting with a man she wouldn't name. The same man Fleming had spotted her with on Sunday?

A special man, obviously—one for whom she'd risk the gallows.

Leah lifted her chin and stared at the delicate designs of the drawing room wallpapers. She would not be cowed. She'd done nothing wrong, nothing to be ashamed of. Not this time. Not in regards to Fleming anyway.

"Thank you for coming so promptly, Miss Vance." The magistrate's bushy brows lowered over narrowed eyes. "I'm sorry for the lateness of the hour, but I'm certain you appreciate the urgency of our investigation."

Fatigue chafed her eyes as she peered at the mantel clock. She didn't often see the hour of two. "I understand, sir."

"Earlier when we spoke, you denied being in Mr. Fleming's chamber at any time today."

"Yes, other than those moments immediately prior to his death."

"Of course. Both Lady Sotherton and Lord Chambelston vouch for your presence then."

Leah fought the urge to glance at the man in question despite her awareness of his presence, of the heavy regard of his stare and the painful weight of his distrust.

"Where were you in the hours preceding Mr. Fleming's death—say, in the time between my interview with Lady Teresa and Mr. Fleming's demise?"

The silence stretched almost as long as those hours the magistrate spoke of—tense moments while Leah's exhausted mind whirled with excuses both impossible and improbable.

"Miss Vance?" Lady Sotherton's frosty tones cut through Leah's concerns. "I pay you good money to educate my daughter."

Not good enough for Leah to care for her sister, let alone

have enough left to provide for herself afterward. Resentment churned in her stomach, making credible lies all the more difficult to formulate. "I—I was…"

"Were you with Teresa?"

To answer in the affirmative would put Teresa in an untenable position—a choice between her mother and her governess, between a lie and a truth and perhaps even between Leah's life and death. For the second time since her mother's death, her mind formed a rusty prayer, a plea for wisdom, help, escape. Leah dropped her stare to the knotted fingers on her lap, knowing she could give but one answer. Much as she disliked Lady Sotherton, much as she feared for her life and Phoebe's future, she couldn't burden Teresa with such a dilemma. "No, my lady. I had an errand to accomplish beyond the estate."

"I thought I had made my expectations clear. You have Wednesday afternoons to see to any personal business."

"I had…personal business that couldn't wait."

"Not even one day? I wonder what could possibly have been so important." Chambelston paced to the fireplace, hands clenched together behind his back. The mirror above the mantel reflected a second, equally forbidding, image of his expression back to her. "By your own admission, Miss Vance, you were not in the schoolroom at the time of Mr. Fleming's death?"

"No, my lord."

"Did you meet with anyone on this critical errand—a shopkeeper, a blacksmith, a milliner—someone who will confirm your presence away from the Abbey?"

Fear roiled in her stomach and ripped the air from her lungs. The room dimmed, the accusatory faces receding into the darkness of her dread. How she could trust Molly's reassurances of a God with a vision for her future when she saw nothing but imminent doom?

"Miss Vance?" The magistrate's voice pierced through the clamor in her head. "Is there anyone who will confirm your absence?"

If she provided Alec's name, what would happen to him? They had no witnesses to her presence in Fleming's room. Was the discovery of her hair comb, combined with her disappearance, enough to hang a murder charge on her? "No, no one." Her whisper echoed through the hostile silence.

"Think carefully, Miss Vance." Mr. Mason peered at her over his spectacles. "Is there anything else you would like to add to your defense?"

"I have only the truth." A partial truth, unfortunately. And therein was the rub. "I didn't harm Mr. Fleming." This time.

The queasiness still fermenting in Leah now touched the magistrate's countenance, coloring his cheeks a sickly green. "Miss Vance, I fear I'm going to have to arrest you on suspicion of Reginald Fleming's murder."

"But I didn't hurt him!" To the contrary, in fact.

"No, she didn't." Chambelston's low, deep agreement reverberated in the quiet and raised prickles of awareness along her arms. "As a matter of fact, I witnessed Miss Vance's excursion outdoors—although she didn't see me at the time."

Leah twisted her head and at last met the scornful bitterness in his glare. Had it been there all along? Had even that twilight kiss been a means to seek her cooperation, or had her reticence tonight quashed what might have been?

An errant lock dangled over his brow, its strands gilded by the light of the wall sconces. His snowy cravat gleamed against the backdrop of his blue coat, the same one of their first meeting. A memory surfaced in her mind of Lord Chambelston marching into Fleming's chamber in his greatcoat, his hair tousled by the wind. Yes, he had indeed been out then. Had he seen Alec with her? Enough to identify him? Nausea bubbled in her stomach where fear mingled with loss.

Mr. Mason straightened in his chair. "What were you doing at the time, my lord?"

"I had gone for a ride. I returned to the house at approximately the same time as Miss Vance. The groom will vouch for my absence and return."

"And you are certain as to the identity of the woman you saw?"

"Absolutely. She was walking, and too far from the Abbey to be in the manor when Fleming consumed the laudanum."

"I admit to a large measure of surprise you didn't inform us of this earlier, my lord."

"I waited for Miss Vance to reveal the truth."

Because he didn't trust her, and perhaps never had. And never would. That truth hit Leah like one of the blows to Fleming's body.

The magistrate's ample girth expanded as he sucked in a deep breath. "Very well, then. It seems we shall have to inquire further to find our murderer. Miss Vance, you are free to retire. However, should you recall any details about your comb or develop any theories about its discovery in Fleming's chamber, I would appreciate your cooperation."

"Of course, sir." Leah pushed herself from the chair, intent on escaping the contemptuous sneer of the man who had saved her from certain arrest and possible death. The room spun with her relief even as her shoulders ached from tension and her eyes burned with fatigue.

Lady Sotherton raised a hand. "Just a moment, Miss Vance."

Leah paused, dread escalating her pulse. "My lady?"

"You have confessed to a dereliction in your duties. I cannot keep you on my staff."

The lump in Leah's throat sealed off any protests she might have made. How would she care for Phoebe with no job, no references, no accommodations, no…anything? But she'd saved Alec. "I understand, my lady."

"You have one hour to gather your belongings and leave."

"One hour!" Leah's gaze shot to the ormolu clock on the mantel again. Only thirty minutes had passed since her arrival in the drawing room. Dawn was hours away. "But how will I say my farewells to Lady Teresa?"

"I will make your excuses in the morning. I suggest you make the most of your allotted time tonight, Miss Vance."

"Yes, my lady." Leah curtseyed, then fled up the stairs to pack. So much for Molly's assurances of a God with a plan.

Chapter Eleven

The cold air stung Julian's eyes and chilled his cheeks as he waited outside the manor door. He set the lantern on the ground and tugged the collar of his greatcoat higher around his neck. The silence of the winter night furled around him, disturbed only by the mournful cries of a dog howling in the distance. The full moon illuminated the snow, creating a world of dramatic grays.

The door latch clicked and the hinges squeaked. Then muted footfalls crept closer.

"Miss Vance?"

Her gasp echoed across the quiet. "Lord Chambelston?" Her arms cradled a modest bag.

"Do you have somewhere to go, Miss Vance?"

"I...I think so."

"How far?"

"The village of Heckton. About five miles to the south. Did the magistrate leave?"

"Yes, but he intends to return tomorrow—or rather, today—to question more of the staff."

"A pity he'll have to find some other convenient scapegoat, now that he can't charge me with the murder."

"You were never in any danger on that score." He scooped up the lantern and clasped her elbow.

She jerked her arm away. "What are you doing?"

"It isn't safe for a woman to be alone at this time of night." Perhaps those who attacked Fleming were associates of hers—but perhaps not. Besides, other depraved, destitute and displaced men roamed the countryside. "Not to mention, you probably shouldn't walk so far on your foot. I'll take you where you need to go."

"You?" Anger flashed from her eyes into the night. "You knew the entire time I was innocent of Mr. Fleming's murder, that I wasn't even in the house. You could have told the magistrate the first time he questioned me and spared me the indignity of being cast out."

"Indignation doesn't suit you under the circumstances. I admit I didn't expect Lizzie to dismiss you quite so precipitously—"

"Why wouldn't she? You let both my employer and the magistrate assume I was a murderer while you knew otherwise."

"I also know you to be guilty of treason. And yet, I let both my sister and the magistrate assume you were merely neglectful, not a traitor."

"So why did you?" Her whisper caressed his conscience.

"Not for your sake." He settled his hand against the curve of her spine and guided her toward the stable. A bittersweet hint of lavender drifted to him on the night air like the faint promise of spring.

"Obviously. You took no great pains to hide your disdain for me."

After her betrayal, she should have expected no less. Given what he'd surmised of Fleming's conduct toward her, he could have forgiven her the man's murder before he could overlook her perfidy to *himself.* Julian hated disloyalty—which is why he would perform this last service for her. "I owe your late brother."

"My brother?"

"David Vance of the *HMS Belleisle,* no? I only recognized the relationship when I saw the comb. We served on the same frigate briefly—a very long time ago. I was a newly minted lieutenant while he was yet a midshipman." The stable crouched before them. Julian slid the door to the side. The twin scents of hay and horse suffused his senses and chased away the memories as he gestured her in, the building's interior darker than the bright night. "In addition to his artistry at carving, I remember your brother as an exceptionally good navigator."

"Yes, as I said, David was the most intelligent of us." A tinge of bitterness colored her tones. Resentment toward the parents who had inadvertently favored their firstborn son over their later-arriving daughters?

"Did you have dinner last night?"

"Not…much."

"I thought that might be the case." He dipped his hand into his pocket and retrieved a small bundle. "We can't have you fainting along the way."

"Where did you get this?" She unfolded the cloth to expose a hunk of bread and cheese.

"Hawkesworth was concerned about you." Julian struck the flint and lit the candle, then hung the lantern on a peg. The small circle of light emphasized the dark crescents of exhaustion that underscored her eyes, the plainness of her coat and bonnet and the meagerness of her bundle containing all her worldly belongings. A new wave of unease washed over him as he considered the incongruity.

What had she done with her ill-gotten gains? Provisioned a destitute invalid during this winter of want? Guilt scratched at Julian's conscience. Would any do the same for her?

"I don't suppose you'll tell me why you left Rowan Abbey this afternoon?"

"It doesn't matter now, my lord."

No, probably not. Not when what might have been would never be.

Leah retreated into the shadows to escape Chambelston's too-penetrating, too-perceptive stare. His gaze lingered on her for several more interminable moments, then he snared a bridle and entered the black gelding's stall.

Leah finished the bread and brushed the crumbs from her fingers.

"My lord?" A disheveled, heavy-eyed Wetherel shuffled his bare feet into the lantern's weak light. "Is there a problem?"

"Miss Vance was called away suddenly because of an emergency. I'm going to see her to Heckton." Chambelston inserted the bit into the horse's mouth.

Wetherel whipped his head around. His bushy brows lowered over his eyes as he caught sight of Leah. "I can do that for you, my lord."

"Thank you, but I have the matter in hand." Chambelston buckled the bridle. "Go back to sleep."

The groom lingered for several more minutes. "Very well, my lord. If you insist." Wetherel's gaze locked onto Leah's as he edged past her. Then the rustle of his footsteps faded and he disappeared.

Despite the lateness of the hour and the seriousness of her situation, or perhaps because of them, a giggle bubbled in Leah's throat. "I don't think he trusts you to suitably manage the matter, my lord."

"No doubt he's met other members of the nobility and fears for his animals." Chambelston smoothed a blanket along the gelding's back. Much as the man's mercurial moods vexed her, Leah acknowledged he displayed a self-sufficiency rare among the aristocracy.

A hand tapped against her arm. Leah peeked over her shoulder as Wetherel crooked a finger and gestured her away from Chambelston. She inched back a step, then another until the darkness of the stable's murky interior swallowed her.

Wetherel pressed a folded note into her hand, then leaned closer to whisper in her ear. "This arrived several hours ago. I had thought to wait until morning to deliver it to you."

"Thank you." Answers from Alec, perhaps about the attack on Fleming and Teresa? Unfortunately Chambelston saddled the black gelding next to the only lit candle in the entire stable. She could hardly examine the note there. But she probably didn't need the message now. Alec could tell her himself once she arrived at his lodgings. She tucked the paper into her sleeve then edged forward lest Chambelston notice her absence.

He secured the girth in place. "See to the candle, Miss Vance." The horse's iron shoes clanked against the floor as Chambelston led the animal outside.

Leah blew out the flame and followed them, dragging the stable door shut behind her. The cold wind tossed snow against her face.

"Quickly." Her unlikely knight-errant climbed into the saddle. "Pass me your bag."

She transferred the bundle containing a few clothes, her mother's shawl, and her father's Bible—unread these many years—without comment. Chambelston balanced it on the front of the saddle before him.

"And now you, Miss Vance." He stretched out his hand to her. "Put your foot atop mine."

She placed her palm against the leather of his glove, braced her sole on the toe of his boot, and let him swing her onto the horse behind him. Sitting astride hiked up her skirt several inches. The cold assailed her calves through her thin stockings.

"Still no gloves, Miss Vance?"

"I—I fear they were quite ruined during the events of the other day."

"Take mine." He stripped them off his hands.

"I can't do that. You need them yourself."

"I'll manage."

Reluctantly she accepted his offering. She pulled the leather over her fingers. The lingering warmth of his touch inside thawed her cold skin. "Thank you."

"Hold on." He urged the horse into motion. "Which way?"

"Veer left. We will follow this road for a mile, then turn right at the crossroads."

"To Heckton."

"Yes." Hopefully Alec could squeeze her into his lodging for the few hours remaining of this night. And in the morning? Where would she go? Her mind swirled with alternatives, each leading to the same conclusion. Molly's words, about a God with a plan, returned to mock her. She had no money and no prospects. No future.

The raw breeze chilled Leah's cheeks. She tilted her head down and sheltered her face from the wind with Chambelston's broad shoulders. The gentle rocking of the horse, the silence of the night and the warmth radiating from his coat promised blissful oblivion from her anxiety and exhaustion. Her heavy lids drifted over her eyes and her drowsy head bobbed.

She jerked and caught herself before she tumbled off the horse.

"Don't fall asleep."

"I won't." And yet, her words sounded soft and slurred even to her own ears.

"You could recite a few of those French conjugations. They kept me awake at night when I was a lad."

"Exacting tutor?"

"Something worse. I didn't want to disappoint my mother, given it's her native language. Unfortunately I proved an inept pupil. Unhappily for me, my little brother has a remarkable ear for languages, and he put my poor efforts to shame."

Rather like her younger sister Phoebe's beauty casting Leah in the shadows. "Say something."

"So you can tease me?"

"Your pride will benefit from a measure of humility."

"Why do I suspect you are more interested in my humiliation than my humility?"

"A good laugh will keep me awake."

"I think I would prefer you sleeping to mocking me."

The indistinct outlines of Heckton's cottages rising before them brought an end to this, their last—unexpected—banter. Longing for the foolish what-might-have-been weighed heavily in her heart as she tapped his lordship's shoulder. The night's ride, like her extraordinary part-friend and part-adversary relationship with Chambelston, had come to an end. "This is far enough."

He drew the horse to a stop, then twisted his head and studied her face through the moon's eerie glow. "Here? Miss Vance, as a gentleman, I would prefer to accompany you to your door."

"But you see, my lord, it isn't my door."

He slid off the horse. "And you believe I would deliver your friend to the government."

She fitted her hand into the one he extended to assist her down. "I think we both have good reasons for not confiding in each other."

"You trust me more than you realize. I wish…"

A pity she couldn't say the same of him. What betrayal

had scarred him? A friend? Family member? A woman? "How so?"

"If you thought me a danger, you wouldn't have directed me to this village. A few well-placed questions backed up with the offer of a bit of silver..."

But she would have bought herself what she most needed tonight. Time. She doffed his gloves and waited for him to pass her belongings.

Instead he reached inside his coat and produced a small purse. "A pity we couldn't have met under other circumstances. I owe you this, I believe." He captured her wrist and plopped the heavy pouch onto her palm. The soft chink of silver echoed in the night.

"I—I..." Pride demanded she refuse—she'd done little enough to earn his coins—but expediency held her tongue. Desperation did not allow for vanity. The money would solve her immediate problems for Phoebe's care. Perhaps more. But... "Why?" The same question she'd asked when he'd insisted on attending her during this middle of the night venture.

"David."

The answer she'd expected, if not the one she'd hoped for. Chambelston would have been pleased she intended to use the funds in the same way David would have—except she had no intention of revealing her family's shame. "Thank you." The swelling in her throat rendered the words subdued and husky.

"You're welcome." He passed her the bundle and swung up into the saddle.

"Would you make my farewells to Teresa and Lady Caroline?" Loneliness pierced her like the wind. "I fear my abrupt departure will unsettle your sister."

"I'll do that." He gave her one last, lingering stare. Then he touched the brim of his hat. "Goodbye, Miss Vance."

He rode off, leaving her holding the bag of silver. And his gloves, still clasped in her other hand. She raised them to her face and inhaled, imagining that sardonic smile as the scent of him filled her one last time.

Leah waited until the muffled clomp of the horse's hooves faded into the darkness before she strolled the span of ageless stone buildings. She'd been to Alec's lodgings but once, and then in daylight. A poor choice would make her decidedly unpopular.

A dog barked from inside a thatched-roof cottage. An angry voice responded, then all lapsed to quiet again. No, there was no dog at Alec's lodgings. She peered at the next building, a modest structure whose warped wooden shingles moaned in the breeze. Alec had been wont to complain about the water seeping through his ceiling.

She gathered a fistful of snow and tossed it at an upstairs window. "Alec." When the silence persisted, she repeated his name, more loudly.

Nothing. Now what? The wind penetrated her coat and the cold breached the slice in her boot. She would freeze if she remained out here until dawn. She tossed more snow at the glass, then ventured a tentative knock on the door.

The dog next door began to bark again. Leah pounded more loudly on the door, if only to get Alec to let her in before the entire village awoke.

A window above—not the one she'd covered in snow—screeched up in its frame. "What do you want?" The petulant alto resonated in the stillness and produced another session of barking.

"I need to speak with Alec Vance. It's a family emergency." Namely, her.

"He ain't here."

"He's not? But then…" Perhaps she had chosen the wrong cottage after all.

"Ain't seen him since yesterday."

"Where did he go?"

"How should I know? I'm his landlord, not his mother."
The window slammed shut.

Why would Alec leave without informing…the note. She
tugged it free of her coat sleeve and unfolded the parchment.
The bright moonlight reflected on a single line in Alec's large
scrawl.

Gone to London.

Why would Alec go to London so suddenly, unless…

Was he in danger? Heart pounding, she flipped the sheet
over but found no additional message on the back. Not visible, anyway, and she'd left her solution—the one that allowed her to see Alec's hidden messages—at Rowan Abbey
in her haste to leave.

The dog barked two more times, then hushed. Leah pivoted
on her heel and began the long walk back to Rowan Abbey, a
journey no doubt made more difficult by the still-sore bruises
on her foot, the souvenir of her confrontation with Fleming.
Perhaps Chambelston would agree to retrieve the solution—
in exchange for Alec's information.

Fatigue burned in Julian's eyes and sat heavily on his
shoulders as he piloted the horse back onto Sotherton lands.
How like those late nights and long watches on his ships. The
moon had sunk low in the sky, creating dancing shadows
of the breeze-tossed branches. In a couple hours a new day
would dawn, yet another new chapter in his life. The loneliness, so recently mitigated, resumed. Intensified.

"Chambelston!"

Julian jerked on the reins as a form rose from behind the
stone fence that paralleled the road. The horse shied, leaving him to scramble to maintain his seat. Once he had the
animal under control, he peered at the intruder. "Harrison?"

"Sorry about that, my lord. I didn't mean to startle you."

"My own fault. I was nearly asleep." But he was awake now. Julian dismounted. "What's happened?"

"I wish I knew. All I heard was talk of London."

"London?" Julian's empty stomach churned with memories of the riot that had caused his father's injuries. "The last meeting there turned violent. Do you know where they intend to assemble?"

"I'm sorry, my lord, but I learned no further details."

So the activity at Wellingborough was a feint, a pretense designed to distract attention from the group's real aims. Did Miss Vance know, even as he carried her to her destination tonight? Even as he foolishly provided her funds to begin a new life? "We can hardly search all of London for them. Do we know anyone who might be willing to assist us? Perhaps for a fee?"

"Your governess…?"

"Has left my sister's employ."

But Harrison stared past Julian, at the road behind him. "My lord…"

Julian turned, his agitation transforming to astonishment at the shadowy figuring limping toward them. He motioned Harrison to silence and the two of them waited as she approached. "Miss Vance?"

"My lord, I…" Her gaze flickered to Harrison before focusing on Julian again.

"Perhaps I should wait for you over by the large tree, my lord." Harrison sidled back.

"Wait!" Julian held up a hand as he deliberated the situation. Miss Vance hugged her bundle, her cheeks pinched with cold. Why had she returned? Their recent conversation about trust—and their lack thereof—returned to him. Alone he and Harrison had little chance of success. Either Miss Vance had come to help, or they would fail anyway. "This is Lawrence Harrison. He is assisting me in my inquiries."

Harrison smiled. "Miss Vance, I've heard much about you."

"No doubt, Mr. Harrison." Miss Vance offered him a graceful nod then looked to Julian again. "My lord, I have bad news. I fear my...contact has left the area."

"For London."

Her eyes widened. "Then you know."

"Alas, no more details than that. Do you?"

"Perhaps." She passed him a folded sheet of paper.

Julian opened the note and peered at the single line in the lustrous moonlight. "But this only mentions London."

"Perhaps not." Her hand shook a little as she flipped the note over to expose the blank back of the page. "Alec and I use special inks to communicate the sensitive parts of our messages—inks that can only be read when the proper solution is applied."

A thrill shot up Julian's spine. "Alec?"

She paused, drew in a deep breath. "My cousin. He...is a member of the...group." That particle of trust for which he'd been waiting.

Her cousin. And perhaps the identity of her gentleman friend? Julian pushed those thoughts aside for a later examination. "When did you get this?"

"In the stable, while you were saddling the horse." A wry smile twisted her lips. "If I had read it then, we could have saved ourselves a lot of effort tonight. At a minimum I'd have known to avoid Heckton."

"Do you have the solution in your bag?"

"No. I kept it in my desk in the schoolroom. I didn't even think to retrieve the bottle when I had to gather my belongings so swiftly."

"May I?" Harrison stretched forth a hand. Miss Vance surrendered the paper. Harrison scrutinized the blank back. "I think Miss Vance might be correct. One of the disadvantages of such inks is that if the writer is not careful, he may leave scratches where none are supposed to be. See these lines? They are possibly those of a quill point."

"Alec was always careful." Miss Vance defended her cousin as Harrison returned the note to her.

"But if he were in a hurry, he might not have wasted time with caution." Julian stretched the tight muscles in his calves, feeling the twinge all the way to his thighs. "Do you have any idea when your cousin might have written this message?"

Another hesitation. And then…another measure of trust glimmered in her eyes. "Tonight. After you saw me walking beyond Rowan Abbey."

After…because she had met with him only this past afternoon? Had he solved the mystery of the unknown gentleman? "We need to determine if Miss Vance's relative conveyed any more information."

"Alec seldom informed me about his actions. He preferred to keep silent—for my sake as well as his." Her hands trembled as she tucked the note inside her coat again. "Such a correspondence is…unusual."

Harrison shoved his hands into his pockets. "My lord, we have kept Miss Vance outside far too long. Perhaps she could retrieve her solution, and then we can determine our next course of action."

"I'll go." Julian offered before Miss Vance had to confess to her dismissal. He shrugged out of his greatcoat and wreathed it around her shoulders. The hem brushed against the snow.

"But my lord, I can't take your coat. You'll get cold—"

"I'll ride back to Rowan Abbey and have Wetherel prepare the carriage while I get the solution. The two of you can wait here, then I'll collect you on the way. Where exactly should I look in the desk?"

"On the left side. In the back. I have both the solution and a bottle of my own ink in there. Bring both and I will show you the correct one when you return. And don't forget to grab a brush from the paints."

"You kept the ink and solution together? That wasn't wise."

Another smile touched her eyes. "I never said they worked together. Alec has the solution for that ink, and—"

"Your solution works with Alec's ink. I grow curious about this cousin of yours. I should like to meet him."

The muscles in her jaw tightened. "That may happen sooner than you think."

Julian shoved a weary leg into the stirrup and climbed back into the saddle. "I shall look forward to it, Miss Vance."

Leah pulled up the collar of Chambelston's coat—only to catch a whiff of warm male drifting to her senses. The pounding of hooves faded in the distance. She glanced at the man standing beside her, caught his scrutiny, then hastily jerked her gaze away. How much had Chambelston confided in this Harrison? How much did he know about her?

How…awkward.

"Miss Vance, is it?"

She peeked at him again. The gray light of approaching day revealed a pleasant enough face below the battered hat that crowned his head. "Yes."

"I understand you were of late the Sotherton governess."

"Yes."

"What do you think might be in this note?"

"Oh, I couldn't speculate."

"I once knew an Alec Vance."

Warning bells clanged in Leah's head. "I'm sure it's a fairly common name."

"During the war."

"Undoubtedly, many men of like age served."

"We had occasion to work together. My position frequently

required the use of unusual…tools of war. Such as invisible inks and their solutions."

The cold lanced through the slash in her boot and sent the wintry chill shooting up her spine. If this Harrison did indeed know Alec, Chambelston would have little enough reason to take her to London. And she must go with them. She must be there if—when—Chambelston located her cousin. "As I said, Vance is not uncommon."

"If you say so, Miss Vance."

Did that mean he wouldn't challenge her on the matter when Chambelston returned? "How long have you known Lord Chambelston?"

"Scarcely more than a year. However, I know his brother very well."

His brother. "The linguist?"

"Yes, Kit."

So, he had known Alec during the war. And he knew a linguist? A picture began to form in Leah's mind. "I don't believe I've ever seen you in this area before, Mr. Harrison. Where did you say you hail from?"

A knowing smile gleamed in his eyes. "I didn't."

"You must miss your home."

"Indeed. But I haven't been gone long."

Only since Chambelston had decided to investigate the activities of Alec's group?

The soft crunch of carriage wheels on snow murmured through the stillness, accompanied by the occasional jingle of a harness. As the conveyance—the same one Chambelston had arrived in that seemingly long ago day—drew nearer, the glow of its lanterns emerged from the predawn gray. The driver reined the horses to a stop, jumped down from his perch and unlatched the crest-embellished door.

Leah drew in a deep breath as she ambled to the vehicle's side. She was entrusting not only her own future, but Alec's life to Chambelston's hands. She passed the coachman her belongings, then mounted the step. The coach pitched, then righted. Or was that her nervous stomach?

Chambelston grabbed her hand and drew her into the dark interior. "After you, Miss Vance." He gestured to the forward-facing seat.

Leah sank into the soft cushion.

"With your permission?" He hovered above the seat next to her.

What could she say? It was his carriage, after all. She nodded rather than force words past the lump in her throat as her mind grappled with the ramifications of many intimate hours beside him.

Chambelston lowered himself onto the velvet upholstery beside her. His broad shoulders occupied more than his fair share of the bench.

She inched closer to the corner, away from the casual brush of his arm against hers. "D-did you have any difficulty finding my supplies?"

"I didn't know where to look for the brush. Fortunately Molly was already awake and at work, and she located the paints for me—without so much as a smirk to betray her assessment of my sanity." A frown tugged down the corners of his mouth. "I only wish I could have clarified to Caro that I will return soon. I fear my absence will distress her."

"Did you ask Molly to convey your apology?" Leah fished inside her coat—under Chambelston's greatcoat—for Alec's note as Harrison joined them inside the carriage.

"Yes, she said she would try to explain."

"My lord?" The coachman paused with one hand on the door.

Chambelston tilted his head and peered at Leah, one brow raised. "Where would you like me to take you this time, if not Heckton?"

"London."

His gaze held hers a moment longer, as if weighing her reasons for choosing that destination. "London it is, John."

The coachman secured the door, and the carriage rocked as he clambered to his seat.

"Now let's see if your cousin left us any clues, or if we have to scour the entire metropolis to discover their plans." Chambelston retrieved the bottles and brush as Leah unfolded the missive.

She glanced up and caught Harrison's bemused scrutiny. "I believe you have some experience with these, sir. Would you like to…?" She offered him the paper.

"You are the expert."

Oh, she highly doubted so. She pressed the note flat on her lap, blank side up, and chose the solution from two bottles Chambelston proffered. Her fingers quivered as she removed the cap and dipped the brush inside. She smeared a streak of the solution across the page.

Her chest tightened around the air in her lungs as the purple lines emerged.

Quickly she applied a thin veneer of solution until she covered the entire paper, then passed the wet sheet to Chambelston.

He held the page to the lantern and read, *"'Oliver to attack Regent en route to opening of Parliament. Gone to stop him. Get help.'"* The deep baritone broke off as he lifted his head and shared a look with Harrison.

"At least we know what part of London." Harrison leaned forward and templed his fingers against his chin. "Miss Vance, do you know this Oliver? I can't say I've ever met him."

Leah searched her memories for the few clues her cousin had provided, but Alec had always been careful. Too careful, it now seemed. "I don't think Alec ever mentioned him before—at least, not by name."

"An attack on the Regent. That would throw the entire government into chaos." Chambelston returned the still damp paper to her. "We'll find someplace safe to take you, Miss Vance."

"No! You need me." And so did Alec. *Especially* Alec. "None of us know this Oliver, but I know my cousin. If we find him—"

"There's a good chance Oliver is nearby. Hopefully your cousin has the good sense to notify the authorities once he reaches London."

"I doubt they'd believe him—even if he can get anyone to receive him."

Chambelston expelled a deep sigh. "I fear you may be right."

"Then you'll take me with you?"

"Yes, Miss Vance. We'll take you to London." Chambelston tucked a lap robe around his legs, reminding Leah that she still wore his coat over her own. But he had already closed his eyes before she could offer to return it. "I'm too old to go gallivanting about the countryside all night long. You should also get some rest, Leah. We don't know what the day will bring."

Leah nestled into the corner of the seat with one last thought whirling through her exhausted mind. Chambelston had used her Christian name again.

Chapter Twelve

Julian peered at the gray light from under heavy lids. Disorientation swirled through his mind while his sluggish brain absorbed the reality of midday filtering through carriage windows. He glanced at the woman beside him, her even breaths marking her as yet asleep.

Relaxed, her face looked more youthful, offering him a glimpse of the young woman who'd entered his sister's employ when she was scarcely past her own girlhood. If Elizabeth hadn't cut her family from her life all those years ago, would Julian have met Leah earlier? Perhaps on a warm summer visit or over happy holiday merrymaking. Would he have appreciated the subtle qualities of her nature then? Would she have turned to him to ease the plight of a desperate friend—rather than resort to treason?

The upholstery rustled as Harrison shifted on the seat across from Julian. "I trust you slept well, my lord?"

"Not particularly." Not if the cramp in his neck was anything by which to judge.

"I expected to find you in your bed when I arrived. Instead, I encountered you—and then Miss Vance—on the road."

"Fortunately for you."

"Oh, I'd have found a way to contact you, even at that time of night." Harrison's eyes gleamed with humor.

No doubt, given the man's background. "Fleming died, shortly after you and I last spoke. Not of the injuries inflicted by the gang of hoodlums, but from poison."

Harrison whistled a soft note between his teeth. "Administered by someone at the Abbey?"

"So it appears—his killer placed evidence suggesting Miss Vance's involvement in Fleming's chamber."

"You are certain of her innocence?"

"Oh, yes. I saw her while returning to the Abbey after our meeting. According to the doctor's estimate as to the time of the poisoning, she wasn't in the manor when Fleming consumed the fatal dose." Julian glanced at Leah again, then leaned forward and lowered his voice. "She was with a man. The mysterious cousin, I presume. Of course my sister was most displeased when she learned of Miss Vance's midweek venture beyond the manor and terminated her employment immediately."

"According to the rumors I heard, Fleming was a nasty piece of work." Harrison folded his arms across his chest and leaned back against the upholstery.

"Yes, we have no shortage of suspects who might want the man dead." Julian pulled the racing form from inside his coat and passed it across to Harrison. "The magistrate found this in Fleming's chamber after his death. Something about it bothered me, so I grabbed it when I went back to the abbey for Miss Vance's solution."

"Quick thinking, my lord." Harrison tipped the page toward the window and squinted as he studied the words. "Are you certain this is Fleming's handwriting?"

"I can't identify it as such, only that we discovered it with his effects."

"But you also believe someone wanted Miss Vance

suspected—or even charged—in the murder. This could have been deposited in the chamber at the same time as the evidence against her."

"To implicate Miss Vance? I highly doubt she follows the ponies."

Harrison glanced at her still-sleeping form and grinned. "A penchant for wagering on the horses could explain her need for money."

So would a destitute friend. Julian tried to recall if he'd seen Leah's writing. If she had been communicating with the radicals, Harrison might have had occasion to see notes from her. "Would you recognize her handwriting?"

"I've never seen a message from her, so I can't be certain. However, if I were to venture a guess, I would say this is not hers. A racing form is a rather subtle clue if one is trying to incriminate a governess. It probably belonged to Fleming." Harrison returned his attention to the page. "Based on the formation of the letters, I suspect if we discover the creator of these comments, we'll uncover the author of your anonymous note."

Excitement ricocheted along Julian's spine. "Are you certain?"

"Do you have the other message? The one about your father's injury?"

"Yes, it's…" In the pocket of his greatcoat. The same coat currently shrouding Miss Vance.

Julian leaned closer to her. A hint of lavender teased his senses, and a few wisps of hair escaped her chignon. He tucked them back in her bonnet, marveling as his knuckles brushed against the soft skin of her face. Her puffs of breath tickled his skin as he carefully extracted the note from the pocket. She stirred, then settled back to sleep with a sigh while Julian handed the note to Harrison.

The former spy pursed his lips while he perused the message. "I can't be absolutely certain, you understand. But a clever gamester would wager the same hand wrote both."

Julian contemplated the implications of two such disparate records being in the same hand. "Who would seek my involvement in the quarrel between the government and antiroyalist extremists? Most certainly not Miss Vance or her allies. Suggesting the radicals had killed my father would attach me firmly to the government's cause." And Fleming? By all accounts the man was a frivolous sort, too absorbed in pleasure to exert himself with the effort of politics. Exactly, in fact, the sort of man who would record his observations about the best betting options on a racing form.

"Once we ascertain the answer to that question, we may unravel the entire plot." Harrison handed the paper back to Julian. "Do you know when Parliament begins its session?"

"Tomorrow morning. We have less than twenty-four hours to reach London and prevent a catastrophe. I didn't realize when we left how momentous our journey would be." Helplessness churned in Julian's stomach. If only they had learned of the radicals' intentions earlier. Even one day would have bought them more time to make the trip, notify the authorities and station men along the roads. Julian glanced toward the window and the clouds that muted the sun. All they needed was for the snow to begin again. "Do you think we'll arrive in time?"

"I think a few prayers are in order."

Prayers. Julian stiffened at Harrison's overt proselytizing. "Then why not just ask God to stop this assassin before we get there?"

"I'm afraid God wants our participation, my friend."

"Even though there is a good chance we will fail?"

"Yes, our participation, our reliance and our trust—trust that He will use whatever happens for greater purposes than we can see with our limited perceptions."

"I suppose, given the prince's ill repute, some might find his death to be God working for good."

"Well, the Bible does tell us God doesn't wish for any to perish. But He can use what is meant for evil for good. For instance, my lord, but for your father's death and the note you received, you wouldn't be here right now making a madcap dash to London to save the prince's life. Miss Vance would be alone on a dark, cold night with no place to go, if not hanged. And I would be hard-pressed to afford sustenance for my family."

Julian pulled his watch from his pocket, surprised to find the hands had climbed past twelve already and well into the first hour of the afternoon. "Speaking of sustenance, we must procure a meal. I don't suppose you know of a suitable inn along our route?"

"Not I. We shall have to make do with the first place we find."

"Yes, you are correct. Time is of the essence." Julian sighed. Despite his sister's initial hostility to his presence, she furnished a fine table—something many an innkeeper would be hard put to match in this winter of want.

Harrison tapped his templed fingers against his mouth. "My lord, have you considered we shall arrive in London very late. You cannot take Miss Vance to your house."

"Why not? I won't have time to be there myself. We have to notify the palace of what is happening, so the prince can make alternate arrangements for his ride to Parliament. It would be best if he sent his carriage along the usual route as a decoy. And then, if I have time, I thought to meet with some of the officers at the Admiralty so we can station men along the streets and hopefully capture our villain before he commits serious harm. A night at my house—with servants present and me absent—isn't going to limit Miss Vance's future employment any more than her dismissal from my sister's household."

"I'm sure London has at least one inn with an available room." The feminine voice cut into their quiet conversation.

Julian shifted to meet the determined hazel eyes. He studied the proud tilt of her chin, so incongruous with the unruly tresses escaping from the sadly crushed bonnet. "A woman alone at an inn would be more unsuitable." Not to mention dangerous.

Harrison cleared his throat. "If I may suggest, Miss Vance is always welcome in my home."

"But as you already said, we will not reach London until well into the night. That is quite an imposition."

"My wife Alice has the gift of hospitality. If she were here, she would insist. Besides," he winked at Miss Vance, "I'd like to think she'll be so pleased I've returned that she will agree to any suggestion I make. For a day, at least."

Julian looked from one to the other. "Well, then, let's hope the matter concludes quickly. In the meantime we must find provisions as soon as possible. Other than a few bites of bread and cheese, neither Miss Vance nor I have eaten since yesterday's nuncheon."

The worst of her hunger satiated and even hastily donned in a fresh—if wrinkled—gown from her bundle, Leah snuggled back into the familiar corner of the carriage as the driver urged the horses into motion once again. A few raindrops clinked against the window and then dripped along the outside of the glass. She let her eyes drift shut, more to save herself from having to converse with Chambelston, who sat mere inches away, than from any real fatigue.

Besides, she could learn so much when the men thought her asleep. Such as Harrison's contention that Reginald Fleming may have written the letter accusing Alec's friends of the murder of Chambelston's father. Why would Fleming even consider such a thing? He didn't know anyone in their group. Unless he only sought to cause mischief—a sick joke to be played on a grieving family.

Now *that* Leah could believe more than the idea of Fleming developing a sudden interest in politics or a sudden concern for the welfare of the nation.

She peeked out from under her lids at the man beside her. He reclined against the seat, head tilted back, eyes closed, his hat shadowing his brow and his greatcoat once again shrouding him from chin to boots. How had the events of the night changed their relationship? Did he still distrust her so, after she had put her life, and Alec's, in his hands? And perhaps even the prince's?

The carriage skidded, lurched and tipped, tossing her against the side and hurling Chambelston atop her. The crack of shattering wood mingled with the coachman's shout, then the entire conveyance toppled and jolted to a stop.

"Miss Vance!" The muffled voice pierced the ringing in her ears as Chambelston scrambled off her.

Leah pushed back the bonnet that had slammed across her face in the melee.

The door flew open to reveal the disheveled coachman. "She slid off the road in the ice and broke the wheel, my lord. Are you injured?"

"Not I." Chambelston took Leah's hand and assisted her from the floor. "Miss Vance?"

"I'm fine." Except for the wrench to her neck and the bruises she could already feel forming on her arms. Legs. Everywhere.

Harrison crawled out of the carriage, then reached back in to help her out. Gingerly.

Once they'd all safely exited, they slogged to the other side of the vehicle. The rain had soaked into the packed snow and created a heavy, miry mess that seeped through Leah's worn, damaged boots to saturate her stockings. Tracks cut through the slush and ended abruptly at a rut littered with pieces of the carriage's wheel. Her gaze slipped from the scattered remains to the carriage where broken spokes jutted out from the axel like a child's sketch of the sun.

"You might want to add this to your prayers, Harrison," Chambelston murmured to the other man before addressing his coachman. "Any idea whether we would do better to return to the inn or take our chances on what lies ahead?"

"Well, my lord, the last village was some ways back, and I suspect we are about halfway between posting inns. I suggest we continue in the direction of London."

Leah pulled her bonnet lower over her brow to shield her face from the cold rain. "Perhaps we'll meet with a farmer or carrier with room on his cart for us."

Harrison accessed the carriage and retrieved his crumpled hat. He shoved it onto his head and surveyed the lonely stretch of road that extended in both directions. "The coachman makes an excellent point about our position. However, I am less optimistic than Miss Vance about our chances for a ride on such a day."

"Then forward it is."

Chambelston extracted the blanket from the coach and draped it over her shoulders. "Not as comely as your mother's shawl, but it will add another layer since I'd like to keep my coat this time. I don't know how long we will have to hike through the rain."

"Or worse." Harrison kicked a pile of water-saturated snow. "As soon as the sun sets, this slop will harden to ice."

Leah glanced at the leaden sky, estimating the time to be well into the afternoon.

Chambelston gestured to the coachman. "Let's unhook

these traces. We'll have to lead the horses. Hopefully we can rent a bit of space for them in the next village."

The two strode off to disconnect the horses, leaving Leah alone with Harrison.

"So you have a house in London then, Mr. Harrison?"

"Not an especially large one."

That was…vague. Not large compared to Rowan Abbey? Or compared to the tiny vicarage of her childhood? "And you live there with your wife?"

"And our five children."

"Five? Well, I suppose that would make any house feel small at times."

Chambelston chuckled as his long strides reached them, one of the horses clomping in his wake. "As the fourth of six children, I will vouch for that. Some days it seemed as if I couldn't find a few quiet moments alone. And then I joined the navy where I got to live in close quarters with hundreds of men."

And yet, he'd always seemed so alone.

"Ready, my lord." The coachman approached with the second horse and Leah's bag.

"Let's go. Miss Vance, you can ride my horse."

"Ride? But…" She stared at the animal's bare, wet back.

"I realize it's hardly as comfortable as my carriage, but we are in a hurry, so we cannot make allowances for your gender should you tire or reinjure your foot."

"Very well."

That sardonic smile stretched across Chambelston's face as he lifted her onto the carriage horse. The coachman handed Leah her bundle of belongings and the motley group set off.

The blanket covering Leah's shoulders grew heavier as it absorbed the drizzle, the aches and pains of the accident swelled with her new bruises, and the water sloshing in her boots chilled her feet into numb lumps.

"Do you yet regret your insistence of making this journey, Miss Vance?" The deepening twilight—early tonight on account of the gloomy skies—hid Chambelston's expression, so Leah could only imagine arch of tawny brows below the dripping brim of his hat, the sardonic gleam in his eyes.

"I won't when we reach the next village. If I am not mistaken, I detect smoke."

"I do believe you are right, Miss Vance."

The smell intensified as they continued, augmented by the sights and sounds of civilization—the occasional flicker of lantern light, the lowing of cattle, even the indistinct tones of human voices. A half dozen shadowy outlines of buildings loomed before them, the windows of what Leah presumed to be an inn glowing with light.

"Obviously too small to be the next posting inn."

Water dripped from the brim of Harrison's hat. "My lord, I suggest you see Miss Vance to a warm fire. Your coachman can find a livery for the horses, and I'll seek a wheelwright."

Chambelston hesitated, then retrieved his purse and passed the other man some coins. "Very well, Harrison. I expect you are better versed in such procedures than I."

"Don't fret, my lord. If we travel by frigate on our next excursion to London, I'll yield to your superior skills."

"If it rains any more, we may need a ship."

Harrison's chuckle echoed through the hazy drizzle as he set off.

Chambelston counted out more money for the coachman. "Once Harrison finds a wheelwright, you can return to the carriage to help him replace the wheel. We'll continue on to the next posting inn. If the repairs go quickly, you will find us there. But if you haven't arrived before the mail coach arrives tonight, we'll try to secure seats to London."

"I hope to see you later tonight, my lord. But if not, I will follow you to London."

"Come, Miss Vance." Chambelston reached up and lifted her off the horse.

Her fatigue and discomfort were of such that Leah almost didn't react to the strong, masculine hands around her waist.

Almost.

"How long do you think the wheelwright will need to make the repairs?"

"I doubt he will finish before tomorrow."

"But we need to get to London."

"We'll warm up here for a few minutes and then leave for the closest posting inn. The mail coach will be passing through late tonight. We can still make London by morning." Chambelston settled his hand against her back and escorted her to a building with bright lights. A faded sign of a yellow crown and red lion dangled above the door. "Let us see if this Lion and Crown has a warm fire and hot tea while we wait for Harrison to perform his magic."

An innkeeper met them at the door, took their wet garments and gestured to an empty table before the fireplace.

"Perhaps the lady would like a seat?"

"Thank you." Leah slid onto the chair and stretched out her feet toward the fire, wishing she could remove her boots.

Chambelston settled into the seat across from her and ordered tea for both of them from the maid who approached the table. He lounged back in his chair. "I wish I had a way to send you back to Rowan Abbey. I doubt the remainder of our journey will be any more commodious than what we have experienced thus far."

Thoughtfulness, or did Chambelston wish to abandon her? "But you need me with you in London to identify my cousin."

"Not if we convince the prince to travel to Parliament on another road or at an earlier time."

"But there won't be time for that if we don't arrive in London until morning." A serving maid brought tea and two cups.

Leah waited for the woman to leave before pouring. "Besides, that will only thwart tomorrow's attack. It won't prevent this Oliver fellow from attempting again because you won't be able to identify him."

"But your cousin can." The blue eyes stared at her over the rim of his cup. "You never did tell me why you were meeting him yesterday."

Leah stilled, except for her madly pounding pulse. "So you did see Alec."

"Only from a distance. Unfortunately I doubt I could find him in a crowd such as the one that will be on the streets tomorrow."

But Harrison could. Leah didn't impart that tidbit of knowledge as she took a fortifying sip of the hot brew. "I met with Alec because I wanted to ask what he knew about the attack on Fleming."

Chambelston wrapped his fingers around his cup as if trying to absorb its warmth into his hands. "And did you learn anything?"

"Not really. Alec claimed his group had nothing to do with the assault. Which I readily believed until…"

"Until you overheard Harrison and I discussing the link between my anonymous note and the papers in Fleming's chamber."

"Yes. Blaming Alec's friends for your father's death does provide a motive for them to wish ill for Fleming." Leah set down her cup. "It occurs to me Alec doesn't know about Fleming's death and the consequences it meant for me. He assumed I would have gotten the note this morning. But what did he expect me to do? I've never been to London. How could I help?"

Chambelston's brows lowered over narrowed eyes. "He intended you to come to me, of course."

"Exactly. Alec didn't mention you by name, but he obviously meant you. You were the one person at Rowan Abbey in a position to thwart this 'Oliver's' plans. You know who to contact, and you will be believed."

"Only if we arrive in time."

"If we don't, I fear I shall lose my cousin forever."

The dray—the only transportation Harrison could procure for their four-mile trip—drew to a halt before the posting inn. While Harrison settled the fee with their congenial driver, Julian uncurled stiff muscles, jumped out of the cart and assisted Miss Vance to the ground.

"I'm afraid your purse is considerably lighter, my lord." Harrison joined them in front of the large inn. "We will have to economize on our meal."

"I still have the money you provided me, my lord." Miss Vance retrieved the pouch Julian had offered so many hours earlier. "We can supplement your coins with these."

His jaw tightened at the idea of accepting assistance. "Thank you. I will replace the funds once we reach London, you know."

"Of course. But I for one will have more energy and better concentration tomorrow if I'm not weak with hunger when we try to stop the assassin."

As if he would allow her involvement in any circumstances. "Very well, you make an excellent argument for investing in our welfare." He clasped her by the elbow, escorted her inside and requested a private room for their dinner.

Once the landlord left, Miss Vance strode to the blazing fire, shed his gloves and struggled with the knotted ribbons of her bonnet.

"Allow me."

"Thank you." She cast her face downward, but not before he'd glimpsed the beginnings of a blush in the cheerful lantern light.

His knuckles brushed the chilled skin of her neck as he disentangled the ties. A streak of warmth whizzed through him that owned nothing to the flames on the hearth. He peeled the wet bonnet off her head. "I'm afraid it is ruined beyond repair." Damp locks cascaded over his hands and down her back, a curtain of dark silk.

"The poor thing hadn't far to fall to those sad depths."

While Julian tugged the heavy wet coat from her shoulders, servers waddled into the room burdened with hefty trays of food. The aromas of roast beef and fresh bread teased his senses. He held the chair closest to the fire for her. As she settled onto the seat, her hair once again tickled his skin. He leaned closer to whisper in her ear. "You will take sick if you insist on wearing those wet boots. Kick them off under the table. Neither Harrison nor I will peek at your toes."

The roses on her cheeks darkened. Or was it only the room's warmth that made her skin flush?

He backed away and hung her coat on a peg, then took the chair opposite hers—leaving the one beside her to Harrison who regaled them with tales of his children. Alas, though the location provided Julian needed distance, it obliged him to observe her throughout the meal. Those rare smiles flashed like sparks, enlivening her face and revealing her dimple. But as the evening lengthened, the crescents under her eyes deepened and the set of her shoulders drooped.

"Miss Vance, I took the liberty of procuring a chamber for you. I thought you might like to rest until the mail coach arrives."

Uncertainty wavered in her weary gaze. "I, ah, yes, thank you, my lord." She rose awkwardly from her chair.

Julian jumped up and guided her up the stairs to a spacious corner room and passed her a key. "Sleep if you can. The mail coach is apt to be crowded and uncomfortable. Or worse. If we find the inside seats already occupied, we'll be consigned to riding on top. In the cold."

"What about you, my lord?"

"I spent over half my life in the navy—where being cold, wet and awake at strange hours is customary."

But she hesitated on the threshold. "You do promise to wake me when the coach comes?"

He captured her chin and tilted her face toward the sconce's dim light. "Miss Vance, much as the idea of you facing an assassin disturbs me, I would never abandon a lady in a posting inn."

"I suppose I should have realized so after you insisted on escorting me to Heckton last night." Her lips trembled, but the shadowy doubts lingering in her eyes suppressed the hoped-for smile. "It occurs to me, my lord, the country would be better served if you were to take a horse and ride to London. Harrison and I could follow in the mail coach."

Julian didn't deny the same thoughts had occurred to him ever since the carriage mishap. "A man alone on the London road? It sounds as dangerous as leaving you here. Are you trying to rid yourself of me, Miss Vance?"

"I might—if the matter weren't so dire. I only thought if you were to reach London before morning—"

"I know. But I'm correct that the roads are dangerous at night. That's why the mail coaches carry armed guards. And besides, I promised to see you to London." Because she wanted to protect her cousin?

"Thank you, my lord."

"Perhaps it is time we put Harrison's trust and reliance to the test."

"Miss Vance?" A deep, masculine voice interrupted Leah's dream about…the same deep, masculine voice. Chambelston.

She blinked, her eyelids still heavy and her mind still

groggy with sleep as she peeked out the window of the stopped coach. "Where are we?"

"Welcome to London. We are at the Swan with Two Necks Inn." Chambelston wrapped his fingers around her elbow. The coach door popped open and the driver lowered the step. "I instructed the driver to deliver your belongings to my house. We need to get to Parliament immediately. We'll start at Westminster and walk toward St. James along the prince's route until we—hopefully—spot your cousin."

"Is it a long way to Parliament from here?" Buildings squatted one beside another as far as her eye could see through the fog.

"Not if we can find a hackney."

The other two passengers, a smiling businessman of middling years and his pinch-faced wife, waited deferentially for Chambelston to exit first. Even with lines of weariness cutting across his face and the same greatcoat from their Heckton ride, his commanding presence engulfed the cramped interior of the coach. He sprang to the ground, then reached back with a hand to assist Leah.

She drew in a deep breath, already discerning the heavy smoke for which the city was famous. London. She took Chambelston's hand and let him help her down.

Harrison joined them while Leah shook out her badly wrinkled skirts. All around, the inn was a hive of activity. The hostler rushed forward to grab horses while passengers entered and exited the large inn.

"I'm sorry you had to ride on top, Harrison." Chambelston threaded Leah's hand around his elbow. "I told you I would have—"

Harrison raised a palm in protest. "I didn't mind, my lord. It was your coin that purchased my fare. I could hardly complain about the accommodations. Now let's see if we can find a hackney, shall we?"

The gray light of a hazy dawn was peeking over the rooftops as they marched to the road before the inn. A surfeit of noise assaulted Leah's senses—cart wheels bumped over the cobbled streets, dogs barked, men shouted and swore.

"This way." Chambelston piloted her through the bewildering maze of streets and buildings. Shop windows stared blankly back at her, their glass reflecting the murky sky and her own disheveled features.

Moments later Harrison hailed a passing hackney pulled by a single sorry horse. "After you, Miss Vance," he said as the driver pulled the animal to a stop.

Leah forced her exhausted muscles to climb into another vehicle. "I could die happy if I never rode in another carriage or sat another horse."

Chambelston chuckled as he settled onto the seat beside her. "It's a long walk back to Northamptonshire."

Where there was nothing for Leah. No job, no home, no future. Only a sister who didn't even recognize her.

Harrison finished his instructions to the driver, then scrambled into the hackney as the vehicle set off. "Perhaps, Miss Vance, you would be so good as to provide us with a description of your cousin so we all have an idea who to look for."

As if Harrison didn't already know. "He is a bit above medium height. Thin, especially this winter. And he walks with a limp from an injury sustained during the war." Maybe that last detail would engender a bit of sympathy from these two men and make them less likely to perceive Alec as a villain.

"Anything else? Hair color? Distinctive clothing?"

Leah glanced at the whorls of fog—smoke?—beyond the hackney that blurred even the buildings looming over the streets. How would they ever find Alec in this gloom? "He wears a gray greatcoat from the army. Rather worn these days. His hair is reddish brown but difficult to see under his hat, of course." Which would be pulled low across his brow, no doubt, to shield his features from his erstwhile confidant.

Chambelston tapped her arm and drew her gaze back to those mesmerizing eyes that pierced even the hackney's shadowy interior. "Is he armed, do you think?"

"I—I don't know." If she gave Chambelston an honest answer, would he suspect Alec of being their mysterious shooter that day she returned from the asylum? She'd never seen her cousin fire a gun, but he'd spent years in the army. In a matter such as this…? She swallowed the lump in her throat before answering. "Probably."

They lapsed into silence until the hackney crawled to a stop. Chambelston glanced at the magnificent building with its many towers and huge windows. "Westminster."

Harrison hopped out of the vehicle and paid the driver while Chambelston and Leah followed.

Already throngs filled the streets—carriages with embossed crests on their doors, simple hackneys, swarms of ordinary folk on foot. Their faces blurred together as Leah's gaze swept across the dozens, hundreds, even thousands. How would she ever find Alec amid such a multitude?

She edged closer to Chambelston lest she lose him. After two days of near-constant travel, even he little looked the part of well-heeled nobleman. Stains sullied his coat while mud and scuffs had replaced the shine of his boots. Indeed but for the bracing smile he wore for her benefit, he easily blended into the mundane mass of humanity. "What do we do now?"

Harrison shoved his hands into his coat pockets. Because he had a weapon there? "My lord, I suggest you and Miss Vance take this side of the street. I'll cross and search the crowd on the other."

"I trust Miss Vance's description will be enough to identify her cousin." Chambelston's brows rose as he glanced between his friend and Leah.

"That, and a few prayers perhaps, my lord." Harrison's serene demeanor contrasted with the fear slithering through Leah's middle. He tipped his sadly crushed hat and strode away with quiet assurance.

"I wish I had his confidence." And his faith? Leah slid a hand through Chambelston's proffered elbow again, loss welling within her and almost driving away her fear. How much Harrison reminded her of her father. And yet, look how badly that had ended. Or had it?

"Come now, Miss Vance. We've made it thus far."

"With precious little time to spare."

"Or perhaps at exactly the right moment." They nudged their way through the crowd.

Leah examined each of the faces—some expectant, many sullen—as she searched for Alec. This "Oliver" would be as close to the street as possible. And no doubt armed. "Harrison's trust and reliance?"

"Precisely."

The mutterings and murmurings swelled, a palpable anger rising in the air. Men jostled each other. From somewhere nearby a woman shrieked. Leah tightened her grip on Chambelston's arm. "Someone is agitating the people."

"I think we can guess why, if not whom."

"A distraction."

"We must be getting close. Do you see your cousin?"

"Not yet. I—" A movement, unaccountably familiar, captured her attention. She peered through the churning mass. There! She spotted the motion again—a gray army greatcoat hitching her direction, the wearer's hat pulled low over his face. Alec? The fear stirring in her belly began to boil. She bit back an instinctive exclamation, a reflexive need to call his name.

Beside her Chambelston's indrawn breath hissed between his teeth. "Where is he?"

Leah looked down the street, at an ornate approaching carriage drawn by matching dappled gray horses. The crowd surged, the noise swelled. Then all receded as Alec—she was certain it was he—approached. She followed the line of his stare to a man in a commonplace brown coat slouching along the street, a humble felt hat drooping across his features.

"There!" Leah dropped Chambelston's arm and pushed past the press of bodies in her way. The man—the assassin—slid open his coat as the carriage advanced toward them. He shouted unintelligible words over the din of the mob as he withdrew something from his coat.

She recognized the pistols at almost the same moment she heard the distinctive blast of a discharge. Glass shattered amid the roars and screams of the people.

"Alec!" Leah sprinted forward as her cousin hurtled into the man. A second detonation ripped through the air, and then the two men crashed to the ground. She plunged into the melee, trying to grab one of the villain's flailing arms and prevent him from pummeling Alec with the pistols' steel barrels.

And then Chambelston joined the fray, pulling Alec away while Harrison with surprising—or perhaps, not so surprising—strength, hauled the shooter to his feet. Other men, including some in uniform, rushed to join him in the capture.

Leah rose to her feet. Her legs trembled and her stomach lurched with the repercussion of her fear. The muscles in her side stung from the strain of her impulse to launch herself into the conflict.

"Leah?" Alec's voice pierced through the dizziness clouding her mind.

Why was he moving away? She fought against the fog

darkening her vision. She tried to say his name, but the words stuck to her tongue.

"Leah!" Chambelston's shout echoed faintly through the mists in her mind. "She's been hit!"

Chapter Thirteen

The candle's glow shimmered on the bedchamber's golden walls. The long hours of stillness and shadows and stress hammered away at Julian's soul, so eerily similar to the days last month when he and Maman had held vigil next to his father's bed. And yet, how much worse. A glimmer of understanding at his mother's paralyzing grief filtered through him. And for the first time in years, he commenced to pray.

To no avail?

Below the pale sheet, the woman he'd admired, distrusted, and—yes—loved fought the infection rampaging through her body and weakening her by the minute. Perspiration beaded on Leah's forehead, and her incoherent mutterings occasionally interrupted the quiet.

"Any change?"

Julian glanced across the bed to where Leah's cousin sprawled on a chair. Dark circles of worry and weariness underscored Alec Vance's green eyes—eyes that snapped with antipathy despite his fatigue. Julian pressed his palm to her face, feeling the frightening heat that radiated from her skin. "None for the better." How much longer? He stared at the window where weak, wintery light filtered through the curtain. Morning again.

And yet, the dark persisted inside him.

"Julian?" Lady Langstern, his father's cousin, joined them in the chamber. "You should get some food and rest. I'll take a turn here."

He smoothed a sweat-dampened lock of hair behind Leah's ear and drooped against the back of the bedside chair. "I'm used to going without sleep."

"You haven't sought a bed the entire time you've been here, not to mention what transpired before. And I have yet to see you approach the dining room so much as once since I arrived. Even the navy doesn't require men to deprive themselves for so long."

Julian ran a hand across his jaw, feeling several days' worth of stubble. But what did it matter? He would have an eternity to seek oblivion if Leah didn't survive.... "When is the physician next scheduled to visit?"

"Ten, I believe." A strained smile tweaked the older woman's mouth. "Unless your appearance frightens the poor man."

Or his attitude. "He said these hours would be critical. If the fever breaks, she will recover." And if not... The horrifying thoughts would not remain at bay. Another plea welled in his mind. In his heart.

"My lord?" A gentle tapping drew Julian's gaze to the doorway where Higgins, the long-time Chambelston butler, waited with impassive face. "Mr. Harrison has called."

"I know you've turned away all other visitors, Julian, but you'd better see this one." Lady Langstern touched his arm, her eyes gentle as she studied him. "I'll sit with Miss Vance. If anything changes, I'll let you know."

He stared at Leah's still form several moments more, committing her flushed face to memory and offering another—futile?—prayer. Perhaps Harrison, with his unshakeable faith, could be of assistance there. "Very well."

"Higgins, usher Mr. Harrison to the breakfast room." Lady

Langstern's command charged through the silence with the force of an admiral's. "Mr. Vance, you should dine with them. I suspect you have eaten even less than Julian of late."

Julian opened his mouth to rescind the invitation—he didn't need this man's presence during his conversation with Harrison. "I don't—"

"If it's all the same, my lady, I would prefer to stay with my cousin." Vance's hard stare challenged Julian from the other side of the bed.

"Very well. Higgins, tell Mr. Harrison his lordship will join him shortly, and have a maid bring a light repast here for Mr. Vance."

"As you say, my lady." The butler bowed and withdrew.

"Go, Julian." Lady Langstern pointed at the door. "And eat."

"Yes, ma'am." He trudged through the hallway to the staircase, realizing for the first time since they'd brought Leah here—bleeding, suffering, dying?—the house and its contents now belonged to him. But what cared he for the future if...

Higgins hovered near the bottom of the stairs as Julian approached. "Has Miss Vance improved, my lord?"

"Not yet."

"The staff have included her in their prayers."

"Please convey my appreciation to them." Julian nodded to the butler then joined Harrison.

"I gather by your rather unkempt appearance Miss Vance is no better." Harrison politely waited until Julian gestured to a sideboard covered with all the necessities for a stout English breakfast in defiance of the famine.

"The fever persists." Julian loaded a scoop of buttered eggs and a piece of toast onto a plate, but he could work up no great appetite for the meal. Perhaps the servants would enjoy what remained.

"And the cousin?"

"He's with Miss Vance. I intend to find him a position."
Preferably one far away where he'd be conveniently out of
trouble. And Leah's life.

"That should bring her comfort."

Julian set down the plate and dropped onto a chair. "That's
the only reason I concern myself with the fellow. I can't help
but consider that had I taken a horse and come alone, she
wouldn't be lying near death now." Given Alec Vance's barely
veiled hostility, Leah's cousin seemed to be of the same mind.

Harrison joined him at the table. "Trust and reliance, my
friend. God has provided for us thus far." The man bowed
his head over his meal for several moments before tackling
his food.

"So you think God will heal Miss Vance?"

Harrison's lips tightened into a straight line as he shook
his head. "Oh, my lord, it is not so simple."

Julian lifted a forkful of eggs, but his stomach foundered
as the smell filled his senses. "It never is." He didn't disguise
the satirical edge on his words that matched the sharp pangs
in his heart.

"Let me try to explain. I've noticed you carry a certain
fondness for Miss Vance."

"I doubt that took any great power of observation on your
part."

"No, you wear your feelings quite openly." A shadow of a
smile flickered across Harrison's face. "There are hundreds,
thousands of women who would gladly be the next Lady
Chambelston—women who are more beautiful, wealthy, accomplished. Why this one?"

"I admire her." Julian bit into the toast. It was as dry as
dust, but at least, unlike the eggs, it didn't make his stomach spin.

"I admire you, my lord, but I have no wish to marry you.

Admiration is essential, but it is not the entirety of a relationship."

"When I am with her, I feel more than what I am. She challenges me. She sees…" The real man, the man behind the title—and yet, she still seemed to care for *him*. "She sees more than an earl and what I can provide."

"A glimpse of God's perspective, my lord. God doesn't want to be loved just for what He can do for us. He wants our love—our trust and reliance—even when His plan differs from ours."

Julian pondered Harrison's words, not certain whether he was yet ready to cede control over his future to some unseen power. What kind of god would be worthy of his trust if Leah failed to revive, would be able to create something good from her death? To think life and death itself held no ultimate meaning, that all was chance and purposeless—even the loss of a simple, impoverished governess—was to face an empty future. An abyss of futility.

"You changed the course of our country's history this week, my lord. But God wants to change the course of your future."

"I spent my entire naval career doing everything I could to avoid surrendering, you know."

Harrison's eyes crinkled with humor. "Ah, but you see, unlike Napoleon, God isn't seeking your destruction. He wants good for you, even if that doesn't always take the form we, with our limited perspectives, think it should. God has always been on your side. All He asks is that you join His. There is no weakness in giving deference to your King. And at least this one is infallible."

"Unlike my earthly monarch, you mean?" Julian conceded the point. Why did he so fear yielding control to God when he had spent his entire life serving a sovereign often motivated by his own selfish desires? "You make a persuasive case, my friend."

"Perhaps because I've been in your position."

The clock on the mantel softly ticked its way through the moments of Julian's introspection, the memories of his parents' gentle faith since their transformation twenty years past. The walls around his heart cracked, crumbled, crashed. Surrender, once begun, grew increasingly easy as he yielded his life, his fortune, his future.

He stared at the sunshine streaming through the window panes, feeling…unburdened.

"My lord!" Higgins rushed into the room. "Lady Langstern insists you come at once!"

Julian's heart stuttered and stopped, then raced forward. He jumped from his chair so quickly it tipped and fell backward onto the carpet.

Harrison clutched his arm before he could dash from the room. "Remember, no matter what, my lord."

Easy words to say, but could he live them now the moment was at hand? Julian nodded and sprinted up the stairs. He burst through the door to Leah's chamber, feet sliding on the polished oak as he lurched to a halt.

Relief poured through him and weakened his knees as he crossed the carpet to the center of the room. From the bed Leah met his gaze and smiled. Her eyes were dull and pain shadowed, the smile weak and wavery. But alive. She'd never looked more beautiful.

Lady Langstern sidled next to him and patted his arm. "Isn't it wonderful? The fever broke."

Julian pressed her hand, then approached the bed. "You gave us quite a fright."

"S-sorry." The breathy words were hoarse and faint. Leah waved weakly to her cousin, and he assisted her with another sip from the bedside glass. A spurt of irrational jealousy flooded through Julian as her only living relative performed this service for her.

"I'm glad to see you with us once again, Miss Vance." Harrison paused beside Julian, a thoughtful smile parting his mouth. "But the sick room is no place for a convention. Perhaps we should let you rest."

She half raised a hand, then let it drop back to the mattress. "Want to know…what happened."

Alec Vance returned the glass to the table. "There will be time plenty for that once you have recovered."

"Please."

Unable to deny her appeal, Julian ignored the gentle shake of her cousin's head. He lowered himself to the chair Lady Langstern had vacated and placed his hand over Leah's. "We'll keep the explanations short. It was Killiane."

The hand below Julian's tensed. Her lips moved but he interrupted her.

"No, don't speak. Rest—else we won't tell you. Killiane told Lord Sotherton he was visiting his friend Warren, but he went to Heckton instead for recruits. He needed a few people to start a ruckus. With the crowd agitated, he could take his shot at the prince."

"But…why?"

"Chambelston told you to lie still." Her cousin leaned closer to her. "Killiane yelled as he fired the first shot."

"Something rather unintelligible, it seemed at the time," Julian answered before Leah took any notion to try to talk again.

"Only to those who don't have the Gaelic." Alec Vance's green eyes snapped his disapproval.

"Your cousin is full of surprises." Julian stroked her cheek as he spoke lowly and softly, hoping the soothing words would lull her to sleep. "You never told me he was half Scots."

"The best half, of course. My mother spoke the language.

I was in the army with several men of Ireland. The languages share some similarities—even words. So, when Killiane yelled, I recognized the language and the sentiments, if not the exact meaning."

"Viscount Killiane was indeed interested in politics—Irish politics. In particular, Irish independence." Had she drifted off? Julian watched her slow, even breaths. "The famine had already thrown the country into turmoil, but he decided to create further chaos by assassinating the Prince of Wales. He hoped to exploit the unrest by moving for Irish independence at a time when the country was too preoccupied with internal matters to contest the situation."

"Fleming? The letter?"

"You already know how the two brothers detested each other and that the writing on the note matched that on the paper we found in Fleming's room. When we questioned Killiane, he blamed his brother for his ruin. We think Fleming suspected Killiane's involvement in the troubles, so he contacted me anonymously with a specious claim about my father's death. By involving me, he brought the full force of the government against the radicals and, by extension, his brother. A charge of murder receives more attention than the claims of a jealous brother. Killiane had other spies at Rowan Abbey. We don't yet know if he learned of Fleming's note, but if so, that would be a strong motive to have someone kill his brother."

"That's enough for today, I think. Any other details can wait until tomorrow." Lady Langstern gestured to the doorway. "It's time for all of you to leave. Miss Vance needs her rest—and so do you men, for that matter."

Julian gave Leah's hand one last squeeze then followed Harrison and Vance into the hallway. "Harrison, you are welcome to take the surplus from the breakfast room home to your family."

"They are well provisioned, thanks to you, my lord." Harrison gave him a bow. "I'll call again tomorrow."

As Harrison marched to the stairs, Julian clasped Vance's elbow before he escaped to a bedchamber. "Not you. I have something to say."

Affront glittered in the green eyes, then the other man shrugged.

Julian led the way to the library, slowing when he realized the other man's limp made descending the stairs difficult. A fire burned in the grate, so Julian took a chair on one side of the hearth and gestured to its counterpart on the other. Mutual antagonism coiled through the room like angry snakes.

"I appreciate all you've done for my cousin." Vance lowered himself onto the seat's green upholstery, and yet, tension remained stiff across his shoulders.

"It was no hardship. She is a woman with many admirable qualities, not the least of which is loyalty." To her cousin. To him? "I expect the Regent will recompense her with a monetary reward for her service—hopefully, enough she will not have to answer to the likes of my sister again unless she is very frivolous in her habits."

For the first time since Julian had met him, Vance's face relaxed. "I can't imagine anyone accusing Leah of extravagance. She will be vastly relieved to have security for her future."

Julian drew in a deep breath. "Speaking of Miss Vance's future, I should like to offer her a permanent position and permanent home. With me. As my wife."

Vance's jaw dropped, leaving his mouth agape in a most comical fashion. "M-my lord?"

"You are her closest relative, I believe."

"Yes."

"I thought to seek your permission before I ask her."

"Leah passed her majority some years back and has been

independent for even longer. If she will accept you, I'll not gainsay her choice."

If? Did Vance calculate that once endowed with the Regent's reward, Leah would find Julian a less attractive prospect? "Very good. I'll ask my solicitor to draft the appropriate papers." Julian rose and offered his hand.

Leah tossed the volume of poetry onto the jumbled pile of discarded books. How quickly forced inactivity dulled the mind, even with Lady Langstern plundering the vast resources of the Chambelston library for her amusement. Her wound itched. Her back ached. And her stomach demanded stronger fare than the physician yet prescribed.

Afternoon light poured through the window and emphasized the room's cheery yellow where her meager bundle of belongings slumped against the wall. Leah flipped back the sheet and edged off the bed. Her muscles protested the movement as she knelt beside the small bag containing all her worldly belongings.

She withdrew her mother's shawl, arranged it on the desk and unfolded it to reveal the three pieces of David's comb and her father's long-neglected Bible. Her finger traced the edge of the worn leather binding, then circled around the cover. Gingerly she returned to her position on the bed and thumbed through the pages.

Her father's neat penmanship recorded the date of David's death. She flipped past sermon notations in the margins to a scrap of paper stuck between two pages. Blank. Disappointment thudded again in her stomach, as if she'd half expected a message from her father. His face flashed across her memories, the picture gray and hazy with the years.

And then she chanced to glance at the typeset words, carefully underlined on some long-ago day.

Trust in the Lord, and do good.

Words her father had quoted—so often she could almost hear his deep, rich voice reading them to her even now. She'd failed on both counts. Indeed her failure to trust had led directly to her poor choices. At this final message from her father, conviction fractured her remaining pride, and she bowed her head.

"Am I interrupting?" Lady Langstern danced into the room as Leah was finishing.

"I was just…soul searching."

"Did you learn anything new?"

Leah tapped the Bible on her lap. "Too many ugly truths about myself, I fear."

"It's always better to face them than to bury them. Falsehoods have a way of rising to the surface." Lady Langstern gestured to the untidy pile of Leah's belongings still littering the desk. "I came to ask if you would like to get out of bed—but I see you already have."

"This is a lovely room, but…"

"It gets smaller with every minute. I understand. When our physician restricted me to bed for the last two months of my confinement with our youngest, I discovered I should very much dislike prison." Leah joined her laughter. "If you promise not to overexert yourself, I'll have the maids bring water for a bath."

"Oh, how lovely!"

Lady Langstern withdrew. Leah clutched the Bible by the cover, then paused to read the words one more time. A curious jumble of emotions assailed her. *Trust*—the lightness of a burden surrendered. *Do good*—the responsibility of new integrity assumed.

"I thought you might enjoy a fresh gown also." Lady Langstern breezed back into the room, three maids encumbered with buckets trailing behind her.

"Oh, you needn't go to trouble on my account."

"Trouble? For the Regent's rescuer? That's how the papers refer to you these days."

"Papers? They haven't published my name, have they?" She'd never get another position with that kind of notoriety dogging her.

Lady Langstern draped a swath of green fabric over a chair and assisted Leah out of the bed while the maids filled a tub. "Julian has kept your identity a secret."

Leah sank into the warm water and enjoyed the blissful moments of a maid washing her hair. Her eyes drifted shut as soothing waves lapped against tense muscles and the angry red wound in her side.

"Come, Miss Vance. The bath seems to have exhausted you. If you are going to sleep, we should get you to bed again."

"Oh, please don't send me back. I'm not weary, just savoring the sensation."

"Very well. If you have the strength, Julian would like to speak with you in the drawing room."

Leah's heart gave an involuntary leap despite her best efforts to restrain her response. "Of course." One of the maids assisted her into the gown while the other two removed the tub. If she were going to stay, she'd have to learn their names. The impossible longings filled her with a fresh wave of loneliness.

"As I thought." Lady Langstern gave Leah a self-satisfied smile. "The green draws attention to the same color in your eyes."

The maid arranged Leah's still-damp hair in a style that made her feel…almost pretty. Perhaps it was only the gown, such a stark contrast from years of the dark browns and grays common to her position.

"Thank you, Violet," Lady Langstern said as the maid curtseyed and backed out of the room. "Miss Vance, if you are ready, I'll assist you. I won't have you navigating those stairs alone."

Together they made their way along the hall to a broad sweep of stairs that pointed to a grand entrance hall lined with family portraits.

"That one is my cousin, the late Earl of Chambelston." Lady Langstern nodded to a picture of a man with a powdered wig and roguish grin. Familiar blue eyes stared back at Leah. "Julian's father."

The beautiful blonde beside him could only be Chambelston's mother. Insecurity intensified the weakness in Leah's limbs—until she focused her thoughts on others. Chambelston's mother. Teresa's grandmother, whom she'd never met. Perhaps Leah's last bit of service to the family could be to narrow the rift that had caused so much heartache.

"Here we are, Julian." Lady Langstern tugged Leah into a restful room of soft blues and whites where Chambelston rose from a chair. Beside him, a fully-laden tea tray awaited. "Miss Vance is still recovering. Don't tire her."

"I shall take excellent care of her." His customary smile flashed. "Won't you sit, Miss Vance?"

Leah crossed to an elegantly upholstered chair. "Thank you."

"I had Mrs. Parker bring tea." Tension sat tightly on his shoulders as he took the chair next to her. "Would you… That is, unless you are yet too…"

"I'm fine. Only a little frustrated from so much idleness." She filled two cups with the steaming brew from the pot.

"I'm thrilled to see you doing so much better. You scared several years off my life." He accepted the cup from her, then set it on the table beside his chair.

"I was a little concerned for my future, as well." She added a bit of sugar to her drink and took a sip. "Rather remarkable how a brush with death focuses the mind. In fact, I have a favor to ask of you."

His brows rose and his fingers tightened around his cup. "Anything—to the half of my kingdom."

Despite the tension swirling around the room, she smiled. Compared to her, he really did live like a king. "I hope it won't come to that, but it may. I noticed a portrait of your mother in the entrance hall, and it reminded me of Teresa's expressed wish to meet her grandmother."

"And you think I could convince my sister to allow that?"

"It strikes me your sister is in your debt for your rescue of Teresa. Yes, I think you might be the mediator your family needs." Another sign of God using something bad to create something good? Amazing how she could see the patterns when she looked for them.

"I have to return to Northamptonshire to fetch Caro. I promise to speak to Elizabeth." His now-familiar smile flashed. "But today, I would like to discuss an offer with you."

Her rapidly pounding pulse impossibly accelerated. "An offer?" She took a sip of tea to calm her agitated nerves.

"I, ah, as I told you before, I admire the way you managed to provide for yourself and the way you protect and care for others like Teresa and Caroline. You might have noticed I hold you in high regard."

"I thought you disapproved of treason."

The steady blue stared at her as if assessing her secrets. "Why did you do it?"

The teacup trembled in her hands as Leah lowered it to the saucer with an audible "chink." She quashed the lies that rose so naturally to her tongue. Trust God. "I needed the funds… for someone else. Someone unwell." Or so she had convinced herself at the time.

"Oh, Leah!" He yanked the trembling cup and saucer from her hand—sloshing tea on the rare rug—and shoved the china onto the tray. Then he wrapped a rough, masculine hand around her locked fists. "Your invalid friend. I long suspected…but why didn't you tell me?"

Tell him, that her sister was crazy? Watch the admiration in his eyes transform to horror like the last time? How much worse would be Julian's rejection.

"Marry me, Leah."

Chapter Fourteen

"I— What?" Leah stared at the startling intensity glowing in the deep blue of Lord Chambelston's eyes.

"My apologies. I meant to go about this properly." He dropped to one knee in front of her. She tried to snatch away her hands, but his grip tightened. "Miss Vance, my regard for you has grown over the days and weeks I have known you, and I have reason to believe you are not indifferent to me. You have within you the power to make my remaining days happy ones. Would you do me the honor of becoming my wife?"

Her breath caught in her lungs, unable to escape past the welling lump in her throat, and her hands warmed inside his, radiating a bittersweet ache into her heart, into her soul. A tawny lock dipped over his brow, beckoning her to stroke it back in place. For so many years she had thought she'd never find this.

Love.

She searched his smile but detected no hint of mockery, only eager anxiety. And a solution to all her problems. Never again need she grovel to a haughty employer or agonize over how she would care for her sister. Except…trust.

His broad shoulders filled his coat as they had that first night, that night when he had discovered her searching his belongings. But unlike that first meeting, today his eyes gleamed with boyish joy rather than scorn. She focused on his face until his visage blurred with the suppressed emotions. Her skin rapidly alternated between hot and cold in the same manner her mind vacillated between the selfish desire to accept and the honorable necessity to decline. As the silence stretched, the light in his eyes dimmed and his grip on her wrists relaxed—as if he guessed her answer before she spoke.

Leah tugged her fingers free. "I can't." The harsh whisper reverberated across the tension in the room.

His smile faltered and emptiness shadowed his eyes. "Can't?"

She fumbled for the words she'd never thought to speak. "While I am cognizant of the great honor you do me, my lord, I must refuse your gracious offer."

The awkward pause swelled, then he rose and retreated with slow, bruised dignity. "In that case, please accept my apologies for any distress I caused you."

Distress was far too mild a descriptor for the bitter grief coursing through her veins. Escape. She glanced at the door so very, very far away, feeling the urge to flee before she rescinded her refusal and brought misery to him. And her. "If there is nothing else, my lord...?"

"No, no. I've said more than enough. Indeed I've presumed too much."

She bounded out of the chair, bumping the table with the tea tray and producing a cheerful jingle of china that contrasted so peculiarly with the shattering of her heart. Did he hear it, the tiny shards splintering across the dreams of her future?

"I'll speak to my sister about Teresa." The quiet words reverberated through the room, through her. "I'll see she meets her grandmother."

"Thank you." Without another glance—a look which

would at any moment break her resistance—she bolted out of the room, past the censorious portraits and up the vast staircase as quickly as her stiff, bruised muscles permitted.

"Leah!" Alec's voice halted her headlong rush to solitude. "I didn't expect to see you about already. I was coming to visit you."

His words drew her attention to the rekindled ache in her side provoked by her madcap dash, and yet, not even the pain of her wound compared to this searing of her soul. "I was feeling better, though I fear I may have overtaxed my abilities."

"Let me assist you to your chamber." Alec seized her arm and half-carried her through the hall.

"Thank you," she said once she'd dropped onto a chair.

"You're far too pale. I'll have one of the maids bring you a drink."

"No!" Leah stopped him before he reached the bell pull. "Why did you wish to see me?"

Alec lowered himself to a chair on the other side of the window. Late afternoon sun poured through the lace curtain and created variegated shadows on the floor. "I wanted to say my farewells. I'm leaving. On tonight's mail coach."

"Tonight! But...where are you going?"

"Lord Chambelston has procured a pardon for me, and a position on the Duke of Sutherland's estate in Scotland."

"Scotland? So far."

"The crown rather frowns on treason, prior service to the country notwithstanding. Lord Chambelston thought it might be best for my future to spend some time away from London."

"Yes, I can see how that would be wise." For Alec, at least. Another fissure opened in her heart and allowed more loneliness to bleed through. "I'm grateful to him."

A wry smile twisted Alec's lips. "I don't think he applied himself on my account."

"But you did save the Regent's life."

"Chambelston would tell you I did right in the eleventh hour—once I had no other option." Alec covered her hand with his. "Leah? Are you certain you are well?"

She brushed her eyes against the green sleeve of the borrowed gown. "I'm only selfishly missing you."

"Aside from Phoebe, you are my last living relative. I won't go if you need me."

And risk the gallows for her sake? "Oh, no. Scotland is a perfect opportunity. It was your mother's homeland, after all. I expect to find another position presently."

"Another position?" Alec's green eyes narrowed. "But Chambelston… That is, he spoke to me, and I thought… I'm sorry. I spoke out of turn. I had assumed he would propose before I left."

"You knew he was going to offer?"

"Well, yes, I'm your only male relative. It's only proper he should consult me first. But I don't understand. Did Lord Chambelston propose or not?"

The crack in Leah's heart widened. "He did."

"Then…" Alec rose from the chair and paced to the fireplace. "Why are you seeking a position?"

"I refused him."

"Refused him? But, Leah, you would never want again. Besides, it's quite obvious the man cares deeply for you—nor are you indifferent to him."

"Not at all." She stared at the floor where a green-gold vine pattern twined its way around the border of the rug, so like the way her feelings for Chambelston had grown to encircle her heart. "Indeed, I love him. And that's why I can't marry him."

"Now you make no sense."

"Once I thought as you. Such a match would solve all my financial problems." Leah raised her eyes to meet Alec's troubled gaze. His face blurred with the depth of her emotions. "But I can't tie him to a woman with a mad sister."

"I see." He fidgeted with a porcelain shepherdess for several long moments, then returned her to the mantel. "Did you tell him?"

"No. But the knowledge would yield the same result. He's an earl. He has responsibilities to his tenants and his family and his future."

"I wouldn't have agreed to Scotland if I'd known I would leave you alone and unprotected."

"Alec, you must go—for your own safety."

His stare was long and level and laden with meaning. "Very well. But promise me you'll tell Lord Chambelston the truth. You—we—owe him that much."

"Miss Vance?" The masculine baritone harmonized with the piano's lingering notes as Leah reached the end of the movement. "I fear I must interrupt for a moment."

Her heart began to quicken even before she raised her eyes from the sonata score to the man who hesitated in the doorway. Morning sunlight highlighted Chambelston's hair and created a manifest contrast with his muted eyes. Because of her refusal? Had she wounded him so? "Of course." It was his house, after all. His instrument. She lifted her hands from the keyboard and swiveled on the stool. "I trust my playing didn't disturb you."

"Not in the manner you mean." He advanced into the music room and paused beside the piano, a letter in hand. "I thought I should give you this before I leave. It bears the Regent's seal."

"The Regent!"

He passed her the folded sheet of parchment and appropriated a nearby chair.

Leah snapped open the page and began to read… Her heart

beat a furious pulse in her ears. "F-five thousand pounds!" The shocking words escaped on a whisper.

"You saved his life, you know."

"But…" Five thousand pounds—from the notoriously parsimonious prince. Never again would she worry about Phoebe's care or about locating employment. "Did you have a hand in this reward?"

"I might have suggested a woman in your position would better understand the depths of his gratitude if he accompanied his thanks with an appropriate remuneration."

Another debt she owed him. First her cousin, and now this. "And Alec?"

"Considering Mr. Vance committed high treason, I don't think he should expect much beyond his pardon and new position."

"No, of course not." But certainly nothing prevented her from sharing her windfall—if her proud, independent cousin would accept a portion. She'd send him some once he settled into his new situation. He'd departed the night before for Scotland and thinking of him elicited fresh loneliness. Perhaps Alec could even resign and return… She glanced sharply at Chambelston, only now becoming aware of the full import of his words. "What did you mean, before you leave?"

The muscles in his jaw tightened and his lashes dipped over the empty darkness of his eyes. "I just received a letter from Elizabeth on the morning post. Caroline is missing."

"Missing! But…how? When?"

"Yesterday. She seems to have simply vanished. No one can find any sign of her. If she wandered outside…"

She'd have surely succumbed to the cold by now.

Chambelston's hands fisted, the skin across his knuckles turning tight and white. "This is not the first time the maid lost—"

"My lord, you cannot blame anyone until we know all the facts."

"I should have expected as much from you, after your clash with the magistrate last week." A droll smile tweaked his lips, though it never found his eyes. "In truth, I blame myself most of all. If I hadn't taken Caroline from Somerset, from all that is familiar to her, to a place where she was barely tolerated…"

But it was worse. He'd stayed in London extra days to await Leah's recovery from the gunshot wound and subsequent fever. In order to propose. If he'd returned to Northamptonshire immediately after Killiane's failed attack… The cold fingers of guilt clamped around her midsection. If Leah had been honest with him from the beginning, if she'd told him about her sister rather than letting pride hold her tongue, he would have returned immediately to Lady Caroline rather than linger here, near her. Trust. Realization dawned in Leah's mind. When her erstwhile suitor—supposedly a man of God—had failed her, she'd transferred that disbelief and cynicism to her relationship with God Himself. And from there, to everyone else.

Chambelston rose from the chair. "You may remain here as long as you like. I spoke to Lady Langstern. As her husband is deceased and her children are grown, she is willing to stay with you until you feel well enough to travel. Indeed I believe she enjoys the assignment."

Finding a purpose for one's life oft imparted that result. But Leah had an obligation to fulfill. "I'll go with you to Northamptonshire."

"But you're still recovering, and the journey will be arduous."

"No more difficult than worrying from so far away."

For several seconds more she thought he would remain

adamant. Then he nodded. "Very well. But I've already given orders for the carriage to leave in thirty minutes."

"I have little enough to pack. I'll be ready."

Julian rested his head against the carriage's plush upholstery. Awkward silence sat beside him, like an extra occupant in the vehicle. How he already missed Harrison's presence, which would have provided him with the gentle reassurances of faith and eased some of the tension of the enforced intimacy with the only woman to whom he'd gifted his heart.

Only to discover she didn't return the sentiment.

He forced the disappointment from his mind—only to have nothing left to occupy his thoughts but terrifying fear for Caro. Where could she have gone? Not far. She hadn't the vigor for a long journey by foot. Dread overflowed from his soul, the sure and certain knowledge only something tragic explained her disappearance. Trust and reliance seemed so impossible. Surely no one could find a greater purpose in his sister's suffering...or worse. Julian sent up silent, awkward pleas.

"What will we do when we get to Rowan Abbey?"

He started and glanced across the carriage to the sympathetic hazel gaze. "As we will arrive very late, probably not much tonight. I pray Elizabeth has already located her. If not, we shall have to make one more examination of the house tonight, and then expand our search to the grounds and nearby villages on the morrow."

"Do you suppose she could be hiding? Perhaps she got angry and hid in a fit of pique."

"No, Caro's mind doesn't work that way. She doesn't have the ability to design that kind of scheme."

"Fear, then. Could someone have frightened her into hiding?"

"Perhaps, but I can't see her remaining quiet and concealed for so long."

"Tell me more about Lady Caroline. If we are to find her, it would be helpful to have a better understanding of her likes and habits."

Julian allowed his mind to draw a picture of Caro's engaging smile. "She likes most food but especially ham. She enjoys dancing—in a pattern all her own, of course—but she tires easily. And she loves music." Like Leah.

"Has she disappeared on other occasions?"

"Not for any length of time. She escaped from her nurse on her first day at Rowan Abbey, but I found her in a chamber near to mine—Fleming's, as it turned out—looking for me."

"Does she prefer solitude or the company of others?"

"Caro likes being with people. She treats everyone, even new acquaintances, as friends."

"A person who tires easily would almost certainly not wander far. But someone who trusts too readily could easily be lured away."

"For ransom? Elizabeth's message mentioned no such request."

"What about revenge? You did foil the plot to assassinate the Regent."

"The credit for that belongs mostly to you and your cousin. I would expect you to be in more danger on that score. Fortunately we've managed to prevent the papers from discovering your identities."

"Then we must consider the possibility someone took her for more nefarious purposes."

Bile boiled in Julian's stomach and burned in his throat as he fought to contain the revolting images. Would any man…? Oh, yes. "If Fleming weren't already dead, he would be my foremost suspect."

Leah's face blanched as she ripped her gaze away to stare

out the window. The dark ribbons of her new bonnet—a farewell gift from Lady Langstern—contrasted with the pale skin of her cheek. London had faded behind them, leaving only snow-covered fields on the horizon. "You didn't hear from the magistrate or Lady Sotherton about an arrest for Fleming's murder?"

"No. Killiane yet maintains his innocence on that score. So as far as I know, Fleming's death remains a mystery."

"I don't know that Fleming deserved to die, but he most definitely deserved any distrust thrown his way. Unfortunately there are others of his ilk."

Julian leaned across the space between them and covered Leah's hand with his. "What did he do?" He hated forcing her to confront the sordid details of her past, but he needed to know if he was to find Caro.

Silence wrapped around them, interrupted only by the steady clomp of the horses and swish of the wheels. "He trapped me in his bedchamber. I knew if I cried out, my reputation would be destroyed."

Was this the reason she had rejected him? Fresh anger, fed by new worries for Caro, mingled with heartbreak—for her, for him, for Caro. "Caro would cry out. She wouldn't understand the need for such restraint." Unlike a poor governess for whom even a suggestion of scandal would be grounds for dismissal.

"I was desperate. I grabbed the fireplace poker, and..."

"Ah, the injury to Fleming's head three years ago. Elizabeth mentioned it to the magistrate. Good for you!" Poor Caro would never be so quick-witted. "That's how you lost your comb."

"I suppose it fell out of my hair in the melee. I looked later but never found it."

"During Caro's explorations, she discovered a locket and ribbon and other baubles among Fleming's affects. The magistrate presumed them to be gifts, but perhaps Fleming collected such objects from his victims."

"I lived in constant fear afterward. Fortunately Fleming never disclosed what happened."

"No man wants to admit to being bested by a woman."

"I suppose not. He preferred tormenting me as his form of revenge. I knew it was only a matter of time until he succeeded in either assaulting me or seeing me dismissed. Probably both." A wry smile curved one corner of her mouth. "How ironic that with his death, he succeeded in the latter."

"And left you with no means to support yourself." Or the mysterious "someone else" whose needs had prompted her foray into treason. "Both for you and your…?"

"Sister. I support my sister."

"Your sister?" Julian recoiled against the back of the carriage seat. "I thought she was dead."

"Her mind is."

Like Caro? "I see."

"No, I don't think you do. Phoebe is…seriously unwell. She lives in an asylum not far from Rowan Abbey. A good place—as these things go. One where the female inmates…"

"Aren't subject to the base lusts of men like Fleming." An asylum. How many times had well-meaning friends and spiteful rivals suggested such a place for Caro rather than burden the family with her existence? At least the DeChambelles had the means to provide for Caro's care at home. How different for Leah. No wonder she kept her sister's very existence a secret. The last clue to the Leah Vance mystery emerged. Like her care for Teresa, like her concern for Caro, love for her sister had impelled Leah's actions—fear that unscrupulous attendants would subject her sister to the exploitation she had so nearly suffered herself. She strove so mightily to protect others. If only she could trust him to do likewise for her.

"Alas, such situations cost dearly. By last year Phoebe's

expenses had exhausted my father's legacy, and my governess's salary didn't cover the fees."

"Hence your need to raise extra funds."

"I suppose I ought to have considered why anyone would compensate me for collecting information from Lord Sotherton. Such actions suggest evil intentions."

"But you were too desperate to heed the warnings."

"Or too cynical. How astonishing to learn Killiane funded my spying."

"I suppose we should take comfort some good came of his ill intentions. You had the money for Phoebe's care until the Regent gifted you with the reward." Another example of God's ability to bring good from evil? "Is your sister's… affliction one of long standing?"

"Phoebe was vivacious and beautiful. Everyone loved her." Was Leah aware of the raw pain that laced her voice even now? "Then when she was fifteen, she fell down the church steps onto the stone walkway and suffered a life-threatening blow to her head."

"Ah, the event ten years ago. You spoke of a sister once before, but I assumed her deceased."

"In many ways, she did die that day. She lost much of her memory and now finds the simplest activities—speaking, dressing, feeding herself—difficult. Even her disposition changed to one of persistent despondency."

"That must have been difficult for your family, coming so soon after your brother's death."

"Yes, my mother already suffered from melancholy. Phoebe's injury—and subsequent impairment—compounded her grief. My mother and I worked to restore Phoebe's mind. Some days we seemed to see progress, only to have our hopes dashed. After my father's death Mother and I had to relinquish the vicarage. Phoebe found the change too distressing and became a danger to herself and others. At that point, we put her in the asylum. Shortly thereafter my mother died of a broken heart."

"And the asylum? Has she made progress toward recovery since her arrival?"

"No. Remember the day you interrupted Fleming's harassment that afternoon?"

"Of course. You claimed to have visited an invalid friend." Along with a man—her cousin, no doubt. "Your sister, I presume."

"Yes, I visit every Sunday. Sometimes I feel as if she remembers me, but most times I am a stranger to her. That week, the staff had discovered her making another attempt to take her life." Leah's troubled hazel gaze dropped to the clenched fists in her lap. "Whenever that happens, they medicate her with laudanum."

"What will you do henceforth, now that you have funds enough for her care?"

"I thought to get a cottage and a nurse. Perhaps in a loving and stable environment, she will improve."

"I hope someday you'll let me meet her." Assuming he couldn't persuade Leah to change her mind about his proposal. For the first time since her refusal yesterday, he allowed himself to hope. Had he at last discovered her reasons? Maybe, after they had found Caro, he could visit the Vance sisters in their cottage and renew his...friendship with Leah. "We aren't so different, you and I."

"A governess and an earl?"

"No, two ordinary people trying to care for the weakest among us."

Moonlight reflected on the hulking outline of Rowan Abbey as the carriage drew around the drive. Lights gleamed in her windows and created shadows of the shrubs around the building. Leah gathered her coat and her courage more closely around her. Would Lady Sotherton accept her return or toss her into the snow? Worse, would she find the cold remains of Lady Caroline already there?

Once again Leah searched the recesses of her mind for a possibly overlooked cranny or crevice where a scared, or perhaps unconscious, child-woman might be trapped. The attic? The cellar? A wardrobe in an empty bedchamber?

The coachman gave a shout and the horses slowed, stopped. The carriage rocked as he hurtled from his perch and yanked open the door.

"Thank you, John. My compliments on the exceptionally brief journey." Chambelston descended the steps.

"I'm most anxious for Lady Caroline, my lord."

Chambelston extended a hand to Leah to assist her. "See to the horses. And then if you like, ask the grooms if they witnessed anything that might lead us to her."

"I shall, my lord. Good night, Miss Vance."

Leah gave him a nod as she accepted Chambelston's escort to the door. The formal front door accessed by honored Sotherton guests—not their recently dismissed governesses.

Hawkesworth's brows barely budged as he glanced to Leah. "My lord, I'm glad you arrived so precipitously. I only wish it were under more felicitous circumstances." Nausea churned in Leah's belly. So Caroline had not yet returned.

"I also. No word yet?"

"Nothing, sir." The butler accepted their hats and coats. "Lady Sotherton awaits you in the blue salon."

"Very good. Please have the housekeeper prepare a guest chamber for Miss Vance."

The butler's pale eyes blinked. "A guest chamber, my lord?"

"Miss Vance is no longer the governess at Rowan Abbey. You can hardly deposit her in the schoolroom."

Was that a smile that touched Hawkesworth's mouth? "Indeed, sir." He vanished with their garments while Leah and Chambelston strode to the blue salon.

"Julian!" Lady Sotherton vaulted from a seat and flew to meet them in the doorway. Unhealthy pallor whitewashed her countenance, but for the red rims circling her eyes. Her gaze flickered to Leah, registering neither surprise nor opposition. "Julian, I'm so sorry. We've searched and searched, and I don't know what else to do."

Chambelston clasped her hand and guided her back to the settee. "Tell me what you have done thus far. You've searched the entire house, I presume?"

"Everywhere! Every room on every level."

Leah claimed a chair some distance from the brother and sister, near to Teresa. Her former pupil leaned close to wrap an arm around Leah's shoulders and offer a whispered comment. "I'm glad you didn't let my mother's bitterness keep you away."

For any other reason, perhaps. "Not for this."

Lady Sotherton pursed her lips. "Did Benedict return with you?"

"He had to complete some business concerning Killiane. He hoped to follow us tomorrow or the next day." Chambelston paused before the fireplace, hands clasped at his back. "Who last saw Caro?"

"Well, that adds to our dilemma. Anna, the nurse you brought, claims Lady Caroline was last with our maid Molly."

"And Molly vows she was with Anna," Chambelston finished for her, his mouth a thin white line. "Whom do you believe?"

Lady Sotherton's frown deepened. "I don't know this woman you brought…"

"But surely she's been here long enough for some on your staff to form opinions."

"Mrs. Anderson and Hawkesworth both defended Molly."

"Miss Vance?" Chambelston swung around and focused those intense blue eyes on Leah. "You probably know the particulars better than the rest of us here."

"I've never known Molly to be anything but competent and truthful." Leah's mind slipped back to those frightening hours when she'd thought she might hang for Fleming's murder. "Furthermore, she is a woman of genuine faith, and she has a sincere liking for Lady Caroline. I cannot imagine her lying to protect herself when such falsehoods put Lady Caroline in danger."

"You don't believe Anna likes Caro?" Chambelston pulled the cord to summon the butler.

"As Lady Sotherton mentioned, we scarcely know the nursemaid." Leah avoided glancing at her recent employer. "I didn't sense animosity so much as discomfort—as if she feared Lady Caroline's condition might be contagious. Many people are like that around those who are...different." Like her former suitor's reaction to Phoebe.

The butler paused in the doorway. "My lord?"

"Send for Lady Caroline's nursemaid."

"Yes, my lord."

"I had thought to hire someone to replace Anna." Chambelston's bleak glance flickered to his sister. "But I didn't want to steal away Molly without first consulting you, Elizabeth. I see I was too late."

The maid shuffled into the room and sank into a curtsy, her posture half defiant and half defeated. As her wary gaze darted around the room, reluctant sympathy welled in Leah at the eerie similarity to her recent ordeal after Fleming's murder. "You wanted to see me, my lord?"

"What I most wish, Anna, is the truth. What happened when Lady Caroline disappeared?"

"Like I told the others, my lord, Lady Caroline was with Molly."

"Lady Caroline was your responsibility, and now her life is endangered. Should we discover anything happened to her—something that could have been prevented had you spoken out in a timely manner—we'll see you punished as an accessory to murder."

Anna's shoulders wilted. "I got a note from William—one of the footmen. He asked me to meet him. Lady Caroline was playing with a toy, so I didn't think she'd miss me."

"And when you returned?

"She wasn't in the room. Truly, my lord, I was only gone a few minutes."

Chambelston glanced at Leah as a chill shuddered along her spine. She fought the rising nausea with a brief petition for Caroline's safety. "Where is this note?"

"I burned it. I didn't want no one finding it and learning he'd made a fool of me. When I got to the kitchen, he weren't there." A moue of annoyance hardened on Anna's mouth. "How do you like that? He played me false and now I'll lose my position and my life."

"Anna, did William send you any other notes? Before this one?"

"No."

"So how did you know the note was from him?"

"He signed his name, of course."

"Of course. Thank you for your assistance." Chambelston paced to the window and looked out into the moonlit night as the maid exited the room. "If we are to believe this iteration of Anna's story, someone planned to get Caro alone. I think we can safely cease any further investigations of the house. We'll begin a search of the nearby villages at first light tomorrow. Tonight, we can only rest—and pray."

As if sleep would come to any of them while their minds whirled with fear. Leah patted Teresa's arm and rose to find her room and a few moments of solitude with her father's Bible.

"Miss Vance, a word if I might?" The quiet command in Lady Sotherton's voice halted Leah's feet with a flinch.

Chambelston turned his back to the window, a frown dragging down the corners of his mouth. "Elizabeth, this is not the time."

"Indeed, I should have said these words days ago. Miss Vance, since Julian seems to fear what I might say in private, I'll make my apologies in public. I regret my impetuous words and indecorous behavior at our last encounter."

Shock dried a response from Leah's throat. An *apology*— from Lady Sotherton?

"I fear my grief for Reggie overcame my gratitude for all you had done, especially the day you rescued my daughter from those hoodlums. I hope you'll forgive my offense."

A week ago Leah would have held her grudge. But then, a week ago, she'd never thought she'd see the proud Lady Sotherton admit to a wrong—any more than she'd thought to see herself return to the faith of her parents.

Tonight, Leah extended her hand.

The sky had barely faded from gray to pink when Julian marched into the stable. "Wetherel, tell the grooms to get ready to ride."

"Already begun, my lord. The bay for you?"

"I'll get him myself momentarily. Tell me—you are in the position to best see the comings and goings around the manor house. We have reason to believe Lady Caroline didn't wander away of her own accord but was abducted. Did you see any unusual activity or unexpected visitors on the day she went missing?"

The groom scratched his head. "Unusual, no. Farmer

Smithy's son made his weekly delivery for the kitchen, but I can't recall any other activity."

A farmer? Hardly a person in a position to plant a false note to the maid. Julian grabbed the bridle from a hook. "Where have the grooms searched thus far?"

"The gardens and near the house. We didn't expect the lady could wander too far, given her condition and all—but we didn't figure her carried off, either."

"In light of the new information, we're going to expand the search to the nearby villages. The grooms are to ask if anyone saw Lady Caroline or observed suspicious activity two days ago. She is a stranger to these parts and therefore conspicuous. In short, gather all the information you can about everything that happened, especially anything out of the ordinary." Julian buckled the bridle in place. He wished he'd thought to ask Harrison to return to Northamptonshire with them. They could have used his expertise. And faith. "Oh, and have the grooms arm themselves in case they encounter...difficulties."

"Where do you want us to go?"

He whirled at the sound of the feminine voice, his heart accelerating even before he met Leah's somber gaze. She stood with his sister and niece, all three of them dressed to ride. "Leah, you are not a competent rider, and you suffered an injury only last week."

She tilted her chin. "You won't keep me here while Lady Caroline is in danger. My discomfort is a small price to pay for her life."

He looked to Elizabeth for assistance, but found only an echo of the same grim determination. "Julian, I know I wasn't welcoming to Caroline when you brought her here, but I never wanted... That is, I would never see her hurt. There are people Teresa and I can question who would never share information with a groom."

Julian knew better to engage in battle when he was outgunned and outmanned. Besides, Elizabeth made a valid point about the local gentility's attitudes. As he settled the saddle on the bay's back, he nodded his acquiesce at Wetherel. "Very well, but everyone is to travel in armed groups. We want no repeats of the mob attack on Teresa and Fleming."

Elizabeth exchanged a glance with Teresa. "We'll start at the vicarage."

As the two women set off to collect their horses, Julian grabbed the bay's reins and led him out of the stall.

Leah tapped his arm. "There's a hamlet in the other direction, near to the asylum where..."

"You go to the vicarage with my sister and Teresa. I'll check your hamlet."

"No, I'll go with you."

As he exited the stable, a chill gusted against Julian's cheek. "The last time I agreed to take you with me, I consequently saw you bleeding on the ground. I'm certain a groom and I can find the location."

"Julian." His heart paused for a moment as his mind cherished this first use of his name. "When my parents died, I left more than my old home at the vicarage. I walked away from my faith. But God has welcomed back the prodigal. I prayed about this decision into the night, and I believe this is something I'm supposed to do."

He drew in a steadying breath, but his mind still whirled with objections. "Leah—"

"'Trust in the Lord, and do good,'" she quoted. "*Trust,* Julian."

A few more silent seconds ticked by before he nodded. "As someone newly come to faith myself, I can't argue with your convictions."

Moments later they set off for the small hamlet near to where Leah had encountered Fleming all those days ago— and near to the asylum she so frequently visited. But for the gravity of their purpose, Julian could have enjoyed the ride shared with a beautiful sunrise and even more lovely companion. The snow clinging to the tree branches reflected the pink of the early morning sky. Birds flitted among the brambles, searching—like everyone else this winter—for food.

They rode in silence past the spot of the incident with Fleming. The impression of that day's event still spoke from the trampled snow.

"Did you ever discover the identity of the person who shot at us?"

Julian glanced at Leah, noting the tightening around the corners of her mouth. Anger welled in him, but he tempered his emotions. He might yet have need of them. "I asked your cousin, but he denied any knowledge of the incident. In fact, he was most displeased you'd never informed him of it."

"The assault on Fleming the next day consumed most of my attention. Perhaps Fleming was the culprit?"

"Possibly. Teresa said he had a pistol when they were attacked. Of course we now know Killiane hadn't traveled to London with Lord Sotherton as we thought—and he also carried weapons."

"At least neither of them will make trouble for us again." A shudder trembled along her shoulders. "What will happen to Killiane?"

"Lord Sotherton was working to have him quietly banished so as not to further inflame the people. He'll keep his life but lose everything else."

A meager collection of humble cottages appeared on the horizon. Julian fought the urge to prod the horse into a faster gait for fear Leah would match his speed—to the detriment of her recovery. Once they reached the hamlet, he alighted from the saddle and strode to Leah's side.

"Careful. We don't want you to break open that wound."

He wrapped his hands around her waist and assisted her from the horse. "How do you feel?"

"Like I haven't ridden for a week. But other than the usual stiffness, I'm fine."

He wound the reins for both their horses around a rail and approached the door of the closest cottage.

A simply garbed matron answered his summons, her suspicious gaze traveling from his heavy coat to the fine horses snorting at the rail. She applied the same scrutiny to Leah's modest apparel. "He's a stranger, but I seen you here before, ain't I?"

"Yes, I travel this road every Sunday to visit my sister. We've come seeking information about a young woman who disappeared from Rowan Abbey two days past."

"Didn't see anyone walk by."

"She was probably taken away by a cart or carriage."

"I haven't seen any strangers in weeks—'cept him."

Julian doffed his hat. "Thank you for your assistance all the same. If you do remember anything, please send word to Rowan Abbey. I'll see your efforts are rewarded."

They tried the three other buildings that comprised the entirety of the village, with the same results.

Discouragement sat heavily on Julian's shoulders. "Perhaps we should return to the Abbey—the others may have made more useful discoveries."

Lines serrated Leah's forehead. "There's one other person we might ask. The gatekeeper at my sister's asylum has always been kind to me. At least we could be assured a truthful answer from him."

Julian led her to the impatiently waiting horses. "Is it nearby?"

"Two, perhaps three miles to our east."

He hoisted her onto the back of the mare, then mounted the bay. "Then as long as we have come this far, let's ask." Since

Leah already had a relationship with the man, she would be more likely to get answers than if Julian returned later without her.

A scrawny ox eyed them curiously as they steered their horses back onto the path.

Julian set a measured pace. "Did you believe the villagers?"

"Not especially. I wonder if they are protecting someone."

"I can't imagine anyone here had the wherewithal to deliver a note to Anna."

"Someone from outside Rowan Abbey assisted her abductor. He couldn't have used a vehicle from the estate without Wetherel knowing."

"When we return, we'll ask him to compile a list of every known cart, dray and wheelbarrow owner in the district."

The horses crested a knoll. The road stretched out below them, wending its way past a redbrick manor house. "That's the place."

The building—even the gatehouse—seemed too remote to be of assistance. "How long has your sister been a patient here?"

"Nearly nine years."

"And for the entire time of your employ, you have visited here?"

"Every Sunday."

An explanation, perhaps, for her refusal to accept either of his offers—that of Caro's teacher and that of his wife? A situation in Somerset would seriously hamper her weekly visits. They reined their horses to a stop outside the high stone fence.

The gatekeeper lumbered out of his cottage, his brows rising with surprise as he approached. "Miss Vance, I didn't expect to see you today. We missed you Sunday." He fitted the key into the lock and swung open the gate.

"We came to ask a few questions."

His gaze paused on Julian for several seconds before returning to Leah. "Of course."

"A young woman has gone missing from Rowan Abbey. We believe her to have been snatched away by someone with deplorable motives. We thought you might have observed a conveyance pass this way."

"When did this happen?"

"Two days ago."

"Two days!" The gatekeeper stroked the gray waves of his beard. "Odd you should say that. We gained a new patient here two days ago. A young woman."

"A woman?" Excitement crackled in Leah's question. "What did she look like?"

"Smallish. Brown hair. Unusual eyes."

Julian's pulse pounded audibly in his ears and relief burned in his chest. They had found her! His baby sister—dear, sweet Caro who'd never harmed another in her life—was here. But…who had brought her here? And why?

Chapter Fifteen

The breath whooshed from Leah's chest as a chill shuddered down her arms. She shared a glance with Chambelston. At least Phoebe's presence provided them the perfect excuse for entering the building to confirm their suspicions. "Did you recognize the person who brought her? Can you describe the carriage?"

"It weren't no carriage, Miss Vance. Just a cart like any of the farmers hereabout use to haul their harvests."

An open cart would have provided him ample opportunity to observe the occupants. "How was she? Did she seem distressed? Or was she…restrained?"

The gatekeeper tilted his gray head and pondered her question. "Confused mostly, I'd say. But that weren't remarkable. Most of the guests here are addlepated in one way or another."

"And the driver? You didn't recognize him?"

"She had a scarf wrapped around her face and a cloak over her head. But I don't think I'd seen her here before."

Leah's fingers tightened around the reins. A *woman* brought Lady Caroline here? "You didn't see any other vehicles traveling the road that day?"

"No, there's been no traffic in this area. We haven't even seen a delivery cart yet this week other than that one."

"Thank you." Leah prodded the mare onto the property. Chambelston nudged his horse to walk beside her.

The clank of the gate closing behind them resonated across the wintry air. Chambelston's gaze snapped to her face. "That sound is more than a little unnerving."

"It's worse when you enter the building. There are more locks." Leah nodded her head toward the hulking structure ahead. "Notice the bars on the windows."

"Will they let us in?"

"Of course. I owe them money. I'd promised to settle the debt Sunday, but then I was in London instead. The more pressing question is will they let us out."

His chuckle relieved some of the tension that normally accompanied her journeys along this drive. "How did you learn of this place?"

"My mother wrote to a childhood friend of my father who ministers to the insane."

"Not a post many men seek, not even the clergymen of my acquaintance."

"No." The power of that response—the care and concern a near stranger evinced for her sister—rushed back to her memory from where it had lain dormant so many years. For too long she had allowed pain to overshadow the glimpses of God's love in human form. If only more people could see others as God did. Beginning with her. "He offered numerous warnings and listed several options. He suggested this establishment because they keep the men and women, both patients and orderlies, on separate floors."

"Good to know that if we do find Caroline here, there was less chance for abuse."

"Precisely our reason for heeding his advice despite the expense. After my mother's death he recommended me for the position in Lord Sotherton's household so I could be nearby."

"A true friend."

And inspiration.

As at Leah's last visit, few tracks marred the snow. Quiet descended on them as they reached the entry. Chambelston swung down from his horse in silence, then assisted her out of the saddle. As they trudged the unshoveled walkway, snow invaded her boot via the slice it had suffered after her last visit—so long ago when she'd encountered Fleming on her return to Rowan Abbey.

The matron answered their summons, her face frowning as she spied Leah—until her gaze chanced to rest on Chambelston. "Miss Vance. And…"

"A guest." The familiar mingling of fear and hopelessness began to pound in Leah's pulse, and she reminded herself she was no longer an impoverished governess dependent on others' good fortune but a woman of means with newly rediscovered faith. "I brought the funds I owe."

"You're late."

"My apologies. I was…indisposed Sunday." Leah withdrew the requisite coins. How long would she need to find new living arrangements for her and Phoebe? "I heard you have a new patient."

The matron's severe face hardened. "Miss Vance, you know we don't disclose information about our patients with any outside their families."

A policy for which Leah had been grateful in the past. "My apologies. How is Phoebe?"

"I'm sorry to report she is much the same as before. We've had to keep her sedated for her safety."

Leah vowed that once free of this place, Phoebe would never again ingest so much laudanum. "We'd like to see my sister."

"Of course." The matron glanced over her shoulder and gestured to a hovering orderly. "Alice, see Miss Vance and her *guest* to her sister's chamber."

Leah's thoughts whirled furiously as the orderly led them up the stairs. How could they search for Caro while locked in Phoebe's room? As the orderly paused before Phoebe's door, Leah drew on the experience of her last visit. "Alice, would you procure a rag and a basin of warm water? We'll wait here until you get back."

The orderly rolled her eyes but obligingly left to retrieve the requested items.

"Quickly! Men are on the floor above, the women here. But the matron has a fondness for laudanum to keep the patients compliant, so your sister may be unconscious."

"I think I should prefer that to finding Caro constrained." A shudder vibrated along his shoulders. "A pity the matron wouldn't answer your question."

"She probably believes she is protecting a wealthy family that wants to keep their shame a secret." Leah tapped on the door across the hallway. "Lady Caroline?"

An unearthly keening responded, the eerie wail wafting from below the door.

Leah backed away and shifted to the next door while Chambelston did likewise to the rooms on his side of the building. She had reached the fourth chamber when a soft whimper answered her inquiry.

"Lady Caroline?" Leah repeated.

"M-Miss Vance?"

"I found her!" Leah motioned to Chambelston.

He joined her in a couple long quick strides, then knelt and whispered through the crack beneath the door. "Caro?"

"Jules!" The knob rattled as she tried to open the door. "I can't..."

"We'll get you out."

The tap of Alice's feet against the steps signaled the end of their parley. The orderly's head rose over the top step, her arms encumbered by a tin basin. Her lips drooped into a frown as her gaze traveled from Phoebe's room to the two people gathered in front of another door. "Miss Vance?"

"Come here, Alice." Chambelston's harsh tones echoed off the bare walls. "Open this door."

"This one?" Alice's eyes flickered toward the steps. "But Miss Vance's sister is over there."

"But my sister is here. Unlock the door." He folded his arms over his chest.

Alice's throat bobbed as her gaze focused on the stretch of fabric over his muscled arms.

"Y-yes, sir." The orderly's fingers trembled as she deposited the bowl on a table and fitted the key into the lock. "M-miss won't like this."

"I'll take responsibility for her displeasure—once I have my sister freed from this prison."

Alice pushed open the door, then Lady Caroline barreled over the threshold and into her brother's chest. He wrapped his arms around her and rested his cheek against her limp hair while whispering soothing words of comfort in her ear.

The ice around Leah's heart cracked and warmth—and realization—flooded in. She'd unfairly assigned another man's faults to Chambelston and assumed he would scorn her because of Phoebe. And yet, he expressed no shame or resentment at being burdened with the likes of Lady Caroline. Only love.

And rage at finding his poor sister in such straits. He drew back a step, tension radiating from the tightly held anger and anguish that darkened his eyes to midnight. "Caro, how did you get here? Who brought you?"

"Lady with gold."

"Lady? Alice, do you know this woman's identity?"

Alice shook her head, causing the tarnished trim of her cap to flutter. "N-no, sir. Only that sh-she paid with a piece of gold jewelry. I saw her give it to the matron when she arrived."

Chambelston met Leah's glance over his sister's head. "A woman who paid gold to keep Caro hidden away. A week ago I would have suspected Elizabeth."

"Lady Sotherton seemed genuinely distressed by what happened. Lady Caroline," Leah spoke as gently as possible. "Where was the lady's gold?"

Caroline touched a hand to the bosom of her wrinkled gown. "Here."

"A gold brooch. We need to see this bauble." Chambelston guided his sister toward the stairs.

The four of them stomped down the steps, the sound of their heels echoing through the cold, empty space. A few plaster friezes yet adorned the ceilings, but the whitewashed walls had long since been scrubbed of any ornamentation.

"Miss Vance, returning so soon…" The matron's voice trailed off as her gaze locked on Lady Caroline. She rounded on Alice. "What have you done?"

"My bidding." Chambelston moved in front of his sister to shield her from the looming confrontation.

"I will not allow you to abduct a patient in my care!"

"I'm not abducting her—I'm taking her home. I am the Earl of Chambelston."

Julian paused as realization sank in. For the first time since his father's death, he had claimed the Chambelston title and not recoiled. "Let me explain. I am Lady Sotherton's brother. And this is our youngest sister, Lady Caroline DeChambelle, who disappeared from Rowan Abbey two days ago."

"Lady Sotherton's sister! She never said… That is, I didn't know…" The resolve leached from the matron's face—along with a great quantity of blood, leaving her mouth but a faded gray line against her ashen cheeks.

"I thought you might understand once I explained the mistake. I would be so grateful if you would identify the woman who confined my sister here."

"She gave her name as Mrs. Keen."

"Mrs. Keen?" Leah shook her head. "There is no one at Rowan Abbey with that name."

"Undoubtedly our nemesis sought to disguise her identity." Julian focused his stare on the matron again. "We understand this woman financed my sister's interment with a gold brooch. We should like to see it."

"Wait here." The matron ground out the words without even moving her jaw. Her feet tapped a tattoo as she left, then returned seconds later with her fist clenched around a dangling gold chain and a swath of dark fabric draped over her arm. She shoved the jewelry into his hand. "Here."

His stomach clenched as he gazed at a familiar gold locket nestled in his palm. Not a brooch but a necklace. "Miss Vance, do you recognize this?"

"Yes, that belongs to the dowager's companion, Miss Godwin."

Julian stared at the object in his hand as his mind tried to draw Miss Godwin's features. Middle years, dark hair...her features once more retreated to the depths of his mind as the locket's details sharpened under his focus. The locket.

"Julian?" Leah's voice intruded on his recollections "If this is Miss Godwin's locket, then—"

He stopped Leah's comment with a squeeze to her wrist and glanced once more at the matron. "Thank you for all your assistance. Please fetch Lady Caroline's cloak."

"I have it here already, sir." She passed him the length of dark wool.

"Excellent. Thank you." He took the garment and wrapped it around Caro's shoulders, his heart brimming with confusion. And...hope? Had Leah even noticed how her intimate use of his given name had slipped out again, seemingly unawares? He led both women to the waiting horses. "Miss Vance, let's get you mounted first. Then you can hold the bay's bridle while I get Caro situated."

Once he had his sister on the horse, he swung up behind and wrapped his arms around her. Riding two abreast on a single saddle was going to be deucedly uncomfortable—and quickly at that. "There. Ready to go, Caro?"

"Scared."

Of the horse, or of the past two days' ordeal? He nudged the bay into a walk. "I've got you now. I won't let anything happen to you. We'll return to Elizabeth's house for today, and then we will leave for Somerset."

"Tomorrow?"

"Soon." As soon as he could arrange his future...whatever that might be.

The gatekeeper met them with a key. "You found her, then."

"It was a misunderstanding." Julian guided the horse outside the stone fence. Still, he didn't breathe easily until the gate locked behind him and they had steered their horses westward toward Rowan Abbey. "Miss Vance, I admire your fortitude in breaching these walls every week. To judge by the undisturbed nature of the snow, I gather not many call on the patients here."

"No, few of them receive regular visitors, no matter how exalted their station or well-heeled their relatives." Only Leah had demonstrated such uncompromising loyalty.

"Are you certain the locket belongs to Miss Godwin?"

"Oh, yes. I've seen her wear it."

"Can you remember the last time you saw it in her possession?"

"Miss Godwin and I never spent much time together, but I noticed her wearing it at that horrible dinner the night your sister demanded my presence."

"Ah, the day Fleming and Killiane and their wordless friend arrived." *Before* he had brought Caro to Rowan Abbey.

"You recognized the locket, too, didn't you?"

"Not from dinner. The day of my return to Rowan Abbey with Caro, you had gone to visit your sister. While I conversed with Sotherton, Caro's nurse carelessly let her slip away."

"Ah, when she went to look for you."

"Yes. When I at last found her, she had the locket."

"Do you know how she obtained it?"

"She found it in Fleming's bedchamber."

Leah started. Her grip jerked the mare's reins, causing the horse to shy. She struggled to regain control of her mount. "Yes, I remember. You thought perhaps Fleming collected trinkets from his victims. Like my comb."

"Caro found this locket with other items. I didn't know who occupied the chamber until Fleming's death two days later. During our searching of his belongings, I noticed someone had removed the necklace. I presumed for its monetary value. I had intended to pursue that line of inquiry—before we rushed headlong to London to save the Regent."

"Such a trifling matter."

"Not to the prince."

The flash of dimple filled Julian with pleasure. Pain. Possibilities? "But it would seem the piece returned to its rightful owner shortly after Lady Caroline discovered it. Your mention of Fleming prompted another memory. I saw Miss Godwin wearing it in Fleming's chamber, immediately after his death."

"Are you certain?"

"It wasn't a day I am likely to forget." Darkness swallowed the green in her eyes, leaving only a shadowy brown that obscured his ability to read his future therein. "I noticed Miss Godwin fidgeting with the pendant when the dowager chastised her for suggesting they leave the room."

They rode past the insular buildings that comprised the hamlet of Norford. Julian felt the suspicious stares that peeked at them from behind shuttered windows. "So Miss Godwin possessed the locket on the day Fleming arrived. The next time we can account for the piece was when Caro found it in Fleming's room. And yet Miss Godwin had resumed wearing it by the time of Fleming's death."

"If Fleming had taken it from her during a..."

"Miss Godwin had a strong motive for wishing the man dead."

"Along with half the women in the Sotherton household. Given my experiences with the magistrate after Fleming's death, I would need more evidence than possible revenge for an attack that might have happened."

Regret lodged in Julian's throat for the part he had played in her distress by withholding the knowledge of her innocence. "But Miss Godwin's involvement in Caro's disappearance also points to criminal intent."

"Speaking of your sister, how is she?"

Julian glanced at Caro's limp head that rested against his arm. "Sleeping. Do you think she will long suffer from the repercussions of her ordeal?"

Leah twisted her head to study the woman slumbering in his arms. The variegated greens and browns of Leah's eyes softened like the promise of spring. "I don't doubt she will experience some ill effects. She'll probably fear being spirited away again for some time. At least she doesn't seem to have suffered any abuse at the asylum."

For that Julian offered a silent prayer of gratitude.

They crested a knoll, and the fields of the Sotherton estate stretched before them, the Abbey sitting in their midst like a ruby pinned to a snowy cravat.

"Caro?" Julian nudged her awake. "We're almost to Elizabeth's house."

"Hungry."

"We'll see you get a meal."

"I like Molly."

"Yes, Molly is very kind." He'd have to ask the maid if she would consider employment in Somerset—especially since Leah wouldn't be working for him.

"But not lady with gold."

Julian fought to maintain nonchalance. "What did she do?"

"Take me away."

"Do you know why?"

Caro said nothing, as she often did when she either tired of the conversation or no longer understood the questions.

"I suspect Lady Caroline saw Miss Godwin with the locket after the murder, just as I did." The dark ribbon of Leah's new bonnet fluttered in the breeze. "But the only time she'd seen it before was in Fleming's chamber."

"And Caro said something that indicated she had seen the necklace in the drawer, which made Miss Godwin fear her secret would be discovered." Julian rested his cheek on the top of Caro's head.

"Miss Godwin spends most of her time with the dowager, leaving her limited contact with Lady Caroline. She wouldn't know her capabilities."

"Thus, she decided she must remove Caro from Rowan Abbey before I returned." Anger and disgust clawed at Julian's gut. "I'll contact the magistrate when we arrive and let him know we discovered Fleming's—"

"My lord, I think it important to remember Miss Godwin didn't harm Lady Caroline. Not physically."

"Like Fleming, you mean."

"But that's it. We don't know she killed Fleming. Her dealings with Lady Caroline indicate planning—distracting the maid, obtaining a cart, transporting her to the asylum—but not hostility. Perhaps she slipped into Fleming's chamber undetected to reclaim the locket, just as Caro did."

"Or perhaps her murder of Fleming was more opportunity than premeditation. Either way, she needs to be held to account for Caro's abduction."

As they reached the house, Wetherel himself came to greet them. "My lord, we didn't— You found her!"

"The credit belongs to Miss Vance." Julian slipped off the horse, feeling every bit of the discomfort of sharing the saddle with Caro. He reached up to assist her while Wetherel held the bridle. "Has everyone else returned?"

"Indeed."

"Good. Send a couple grooms to fetch Mr. Mason. And pass along my gratitude to those who participated in the search." He'd send a more tangible expression of his thanks later.

"Immediately, sir." Wetherel led the horses away while Julian helped Caro to the house.

"Lady Caroline!" Hawkesworth's face lost its requisite severity in a rare smile. "We were so worried. We're glad to have you home."

Julian helped Caro slip the cloak off her shoulders. "Hawkesworth, please see Miss Godwin is confined to her room, with a footman posted at the door. And notify me when Mr. Mason arrives."

"I shall see to it, my lord."

"I'll be with Lady Caroline in—"

"Caro!" Teresa sprinted into the entrance hall and wrapped her arms around her aunt.

Teresa's mother approached more slowly, hesitantly, warily—a woman of uncertain welcome in her own home. Her hands fluttered as if expressing an unconscious desire to join the embrace, and yet fear and ignorance restrained her. "G-good afternoon, Caro. I'm relieved you are well—and home. Are you hungry? Cook prepared a meal for Julian's return. Perhaps you would like to join the family in the dining room."

Caro tilted her quizzical expression toward Julian. "Hungry."

Emotion clogged his throat at this, Elizabeth's first attempt to include her youngest sister in her family. Julian squeezed her hand like he used to do all those years ago when he was a boy and Elizabeth a doting older sister. "I appreciate your thoughtfulness, but after her ordeal, I think Caro will feel more comfortable in the schoolroom this afternoon. It is familiar to her. Would you please see her lunch is sent there? And then perhaps you and Teresa would care to join her…"

"I—I should like that. I shall have the entire meal transported to the room. That is, if you think it…"

"It is very appropriate." He snagged Leah's sleeve while Elizabeth and Teresa conveyed Caro to the schoolroom with promises of the delightful treats to come. "I'll stay with Caro for a few minutes, but I have to confer with the magistrate as soon as he arrives. Would you remain with her this afternoon? She needs the comfort of familiar faces, and no doubt I'll be occupied for some time."

"But won't you want my testimony about the times I saw Miss Godwin wearing the locket?"

Perhaps not if the woman confessed. "I'll send for you if we have need of you."

"Mr. Mason. How good of you to come again so precipitously." Julian shook the magistrate's hand, then gestured to Elizabeth. "I thought that in the absence of Lord Sotherton, my sister should attend this discussion about Lady Caroline's disappearance since it concerns a member of her staff."

"My lady, I trust you are well now that your sister is returned to you." The magistrate offered Elizabeth a bow before he lowered his bulk onto a delicate chair. "You have identified Lady Caroline's abductor, my lord?"

"And possibly Fleming's murderer. Hawkesworth has gone to fetch her."

"Her? Another woman, then."

And not so different in circumstances from the last one—a reminder to use caution in their accusations.

"My lord?" Miss Godwin entered, flanked on either side by a footman-turned-sentry. Resignation dimmed her eyes like the faded beauty that languished on her face. "You wished to see me?"

"You'll be happy to know I recovered an article belonging to you this morning." Julian withdrew the locket from his pocket and waited. The gold chain twinkled in the midday sunlight that streamed through the drawing room's tall windows. "I believe this is yours."

"Yes, it is mine." She offered no excuses or lies, but stood calmly before him.

Julian's respect, even sympathy, rose another notch. "I assume you know where I stumbled upon this—and my sister. Would you tell the magistrate? Or should I?" The unspoken threat hung in the room.

"May I?" She extended her hand. Julian deposited the necklace in her palm. She wrapped her fingers around the piece as if to draw strength from its presence. "My late fiancé gave me this as a betrothal gift. I wore it ever afterward, until…"

"Fleming took it from you."

"And more." The mention of Fleming's name at last elicited emotion. The dark eyes flashed with loathing above lips that twisted with unforgettable horror.

"Reggie?" Elizabeth's voice wavered with uncertainty. "But he was…"

"A fiend."

"Miss Godwin, you needn't disclose personal details which distress you." Julian shared a look with the magistrate. "I'm certain we all comprehend your predicament."

"After he was laid low from the assault, I resolved to retrieve my property. When I saw William administer a dose of laudanum and depart to make ready for dinner, I thought I could recover my locket with none the wiser. Except Fleming wasn't insensible as I'd supposed."

"He was conscious enough to recognize you?"

"I spotted the laudanum bottle beside the bed. All I wanted was to silence him lest the dowager learn of my shame." Her knuckles tightened around the necklace she yet clenched in her fist. "I offered him a glass of brandy—he had a decanter on the desk—and I added a copious amount of laudanum."

"Did you mean to kill him?"

"Yes. No." She shrugged as if the answer was of no importance, as if she no longer cared her response might very well determine whether she lived or died. "I don't know."

Elizabeth dropped her chin onto her folded hands, her eyes sealed shut as if to blot out the truth she'd so willfully refused to see, until too late.

The magistrate shifted on the chair. "Tell me about Miss Vance's comb. I presume you stationed it in Fleming's bed."

"After he consumed the brandy, I searched the room for my locket." Miss Godwin stared at her fist for several long moments, then uncurled her fingers to expose the rose pattern etched into the gold. "I finally located it, along with several other curious items."

"Including a green ribbon and Miss Vance's comb."

Her eyes flickered to Julian before returning to her hand. "You knew about your sister's discovery."

"I accompanied her to Fleming's room to return the item to the armoire. Implicating Miss Vance for murder was unwarranted." And the action Julian found most difficult to understand.

"By the time I found the locket, I'd concluded I gave him too much laudanum and he was like enough to die." For the first time her shoulders slumped. "I panicked."

"Then when you realized Caro knew about Fleming and the locket, you abducted her and conveyed her to an asylum." The clock on the mantel chimed the hour, reminding Julian he had yet one other task to accomplish. "How did you transport Caro? Where did you get the cart?"

"I borrowed it from a friend."

"In Norford." The hamlet where no one would speak to him.

"Please do not hold him responsible for my wrongdoing. Norford was my home once. Long ago."

But never again. The unspoken words lingered in the air between them. Her admission had sealed her fate—either transportation or execution. And yet…Leah was right on another account. "Wouldn't it have been easier to kill Caro to cover your earlier crime?"

"No, I couldn't. She harmed no one."

"Neither had Miss Vance."

Mr. Mason rose from his chair. "I think we have what we need, my lord. Miss Godwin, I fear I must arrest you for the murder of Reginald Fleming."

"Was that an evil deed or a valuable service?" She tilted her dark head and waited until he reached her side. "My lord?"

Julian's head snapped to meet her gaze one final time.

"I hope you will convey my regrets to Miss Vance. I'd like to believe I wouldn't have allowed her to hang for my crime."

Then the two exited the drawing room together.

Julian surged to his feet.

"Julian." Elizabeth paused before him, her blue eyes troubled. "I'm glad you were here during this ordeal."

"I've missed you, dear sister." He wrapped his arms around her for the first time in nearly twenty years, marveling at the divine plan that had at last brought healing and reconciliation to his family.

"Would you...would you like me to order tea? You could tell me about your life in the navy."

Julian found a smile as he tweaked her hair. "I have yarns aplenty I'd love to share, but they'll have to wait until tomorrow. I have a favor to ask of you and one final damsel to rescue."

Leah turned the page and tilted the book more closely to the candle. The shades of sunset shimmering through the window panes colored the schoolroom's walls with oranges and purples, and cast shadows about the corners. Eyes drooping with fatigue, Caro snuggled closer as Leah began to read again.

"Miss Vance!" Teresa burst into the room, her face glowing with her smile. "You are needed in the entrance hall. I'll wait here with Caro."

"We were reading—"

"Yes, yes. I'm certain we'll be fine." Leah's one-time charge hauled the book from her hand and tugged her to her feet. "Now go. They need you."

To give testimony to the magistrate? According to Lady Sotherton, Mr. Mason had left hours ago. But then, why the need for her now? Leah hiked through the hallway, then paused at the top of the staircase and stared at the commotion below.

Chambelston's greatcoat swirled with his brisk, efficient movements while he issued orders from the doorway. Then two footmen followed him into the manor, a litter balanced between them. Leah's heart lurched. Had someone else been injured or even attacked, like that day the same footmen conveyed Fleming's battered body to his bedchamber?

"Leah!" Chambelston's exclamation recaptured her attention. He swept off his hat, and the chandelier's glow gilded his hair and highlighted a hesitant—hopeful?—smile as he strode to the stairs. "We brought someone to see you. Wait there. We'll bring her up."

Her? Leah studied the contents of the pallet more closely... "Phoebe." The name slipped out on a whisper. Nine years. The day she had yearned for, despaired for, had arrived after nine long and lonely years. Her sister's motionless form wavered in the onslaught of emotion.

Chambelston vaulted up the last few steps and stood before her, hat in hand like a pauper petitioning a contribution. "I had a conversation with Elizabeth after the magistrate left. She instructed Mrs. Anderson to prepare the room next to yours."

The footmen reached the landing with their burden. Leah followed their slow procession to an empty chamber and waited as they slid her sister's form onto the bed. Only the faint rise and fall of Phoebe's chest indicated she lived.

"The matron must have administered another dose of laudanum." Leah ran her fingertips along the waxy coldness of Phoebe's cheek.

"Not surprising. She has limited staff, so their choice would be restraints or drugs when patients become unmanageable."

Unmanageable. What would happen when Phoebe regained consciousness—if not her senses? How long would Lady Sotherton consent to the presence of two unwelcome guests, especially one not quite sane? "I'm not certain this was a wise idea. I have no claim on your sister's hospitality. Perhaps we should return Phoebe to the asylum until I have a permanent situation."

"Miss Vance?" Lady Sotherton inched closer to the bed.

The familiar agitation stirred in Leah's belly, eight years of always being on edge before this woman. "I'm sorry, my lady. I didn't realize you were here also. I was only just suggesting to Lord Chambelston that perhaps we should find an alternative placement for my sister as quickly as possible."

"Miss Vance, you saved my daughter from dangerous ruffians, and you returned Caro to us despite my harsh words and rash actions at our last encounter. Your sister is welcome to remain in my home as long as you need."

"But Phoebe might—"

"We'll deal with it." Lady Sotherton tapped the back of Leah's hand. "Now if you'll excuse me, I'll speak to Mrs. Anderson about a schedule so that we have a maid with her at all times."

"Y-yes, of course." Leah waited until her erstwhile employer had departed before she turned to Chambelston. "She seems much changed."

"As are we all. And for the better."

A most accurate statement for Leah's new perspective on life. And love?

"Now come." Chambelston gestured toward the door. "We have much to discuss yet."

"But Phoebe…"

"The maid will let you know the minute she regains consciousness."

"Indeed, I will, Miss Vance."

"Very well. She…" Leah hesitated, suddenly aware of how little she knew her sister anymore. What did she eat? What did she need? Oh, the missing years—

Chambelston enveloped her shoulders in an embrace. "You have the rest of your lives."

"Thank you." She said the words to Chambelston, and then winged the same thought heavenward as she rested her cheek against the fabric of his coat and inhaled its comforting scent.

"All will be well." The scones flickered against the walls as he escorted her through the hallway.

"Did Miss Godwin confess?"

"Yes, it was much as you surmised." He preceded her into an empty salon. "And I believe her claim that she didn't enter Fleming's chamber with the intent to kill him. The footman had recently administered a dose of laudanum, and she thought that a prime opportunity to retrieve her locket with none the wiser."

"Except, seeing him…"

"Exactly." Chambelston led her to a gracefully proportioned chair with blue-and-white-striped upholstery. "I'm going to speak to the judge on her behalf—to request leniency. Perhaps she can begin a new life in Australia. Harrison was right. We all need the chance to find redemption."

"Well, I can't fault anyone in need of a fresh start."

"Your comment gives me hope." He knelt before the chair and took her hand as her pulse began to pound in her ears. "Miss Vance, I do not mean to distress you with repeated importuning, but I am also looking for a fresh start—with you. I love you too much to not try again, and I have reason to believe you are not indifferent to me. Will you reconsider my offer of marriage and agree to become my wife?"

Light and joy bubbled in her heart until the room practically spun with her elation. "I should refuse again, I know." Leah leaned forward and brushed her fingertips against his brow, pushing an errant lock of soft hair to the side.

"Then I'll find myself harassing you again. And again and again until you yield. I can be quite annoying, you know."

"As a matter of fact, I do." She started to giggle, but her laugh caught in her throat. "My sister…"

"Will be cared for by the best nurses in Somerset, in all of England if you find no local women to your liking. Leah, how could you believe I, of all people, would reject you for such a reason? I, who love and value Caro."

Leah drew her finger down along his temple to the rough stubble on his chin. "I had allowed myself to doubt God loves all people equally for so many years, and I wouldn't—couldn't—trust anyone until I repaired my relationship with Him. I was certain you would spurn me if you learned about Phoebe."

"And so you rejected my proposal."

"Because I had fallen in love with you—but not enough to trust you. I was still certain you would never accept a woman with such a family member as Phoebe."

His grip tightened around her fingers. "And now? I know my distrust in the past hurt you, but the trials have led me to a deeper understanding of God's provision."

As with Leah. "When I observed you with Caro at the asylum, I finally realized I'd misjudged you, as if God had at last opened my eyes to your true character. I owe you an apology."

"I'd rather have an affirmative answer to my question. Leah, you are now a wealthy woman in your own right. You don't need my money. But I need you. No other woman of my acquaintance understands my love for Caro as you do. We are both people who have learned God loves and cares for even those the world considers imperfect—and I believe He brought us together at just the right moment. I love you, Leah."

She stared into the earnest blue eyes—not a hint of mockery today therein—and considered how he had arrived in her life at precisely the moment when she'd been most desperate, when her future had seemed most hopeless. God's provision. The last of the ice in her soul melted and washed away her doubts. "Yes. Yes, I should like to be your wife more than anything, Julian."

He caught her in his arms as he bounded to his feet. "Good.

I thought my knees would break before you answered." And then he lowered his head and spoke without words for several thrilling more moments.

"There you are, Uncle Julian." Teresa's voice sliced through Leah's blissful oblivion. "And Miss Vance also."

Julian glanced over his shoulder, smug smile firmly in place. "But not Miss Vance for much longer."

Teresa blinked. "You mean… Oh, I'm so happy for you both!"

"Then you won't be offended if I ask you to go away."

Teresa's grin widened. "You'll have plenty of time for that later. Come with me now. There is something you must see."

Julian met Leah's gaze, one brow lifted quizzically. "What do you think?"

"We'll be leaving for Somerset soon enough. We should accommodate her."

"Very well. This once." He lowered his arms and threaded Leah's hand through his elbow. "Lead the way, Teresa."

Teresa fairly danced through the hallway to the drawing room where a crowd gathered—Lady Sotherton, Lady Caroline and…someone else.

"Maman?" Julian's harsh whisper rumbled across the room. Leah paused in the doorway while he joined his family.

The elegantly coiffed blonde turned her head to reveal the serene features of an older woman. A woman who looked remarkably like Julian and Lady Sotherton and the portrait in Julian's London town house. "Elizabeth wrote that I must travel immediately to Northamptonshire. I came as quickly as I could."

"You wrote her?" Julian's voice rose in disbelief as he stared at his sister.

"I didn't know what else to do. I sent her another note tonight telling her all was well, but of course, she'd already departed."

"You did the right thing." Julian's mother settled a hand on her long-estranged daughter's shoulder.

"Maman, I'm sorry I let you down." Self-recrimination laced Julian's words and replaced Leah's feelings of awkwardness with sympathy. "If I hadn't—"

"Julian! You found her. That is all that matters."

"Not exactly my doing." He motioned Leah to his side, his eyes soft, his smile warm. "Maman, may I present Miss Vance, the woman who discovered Caro's whereabouts? And my future wife."

"Wife! Elizabeth, you did not tell me of 'zis." The inflection of her native France colored her speech.

"She didn't know. Miss Vance, this is my mother, the Countess of Chambelston. Maman, you may be the first to wish us happy."

"Second," Teresa corrected. "I was the first."

"And a good thing she didn't chance upon us sooner, else I'd still be on my knees begging for an answer." That sardonic twist reappeared on Julian's mouth as he glanced at Leah, but this time, he included all of them in the joke. "Miss Vance is not an easy woman to persuade. Fortunately for me, she decided to lower her standards for once."

"Uncle Julian, she hasn't any choice. I found the two of you alone in the blue salon in a most compromising position."

"All part of the scheme to be certain she didn't change her mind. Did you hear that, Caro?" He tweaked his younger sister's hair. "Miss Vance will be coming to Somerset with us."

"Now?"

Julian's laugh reverberated against the walls. "Soon."

"It is so good to see you laugh again, Julian." The Countess of Chambelston clasped Leah's hand between both of her own. "Miss Vance, I pray God grant you and my son every blessing."

He already had.

Epilogue

Somerset, England
June 1817

Julian stared out the study window where the afternoon sun drew shadows on the grass. Lush green stretched toward the horizon and promised new chances, new life.

In his fields, in his heart, in his home.

"My lord?" The butler interrupted his reverie from the doorway. "A message arrived on the post. From America."

His heart skipped a beat as he slipped the paper off the salver. "Is my mother about?"

"I believe the ladies are in the garden."

"Very good. I'll share this with them when they return." He snapped open the wax seal and began to read. Oh, Maman would want to see this! He started to rise from his chair.

"Learn anything interesting?" Leah quoted those familiar words from the doorway. He waited by his chair while she sashayed into the room and next to his desk.

"As a matter of fact, yes. From my brother."

"Are you going to tell me what he said, or do I have to sneak into your room tonight to learn your secrets?" Her charming dimple flashed beside a saucy smile.

"My door is always open to you, Lady Chambelston." He winked and passed her the letter. "A girl, Kit says—with lungs powerful enough to ward off any future English invasion."

Leah's soft chuckle rasped against the quiet. "It sounds as if he has truly acclimated to his new country."

Or perhaps the bonds of family gave a man the drive and determination and dedication to make anywhere a home, so long as he was with the ones he loved. "I thought you'd be outside with Maman and Caro."

"I was. Phoebe seems to especially enjoy the sunshine— not surprising after so many years confined to a single room—but I tired. I left her with Molly and returned to the house."

"Forgive me, my dear. I left you standing. How thoughtless." He nudged her into the chair he'd vacated moments before. "I can't believe the maid let you return by yourself."

"Stop fretting, Julian. It's a child, not some dreadful disease."

A child. *Their* child. His mind sketched a little girl with bows in her hair, a dimple on her cheek and her mother's compassion in her heart. "I bought you a gift." He retrieved a paper from the desk and offered it to her.

"A deed?"

"You once told me that if you ever suffered an excess of funds, you would use them to help others."

Her brows drew together. "But land? What am I to do with a piece of property?"

"Put a building on it and hire staff."

Understanding kindled in the wide hazel eyes. "An asylum! Oh, Julian." She launched herself from the seat straight into his arms.

"An asylum that treats the patients humanely and accepts even those who cannot pay." He rested his cheek against her hair and breathed the soft fragrance of lavender. "I thought perhaps you'd like to go with me tomorrow to look at the property."

"Anywhere, Julian. I will go anywhere with you. God has blessed us beyond measure. It's only right that we should share our bounty and joy."

* * * * *

Dear Reader,

I love history, so when I decided to write Julian's book, I researched the major events of the late Regency to see what real events would have had an impact on the characters.

Historians identify 1816 as the Year Without a Summer. A convergence of unusual solar activity and a massive ash cloud from the eruption of Indonesia's Mount Tambora created a "volcanic winter" throughout much of the northern hemisphere. The unusually cold, wet summer caused poor harvests and scarcity by the winter of 1816–1817. Famine engulfed much of Europe and North America. With Europe still reeling from the devastation of the Napoleonic Wars, civil unrest soon followed.

It was against this turbulent backdrop that I set a story about two lonely people caught up in the events of the time. Of course, I took a few liberties. No one knows the identity of the person who fired on the Prince of Wales's carriage in January of 1817, but since conspiracy theories do make for fun stories, I let my imagination loose.

I love to hear from readers and can be reached through my website at www.cjchasebooks.com.

Questions for Discussion

1. Leah felt her secret was too shameful to share, so she wouldn't confide in anyone beyond her cousin. If she'd trusted friends, would she have been as susceptible to despair and bad choices? What are some steps we can take to alleviate the loneliness of the people in our sphere of influence?

2. Julian was a younger son until his brother died, several years before the beginning of the story. He felt unprepared to inherit his father's properties and responsibilities. Has God given you an assignment you never expected? Looking back, can you now see how God prepared you for that role?

3. Leah believed God didn't hear her prayers because her sister never got better. She saw no purpose to her sister's suffering. Does any suffering have a purpose?

4. Leah's sister, Phoebe, suffered from a traumatic brain injury during a time when resources to treat such injuries (speech therapy, physical therapy, etc.) were limited. Consequently she ended up in an asylum with people suffering from other injuries and mental illnesses such as schizophrenia and bipolar disorder. Today, we know chemical imbalances in the brain cause many of these disorders and they can frequently be treated with medications, yet the stigma against mental illness remains. What are some things your faith community can implement to support families touched by mental illness?

5. For many years, Leah refused to consider God might have a plan for her life. When she at last opened her

mind to the possibility, she could see how God had been working. When have you been surprised by God's plan for your life?

6. Leah finds Psalm 37:3 marked in her father's Bible, and it comes to have special meaning for her: "Trust in the Lord, and do good; so shalt thou dwell in the land, and verily thou shalt be fed." What specific verses or passages have been especially encouraging to your during difficult times in your life?

7. Today Caroline's disability would be labeled as Down Syndrome. Matthew 25:40 tells us "whatever you did for one of the least of these brothers [and sisters] of mine, you did for me." And yet upwards of 90 percent of those with special needs do not attend church. What are some things you and your church can do to reach the special-needs community?

8. Julian and Elizabeth had been close as children until his sister's estrangement from their parents. Even after his retirement from the navy, he waited two years to visit her, during which time their father died. Could—and should—he have attempted anything sooner to bring about reconciliation? What should be our response to discord between people we love? How can we be instruments in reconciliation?

9. Both Julian and Leah found themselves in difficult situations where they tried to take charge of things on their own. How might their lives have been changed had they put their trust in God and sought His guidance? How hard do you find it to cede control of your life to God?

10. The winter of 1816–1817 was a time of unemployment and scarcity. People responded in different ways. Rioting was all too common and led Parliament to pass the Gag Acts, which cracked down on dissent. What would you do if your family and friends couldn't get adequate food? What response should we have to hard economic times?

REQUEST YOUR FREE BOOKS!

2 FREE INSPIRATIONAL NOVELS
PLUS 2
FREE
MYSTERY GIFTS

Love Inspired.

HISTORICAL
INSPIRATIONAL HISTORICAL ROMANCE

LIH13

Love Inspired HISTORICAL

Matchmaker—Matched!

For Ellie O'Brien, finding the perfect partner is easy—as long as
it's for the other people in the town of Peppin, Texas. When her
handsome childhood friend Lawson Williams jokingly proposes,
the town returns the favor and decides a romance is in order for
them. But when secrets in both their pasts threaten their future,
can the efforts of an entire town be enough to help them claim a
love as big and bold as Texas itself?

A TEXAS-MADE MATCH

by **Noelle Marchand**

Available in March wherever books are sold.

To Trust or Not to Trust a Cowboy?

Former Dallas detective Jackson Stroud was set on moving
to a new town for his dream job, until he makes a pit stop
and discovers on the doorstep of a café an abandoned
newborn and Shelby Grace, a waitress looking for a fresh
start. He decides to help Shelby find the baby's mother,
and through their quest he believes he's finally found a
place to belong, while Shelby's convinced he will move on
eventually. What will it take to convince Shelby that this is
one cowboy she can count on?

Bundle of Joy
by
Annie Jones

Available March 2013!

www.LoveInspiredBooks.com

LI87801